ENEMY AT THE WINDOW

BY

A.J. WAINES

'No more tears now; I will think upon revenge.'
Mary, Queen of Scots

Chapter one

15 February 2018

When Sophie opened her eyes everything was wrong. Someone had tucked her into bed, but it wasn't hers. She wasn't in the right place. This wasn't home.

The last thing she remembered was the sound of a police siren. Someone further up the street must have had an accident or maybe it was coming from the television. She wasn't sure. Before that, the childminder had let herself in and was holding her phone, looking horror-stricken. Then there had been a woman wearing green pulling at her arm. She looked like she'd just hopped out of a helicopter or been sky-diving.

What was Daniel doing lying there on the floor under the kitchen table like he'd fallen asleep? And who had spilt all the red paint?

She needed to get out of here; to start clearing it all up.

She struggled against the crisp white sheets. They were too tight. As if she was strapped down. Looking over to her right there was another bed, and then another next to that. *Wait a minute – there are other people here. What's going on?*

The curtain on her left was pulled aside; the rings rattling along the pole like coins spilling from a fruit machine. A woman dressed in a blue uniform looked down on her.

'How are you, Sophie?'

'Where am I?'

The nurse smiled and held Sophie's wrist as she focused on her watch. 'Do I know you?'

Sophie read the name 'Rose' on her name tag, but it didn't mean anything to her.

'You're in hospital – you're safe.'

Rose leant over to plump up her pillows and Sophie flinched. 'Don't worry… no one is going to hurt you.'

'This isn't right. I'm not…'

'Rest for now. There's some juice on the table if you want it.'

Sophie narrowed her eyes. There was a persistent throbbing sound. Too loud. Trapped inside her head. Clanging and banging. She jerked from side to side to try to find the source. *They're trying to electrocute me. They're trying to kill me.* Her bones felt like they were on fire beneath her skin. She called out.

'Help… help me!'

The same nurse returned to her side, looking inconvenienced.

'What's the matter?' she said, her hands on her hips.

'That noise? What are you doing to me?'

The nurse glanced at something above Sophie's head and gave her the kind of smile reserved for someone who has already made too many claims on one's patience.

'It's your heartbeat,' she said. 'It's nothing to worry about.'

'My heartbeat?'

'Yes. You're hearing the blood pumping inside your head, that's all. It's normal.' The nurse turned, her soft soles squeaking on the linoleum.

It was starting to become clear. Daniel had told lies to make these people keep her here, so he could shack up with that slut he's been seeing behind her back. She tried to rear up again, but her head hurt and things started to swim out of focus.

Her body shook uncontrollably and a burning sweat encased her, followed by a chill that made her teeth rattle. *Oh God, I'm dying.*

For a moment she wondered if she was in fact already dead and her body was making its journey towards an everlasting black hole. She tried to call out again, but nothing happened. No sound came out. She was locked inside the tomb of her own body. Then suddenly, as if a switch in her brain clicked off, she started to drift into a hazy calm.

Don't panic… it's only a dream… you'll wake up in a minute.

Chapter two

Only it wasn't a dream. When she woke again the room was lighter and there were more nurses busying about. Sophie had no idea what day it was or how long she'd been there, but at least the banging in her head had calmed down.

Her mind now felt like a vast expansive landscape, with fluffy clouds and misty mountain tops filling up the space. It was as if someone was playing a children's Disney cartoon inside her brain; serene, gentle, sweet.

Then she heard a woman beside her moan and she shook herself back to reality. She was in bed, in a ward somewhere, with no idea what had happened or what was wrong with her. Had she been taken ill? Had she been involved in an accident?

'Nurse, nurse…'

A face she hadn't seen before came to her bedside. 'Why am I here? What's happened?'

'You'll see the psychiatrist soon. He'll explain everything.'

The nurse had gone before Sophie could take in what she'd said. *Psychiatrist? Why would I need a psychiatrist? Aren't they meant for deranged people?*

She tried to sit a little higher in the bed to see more of what was going on around her. The mound under the bedclothes next to her was writhing, buckling the sheets, bubbles forming at her mouth. Another figure was curled up in a foetal position, another crying out, using words that were unintelligible.

I'm in a ward with crazy people. There must be some terrible mistake.

Then she remembered what the nurse had just said to her. *He'll explain everything – the psychiatrist will explain everything. So there* was an 'everything' was there? *What did that mean? Everything.* She repeated the word under her breath, saying it over and over as if her saying it enough times would reveal its secret. But nothing came into her head – it was blank, floating. Empty.

She started to panic. *What has happened? I need to know. I can't remember.* She called out, but no one came. Nurses went by, but none bothered to stop. She huddled under the covers, her fingers in her mouth, frightened, alone. Waiting.

Sophie dragged herself into a slumped sitting position when a man in a white coat came to her side. He shone a light into her eyes, asked her to follow the path of his finger, then pressed and prodded her as if she was an avocado at a market he was thinking of buying.

'What's happened? What am I doing here?' Her mouth was dry. She was fighting to make the words come out in the right order.

'Don't distress yourself. Try to get some sleep.'

Sleep?!

'I need to know what's going on. I can't *sleep!*'

The doctor turned away and was gone.

What is wrong with these people? Why can't I get a straight answer?

She drifted in and out of a shallow unsatisfactory doze until a few hours later, when Rose came to help her out of bed.

'Can you walk or do you need a wheelchair?'

Sophie got unsteadily to her feet, determined to walk. It took her an age to get her arms into the sleeves of her dressing gown and while she struggled, the nurse gathered her things together. It took Sophie that long for her brain to grasp that she was leaving the ward and being taken somewhere else. Her heartbeat was thudding inside her ears again. *Someone must have come to take her home. Thank you, thank you!*

After they'd traipsed along several corridors it became clear that they were burrowing deeper into the heart of the hospital, not making their way towards an exit.

'Where are you taking me? What's going on?'

'You've been under observation for a while. Now we need to take you to a new unit where you can get better,' said Rose.

'Get better? I don't understand. I want to go home.' Her legs felt like they were made of paper; every step was like wading through jelly.

Entering a large room, she saw other women sitting in high-backed chairs staring vacantly out of the window. It was like an old people's home except not one of them had grey hair. Rose indicated an armchair by the window and helped Sophie to sit on the edge of the seat. She shivered. The place stank of urine; it seemed to be embedded in the carpet and in the cushions.

'You're not leaving me here…' cried Sophie.

A drawn out moan behind them was punctuated by jolly chatter from a game show on the television.

'Someone will come for you in a minute,' replied Rose. 'You won't be on the ward any more – it'll be much better.'

Sophie blinked and when she looked up a new stranger had appeared, holding out her arms ready to lift her to her feet again.

When Sophie reached her room it was already occupied by a younger mixed-race woman, who had hair cropped so short that patches of her scalp showed through. Her skinny arms were a blue tangle of serpent tattoos. She watched Sophie furtively from her bed.

'Shareen, this is your new room-mate, Sophie,' said the nurse.

'Welcome to hell, darlin',' said Shareen with a leering grin. She looked down. 'Nice bag.'

Sophie thought she looked like a 'Shareen'; her name falling somewhere in that working class wasteland between Sharon and Eileen. Then she cursed herself for being so mean.

Rose pointed out the shower and toilet in the connecting cubicle. There was a case on the second bed.

'Someone brought some things in for you,' said the nurse. 'It's locked so you can't unpack just yet,' she added, before pulling the door closed.

Sophie hovered over the case, trying to ignore the figure behind her. She then realised that keeping her back turned wasn't going to be possible in this narrow space for long. She turned round and sat down on the mattress. It was all wrong. Shareen looked like she'd come straight from cardboard city under Waterloo station. *What am I doing in a room with this… down and out?*

Shareen was picking her toenails. 'What you in for?'

'I've no idea. There must have been a mistake.' The top blanket was coarse under her fingertips. She still had no sense of how long she'd been there or why she'd been dumped there in the first place. She didn't feel safe. This had to be Daniel's idea – to get her out of the way. So he could be with that… bitch.

'You're posh. They're gonna eat you up alive when you get to prison.'

Sophie shot upright. *'Prison?'* she yelped, almost choking on the word. 'I'm not going to prison. I told you. There's been some dreadful mix-up.'

Shareen snorted.

Sophie noticed a pair of socks floating in water in the sink.

'Why are *you* here?' she asked.

'My dad's flat caught fire and the corner shop where I worked went up. And other places… got burnt down.' She was now checking her fingernails and sounded like she was describing a boring weekend. 'Some people died.'

Sophie's mouth fell open and she tried to hide a shudder. *Why have they put me here… with this crazy lunatic?* She glanced at her suitcase and imagined all her designer clothes going up in flames, the room filling with choking smoke.

'I haven't done it for a while, so don't worry,' Shareen added.

Clusters of posters and photographs were stuck to the wall above Shareen's bed with sticky tape. 'How long have you been here?' Sophie asked.

'Dunno. I've been here and in prison and back in here again.' She turned her wrists towards Sophie, exposing the criss-crossing of old and recent scars that were competing with the swirls of her tattoos. 'I do… other stuff, as well.'

Sophie felt her head begin to spin and leant back against the wall as Shareen continued, 'It's not bad in here, though. You can play pool. I'll give you a game.'

'What day is it?' said Sophie.

'You *have* been on a blinder, sugar,' said Shareen. 'It's Friday, February the sixteenth. That's 2018, in case you're wondering.'

Sophie tried to backtrack to the time before she found herself here. There had been some kind of incident in the street near the house. Daniel had been lying on the floor in the kitchen. She knew that much. But linking up the events with what was happening now was impossible. It was like looking out over a sea of fog. There were swirling shapes, faces, people in white coats, but no sense of time passing and no solid memories. Then she felt something tugging inside her mind, trying to get through; something important.

'Ben! Where's Ben?' she said, clawing her way to the edge of the bed. 'Where's my son?'

Oh my God – why hadn't I thought of him sooner? Has something happened to him? Is he hurt?

Shareen shrugged. 'Dunno, darlin'. He's not in here, that's for sure.'

Sophie put her hand over her open mouth.

'He needs me. He's only three and a half. He needs to know where I am.' She began pacing up and down, turning every three steps because the space was so small.

'Sit down, you're giving me a headache.'

'I don't know why I'm here.'

Shareen laughed. 'It must be something bad. They don't put you in here for minor offences.'

She tossed the final word around in her mouth.

'Offences? What do you mean?'

'You really have been out of it, sunshine. This, here, is a secure psychiatric unit.' She sniffed loudly. 'You're here because you're too nuts to go to prison. This is rehab, sugar. You must have heard of that.'

'Rehab. Rehab.' She played with the word, knowing it was something she'd heard of, but unable to work out how it could possibly play any part in her life.

'You must have been arrested and they realised you weren't right in the head. That's how it happened with me. You'll stay here until your case comes up in court. You'll get to see a psychiatrist and a little nurse will follow you around.' She walked two fingers through the air, by way of demonstration.

'But I haven't done anything…' protested Sophie, screwing up her eyes, pulling at her hair, trying to reach into the past. *February the sixteenth? Is that what she said?*

She sat on the edge of the bed, staring into space, waiting for something to fill up the vacuum of the days she'd lost.

'I'm looking forward to seeing what you've got,' said Shareen, pointing to the locked suitcase. 'You look like my size.'

Even if she could open it, unpacking was the last thing on Sophie's mind. That would mean she was *staying* and that couldn't possibly be happening.

She sat on the bed staring into space while trying to recall what had happened, wringing her hands together, scared, frantic about Ben. She tried to picture the house when she'd last seen it. The kitchen. She'd been in the kitchen. There had been all those people in the house. They'd turned up suddenly from nowhere. Their faces… they looked concerned, shocked… something bad had happened. Something *bad*… maybe it hadn't been down the street.

Her train of thought was broken as another nurse came in to unlock her suitcase and check through the items. Sophie folded her arms and watched as the woman drew out tweezers, scissors and nail clippers and put them on a small tray. Everything sharp. She looked as if she was equipping herself for emergency surgery somewhere else in the building. The nurse also checked the existing contents of the room, and as she watched, Sophie noticed that even the mirror above the sink was made not of glass, but of reflective metal sheeting, the kind you find in public toilets.

That night, Sophie was aware of every minute sliding by; night-time taunting her with its silent, timeless, never-ending void. She fretted, jolting from side to side, trying to remember what had happened. She could hear the other woman opening containers under the bed as she fingered Sophie's belongings, but she didn't care. Shareen could have everything she'd got.

The fluorescent light from the corridor forced itself under her closed lids without respite, turning what should have been an enveloping darkness into one long bright tunnel.

Chapter three

Dr Marshall was staring out of his office window when she walked in. He swung his seat round and without speaking, indicated she sit opposite him on a simple soft chair. His seat, she noticed, was tall and leather and encased him like the shell of a beetle. If she'd met him in other circumstances, she might have assumed he was a barrister or court judge. Impassive, even aloof. More at home with books than people. He opened a file and read to himself through half-moon lenses.

'How are you settling in?' he asked, peering over the glasses.

'*Settling in?*' He made it sound like her first week at boarding school.

'Do you know where you are? How long you've been here?'

'I think there's been a mistake.'

Dr Marshall smiled and removed his glasses. He rested them on his notes and made a bridge with his fingers.

'Let me give you the facts, Mrs Duke. Sophie, if I may?' he said, not waiting for her consent. 'You're in Maple Ward, part of a secure unit in Moorgreen Hospital in Croydon. Two doctors agreed that you have been suffering from mental disorder. You were delirious and unable to walk or talk. You have been remanded here by the Court, under section 36 of the Mental Health Act.'

'I've been sectioned?' She'd heard the word, in connection with people who were seriously deranged or suicidal. *Not me*, she said to herself. *I'm not one of them.*

'You were initially admitted to Keeley Ward on February the fourth, for observation and initial treatment,' he continued, 'and you've been here at Maple Ward for the last ten days.'

Sophie stared at the calendar on the wall behind Dr Marshall's square head. *Over two weeks in all.*

'Did I black out? Did I collapse? I don't understand. I don't remember.'

'Mmm…' he said unhelpfully. 'Like last time, I'd like to record the session. Are you happy for me to do that?'

She couldn't remember a 'last time'.

She nodded and watched as he clicked the touchpad on the laptop on his desk. 'I need to know what happened… can't you tell me?'

He shook his head.

She jumped to her feet. 'I can't remember anything apart from strangers suddenly rushing into the house.' Her voice rose sharply in pitch, edging close to hysteria. 'Were we burgled?'

She cleared her throat. *Stay calm.* She'd got this far. She didn't want him sending her back to the ward.

He flapped his hand, directing her to sit down. 'You know that we have to speak again about the crime you committed and find out a bit more about why that happened. Do you understand?'

She sank down with a frown. 'Crime? No, no, I don't understand.' She reached forward and snatched a tissue from a box on his desk.

'When we spoke before, you said you couldn't remember what happened to your husband on the last day you were in the kitchen with him. I wanted to ask you again about that time. Just try to answer my questions the best way you can.'

Although Sophie was silent, inside her head it sounded like an orchestra was tuning up.

'Your husband was in the kitchen, wasn't he? Do you remember how you were feeling at that time?'

Sophie stared ahead of her, desperate to bring the kitchen to life in her mind. Her husband. Daniel. She heard her own breathing; heavy, laboured. Something was clawing at the closed door of her memory, trying to break through.

'Angry,' she said triumphantly, screwing the tissue into a ball.

'Ah, good.' He sat back. 'Angry about what exactly?'

'That he'd been… that he is… you know, having an affair. I was shouting at him.'

There was something else. Something much worse than shouting, but she couldn't see it, grasp it.

'And the anger you felt – tell me about it.'

'It was very intense… I could hardly see. I couldn't think… I was shaking. It was all a blur.'

'Then what?'

She sent out her bottom lip, thinking. 'There were people suddenly in the house. I felt sick. I was crying. Feeling dizzy.'

'Something happened before that though, didn't it? Before all the people arrived.'

She bit her lip, feeling like the one child in class who hadn't done her homework.

'Do you remember picking up the knife?' he asked.

She didn't hesitate. '*Knife*? No!' She planted her feet down, ready to launch herself upright again, but rocked forward instead. *Hold on.*

'You don't remember turning to face your husband with the carving knife in your hand?'

She let out a tiny pained squeak.

He leant closer and in a softer voice asked: 'Do you know it was *you* who stabbed your husband?'

Stabbed your husband.

The words punched the air. Had she heard him correctly? *Is Dr Marshall talking to me?* His voice seemed to be coming in and out as if someone was playing with the volume control. *The carving knife. Stabbed your husband.*

There was red paint on the floor. No. Maybe, it wasn't paint.

'Oh, God,' she said, a band of sweat creeping across her forehead as she spoke. She bowed her head and started to sob.

New shapes straightened out inside her head, like jazzy pixilation on a screen clearing into recognisable shapes. Dreadful, terrifying images that should only belong in horror films.

'I can… see something… now,' she whispered, in breathy tearful bursts. She sat on the edge of the chair, her hands pressed to her face. 'Pictures in my mind. Pictures of Daniel on the floor with… blood everywhere. Blood on my hands. In my hair. The knife in my hand.' She snatched a breath. 'Did I do that? Was it really me?'

'You recall seeing the knife in your hand?'

She let out the loud howl of an animal caught in a trap. 'It's a picture in my head. I can see it, but it's not real. I don't remember… doing it… holding it.' She began to find it hard to breathe, wanting him to stop.

Her fingers were hooked over the desk in front of her, clutching on as if afraid she might take off and be hurled into space. Her head was throbbing. The images in her mind were pretending to be memories – hounding her, taunting her. *It wasn't real. Was it?* Surely it can't have happened the way Dr Marshall said?

'It's like a dream, not a memory,' she added.

Then came a moment of ice-cold clarity, the first she'd experienced for days. 'Are you saying I *killed* my husband?'

'No,' he said, tentatively.

I knew it! Someone else was responsible for whatever he was making a fuss about.

She *saw* something. That was it. She was a witness to a dreadful attack, but she didn't *do* anything. It was someone else.

'Your husband isn't dead, Sophie, but it was a close-run thing.'

Chapter four

Sophie wanted Dr Marshall to stop. She needed to put the whole day on pause and get away. Run. Hide. Escape. But still his voice went on and on.

'... and your husband had luck on his side, but he's still in intensive care.'

Her forehead crumpled. It was too much to take in.

Close-run thing. Intensive care.

The walls of the cramped office shifted inwards a fraction. The yucca plant, crippled through lack of light, slid a little closer. So too, the wastepaper basket, the standard lamp and the bookshelf. Her whole world was shrinking. Dr Marshall didn't appear to notice.

He carried on. More questions. Endless probing. 'You said your husband was having an affair. How did you find out about that?'

'The letter...' Sophie was fighting to get the facts straight and in the right chronological order. It was like trying to catch bubbles floating past in a strong breeze. 'It was September. I came across the love letter first. It was in the pocket of Daniel's gardening jacket, hanging inside the shed.'

As she spoke, her memories from before the incident tumbled back in a rush of complete and utter clarity. Like watching scenes from a film. She sat up straight, blinking fast.

'We had a few people over and I was looking for tea lights for a dish on the patio. Daniel is always putting things in the wrong place – he's very disorganised like that. I knew he'd bought some; I'd seen them on the kitchen table.'

'And you confronted your husband with this letter?'

'It wasn't as simple as that. I was in shock and my first instinct was to stuff the letter back, because all these people were there. At bedtime, when I went back to retrieve it, it had gone. I started checking through his things after that, and a few weeks later I found a sexy bra and pants he'd bought – not my size. He happened to be away at a conference, so I left them in his drawer until he got back.'

'Did you tell anyone?'

'No, I didn't want to say anything to anyone until I'd had it out with Daniel. I was humiliated and kept hoping there'd be some misunderstanding. But once he was back, I went to his chest of drawers and they'd gone.' She huffed a little sigh. 'There was a signed photo of a woman in his suit pocket and condoms in his gym bag, too. The same thing happened. Before I had the chance to confront him with them, they'd gone.'

'And this happened over a period of weeks?'

'Yes.'

'But you had nothing to show Daniel. There was no actual proof in the end.'

'That's right, but I'd *seen* everything. He must have known I was on to him. He must have hidden things, taken them to work, maybe. I kept going on at him… wanting answers, telling him what it was going to do to Ben. But – and this is the thing that *really* gets me – he kept saying he didn't know anything about it! Every time.' Sophie could feel her cheeks burning and her palms getting sticky.

'And, how did you feel about that?'

'I told you, I was angry. Furious. Of course I was, wouldn't you be? I still am. Why didn't he just admit it, so we could deal with it?' She was starting to feel self-righteous now, resolute. 'All the arguing. It wasn't good for Ben. I didn't want him finding us lashing out at each other.'

'Lashing out?'

'Well. Only verbally…' She avoided his eyes.

'Did your husband ever hurt you? Get physically violent with you?'

'No, never.'

'And you'd never tried to hit or attack him, before?'

'Absolutely not. Never. I'm not that sort of person.' She realised her claim sounded stupid in the light of what Dr Marshall was accusing her of.

'You have no history of violence,' stated the psychiatrist, 'in fact your family say quite the opposite. They describe you as warm, generous, devoted, self-disciplined and always concerned for others.'

Fresh tears flooded her vision. *Yes – that was who she really was.* The faces of her parents flashed into her mind; confused, mortified, trying to make sense of what had happened.

He frowned as he closed her file. 'There is something I really don't understand about this.'

Her mind shuttled on to a new thought. 'When can I see my son?' She reached out a twisted hand towards him.

Dr Marshall smiled, but the gesture wasn't warm. It was the dry smile of a man who wasn't about to give her what she wanted.

'Soon…' he said. 'You'll be able to see him very soon.'

She ground her teeth, but stayed quiet. There was no point in causing an uproar. It wouldn't help her – she knew that much.

'Okay. Just one more thing before we finish.'

He stood up and pulled out a drawer in the filing cabinet. 'I've got some sheets here I'd like you to look at. I'm going to put them in front of you and I'd like you to tell me what you see. Tell me the first idea that comes into your head. Here's the first one.'

He placed the card showing a haphazard black inkblot into her hand. She gazed at it. For a moment she forgot what they'd just been talking about. She looked at the card. It reminded her of the boards they'd used in a psychology class once at university.

'I've seen this before,' she whispered. 'It's blood.'

'Okay. And this one? You can turn it round if you like.'

'It's obvious. That's more blood.'

'And this?'

Sophie cocked her head on one side. 'That's a pool of blood.' All ten shapes looked the same to her. Blood and nothing but blood, everywhere.

'Let's leave it there, today.'

Sophie breathed a heavy sigh and pushed the damp tissue back up her sleeve.

Chapter five

Daniel stood in front of the hall mirror examining his ribs. Or more to the point, the new pink snake of skin running between them. Half an inch to the left and he would have been in the company of angels, the specialist had told him. Half an inch that separated life from death – about the width of Ben's thumb.

The phone rang and Ben padded out of the lounge. 'Dingy-Dingy, Daddy…'

'All right, Ben, I've got it,' he said.

Daniel hadn't been able to pick up the phone until today. Since he was released from hospital, he'd let the answerphone do the job for him. He'd selectively called people back, but to be honest, not many. He couldn't bear to face the questions, the gasps of disbelief as he stumbled through what had happened.

'Hi, Dan, how's it going?' Daniel knew it was Rick straight away. He was the only person who called him Dan since school, and he hated it.

'Okay… you know. Sorry I didn't return your calls.'

'No worries, mate.'

'Mum said you came to see me in intensive care.'

'You weren't very chatty.'

Daniel blew out a heavy breath and realised how tired he was. A thick, heavy exhaustion he'd been unable to break through since the attack.

'How are things… since you… since she…?'

'Getting used to things – sort of.' Daniel was lacking the energy to put on a brave face. 'Actually… pretty grim, I still can't get my head around it.'

'It did seem… a bit out of character. Your mother filled me in at the hospital.'

Daniel laughed out loud at Rick's understatement. He sank to the bottom stair in the hall and felt the wash of truth threaten to drown him once again. He'd never seen Sophie's eyes on fire like that before. It wasn't her at all. It was an impostor, a demented demon who'd climbed into her skin the second he'd turned away to butter the toast.

'What happens now?' came Rick's voice again.

'I have no idea.'

Daniel still found the entire episode too far-fetched to process. She'd wanted him dead. There was no question about it. His beautiful, elegant wife. The woman he could always spot in a crowd, no matter where they were. Not because of her height – at five seven, she was barely above average – or even her hair, a curtain of tumbling gold. It was something about her presence. There was a grace and glow about her, a mystical aura like a special spotlight around her that he'd never witnessed with any other woman.

He gripped the rung of the banister. She wasn't the Sophie he'd encountered that afternoon. In their own kitchen. He hadn't recognised the feral screams that spewed out of her distorted velvety lips. That face. All contortion and ugliness. He'd never seen those angular, robotic movements before; the savage hatred driving the muscles in her slender arm as she lunged at him, the carving knife twinkling in the sunlight.

He pulled himself gingerly to his feet and walked into the lounge. He was never going to shake those images from his memory.

'It's all been some dreadful misunderstanding,' he said, his voice weighed down with a sigh.

'Bit more than a misunderstanding, mate. I mean, let's face it, she tried to—'

As usual, Rick had rushed into a sentence without thinking about how it would end. He stopped himself in time and changed the subject. 'You back at work, yet?'

'No. Next week. It'll be good to get back. Establish some kind of normality. Just mornings to start with, then I can collect Ben from nursery and make sure I spend lots of time with him.'

'Have you seen her? What's the latest?' Rick kept picking. He wouldn't let it lie.

Daniel sank onto the sofa and watched Ben setting wooden blocks on top of each other. Since his brush with death, it was hard to let Ben out of his sight.

'She's in a secure unit for the time being. I've asked to see her but the specialist said leave it a day or two. She's seen various doctors, psychiatrists. She's on some sort of antipsychotic tranquillisers.'

'Ah, man, that's tough.'

'Well, it's the right place for her at the moment.' He pulled a cushion onto his lap and cradled it. 'It's not so much that I ended up in intensive care – it's the fact that she could attack me in the first place. That's what really hurts.'

'Too true, mate. It isn't how Sophie is… *who* she is…'

'I don't know where she got the idea from in the first place.'

'Idea?'

'She got it into her head I was seeing someone else. Claimed she'd found things to prove it.'

'What things? Did she show you?'

Daniel rubbed his forehead. 'No, that's the point. When I asked to see all this so-called evidence, she didn't have a thing. She raked through all my gear, my wardrobe, my cupboards. She pored over my phone, my laptop, convinced there was something there, but she couldn't come up with anything at all. It was all in her head.'

The line crackled for a moment and Daniel wondered if they'd been cut off.

'She's clearly got problems, mate. We just didn't see it.'

The wooden tower toppled over with a clatter and gave Ben a shock. He looked like he was about to cry, but instead he dragged the blocks to one side and started again. Daniel leaned forward and ruffled his son's hair.

'You spoken to Sophie's friends about it?' Rick asked.

'One of her close friends, Greta, is also a work colleague. Seeing her every day, she'd started getting worried about her, but Greta never bothered to mention it to me.'

Rick tutted.

Daniel stared into space. How could he ever put this behind him? He'd seen a vicious, vile side to Sophie that would be impossible to erase.

'You sleeping okay?'

'Not really.'

'Well, we need to get that sorted. I've got some fabulous tablets.'

Daniel shook his head at the phone. 'Nah, I don't like taking anything.'

'These are just herbal, over the counter jobs. Definitely not addictive. Honestly, they're brilliant. I'll get you some.'

Daniel let the air out of his nose in a sigh. 'Maybe. I'll think about it.'

He hadn't meant to confide in Rick to this extent, but he'd felt so emotional and lost lately, it was a relief to pour it out to a familiar voice.

'What you need is something to take your mind off it,' said Rick. Daniel braced himself. 'Like a night at the Stag's Head.'

'That's the last thing I need!' he said, unable to keep the smile out of his voice. Since they'd been teenagers, Rick's answer to everything was to have a drink.

'Oh, mate, come on, it'll stop you being miserable. How about tomorrow night? A couple of bevvies, just the two of us.'

'It's a bit soon.'

'Next week, then, once you're back at work.'

'I'm not sure I can get a babysitter. My mother's been brilliant, but I can't keep asking her. Not when she's had Ben 24/7 so much, lately.'

'Louise'll do it. My sister, remember?'

Rick's sister must have been about seventeen when Daniel had last seen her. She was going out with a boy from Aberdeen and was trying to impress him by learning the bagpipes. She'd got about as far as making the bag wheeze.

Rick had mentioned that she also lived in South London and was producing games for children, which seemed exactly the right job for someone with her natural leanings towards all things immature. She was similar to Rick in that respect – unruly and a bit silly – although he did recall she used to have a way with children. Always in demand as a babysitter, back then. Unlike most teenagers, she wasn't afraid to clamber around on the floor and get her hands dirty.

'She'd be stoked to look after Ben,' said Rick. 'And kids always love her.'

'I'm sure,' he said. 'Only I don't want Ben with someone he doesn't know. Not when things have been so difficult.'

'Get whatshername from next door to do it, then – she's always around, isn't she?'

Daniel knew Rick was trying his level best. When the stabbing news first broke most of his friends and family rallied round to start with, but now that the 'thinking of you' cards had tailed off, he wondered how much of people's concern had simply been curiosity.

Rick, however, was one of the few who'd been several times to see him in hospital, even though Daniel was too sedated to speak to him. Rick was annoying, but at least he was making an effort.

'Have a think about it,' said Rick, when his option for a babysitter was met with silence. 'Ring me back, okay?'

Daniel put down the phone and watched Ben build his tower again. This time it looked like it was going to stay put.

Yeah, maybe it's time, he thought. *Surely, the worst must be over by now.*

Chapter six

Sophie was lying in bed, sticky with sweat and drowning in feverish images. Pictures of Daniel, smiling, with blood oozing from his eyes, kept coming at her. Visions of Ben pushing her away, screaming at her and moments when their two faces blurred together into one; pointing at her, shouting at her, laughing at her. She'd tried putting her pillow at the other end of the bed to avoid facing the harsh square of light in the middle of the door, but the pillow kept slipping onto the floor. *I've got to blank all this out. I'm going to go mad if I don't sleep.*

The next afternoon she was granted stronger sleeping tablets, which took her to a foggier place during the day, but with the redemption of blackout at night. The daylight hours became waking dreams, where she shuffled from place to place and watched her feet move across the floor as though they belonged to someone else.

You've done something terrible, unimaginable.

She could hear the words in her head, but she didn't dare hold on to them. They were just sounds, like someone humming beside her ear.

Walk away.

She wandered into small corners in her mind and allowed the visions she found there to carry her along.

Best not to think too much.

Or try to work anything out.

'Are you going somewhere?'

It was Annie, the nurse who'd been assigned to her, popping up everywhere, acting like Sophie was a shoplifter.

'I wish I was,' Sophie replied.

Annie was short and squat; her black hair that flat unnatural colour women get from trying to cover grey. It was thick and blunt-cut, giving it the texture of brushes you find inside a letterbox. Sophie kept finding her gaze returning to the furry boil on her chin.

'Why don't you watch some television before your husband arrives?' It was more like a command than a suggestion.

Sophie had forgotten Daniel was coming. How could that have slipped her mind? Her memory had been dreadful lately. It was like trying to hold water in her hand – everything kept slipping through her fingers.

Annie pointed in the direction of the dayroom and Sophie had no energy to protest otherwise. She looked like the sort of woman you'd find teaching hockey in a girl's school, thought Sophie, the kind who'd force you to take cold showers in the middle of winter.

Daniel knew he couldn't keep putting it off. Greta had rung to say his wife was in better spirits and was prepared to see him – and today was as good a day as any. He left Ben with Edith, the super-reliable next-door neighbour, and drove over to Moorgreen Hospital in the rain.

As the shiny, wet street corners shuttled past, he began to reflect on living in East Sheen. It was upmarket, innocent and with a lively character of its own. Rather like Sophie herself, he thought, before remembering that what he thought he knew about her was wholly out of date.

Buying a property there had been Sophie's idea and they had a running joke about it being '*Sophie's Choice.*' It was mainly because she'd put in the lion's share of the vast amount of money required. Daniel would never have considered the area, otherwise.

Sophie worked as an editor at Otterbornes, a prestigious publisher of children's books, but although the salary was very respectable, it wasn't the reason for her wealth. She would readily admit to being spoilt growing up. With a diplomat for a father and a mother well-paid as a fashion designer, she'd had her every material whim catered for: a doll's house at the age of five, a swimming pool at seven, a horse at sixteen. Things.

Sadly, however, the one thing she wanted more than any other was her father's attention, his presence, his love, and it was the one thing she never got. He was always away, travelling. It gave her the muted sadness that Daniel saw in her the first time they met. From the start, he'd made it his mission to be the one to change that. He'd been determined to wipe away the melancholy and wrap her in devotion, intimacy, a sense of family and shared joy.

On her account, they didn't even need a mortgage for the double-fronted period property, but she never mentioned the fact to anyone. In her eyes, everything was shared. If they ever had to divide it up in proportion to their actual contributions, he'd barely own the shed, the size of a small wardrobe, in the back yard.

The windscreen wipers batted the rain from side to side in an uneven rhythm as he got caught up in traffic near Morden Underground station. Since the attack, Daniel's feelings about the house itself had changed. For one thing, the interior seemed darker, seemingly robbed of daylight and even though it was early spring, he was forever having to switch on the lights.

A thickset male nurse guided Daniel into a small private room and he was asked to wait. When the door opened again, he gaped at her, his mouth open. He barely recognised her. She had on a loose-fitting tracksuit and trainers; items she never wore. She tottered slightly as though the ground was sloping away from her and she'd lost weight, making her already size eight frame appear verging on anorexic.

When they first got married, Sophie used to wander around the house in a permanent state of virtual undress, in flimsy, see-through négligées. It had him constantly aroused as she brushed a chiffon sleeve or loose belt against him with a coy smile. Everything about her was sexy. The way she swung to one hip to wash the dishes, sashayed upstairs or leaned over to draw the curtains. Even her handwriting was seductive, which curled and looped like the lettering on a luxury box of chocolates.

But there was none of that allure now. She looked like an older sister who'd spent weeks lost at sea.

She tilted her head as if listening to the rain outside. She'd always been excited by heavy rain. She said a storm always took her back to when she was small. She would sit with her mother in their conservatory while raindrops pattered to a hammering din on the glass, then slid down making feathery waves into the gutters. Even recently, at the sound of rain, she'd stand wherever she was, indoors or out, to listen as it crescendoed into a roar, revelling in the noise.

Now, she seemed slightly flustered by the commotion.

They were directed to sit on hard wooden chairs on either side of a yellow table, the functional type you'd find in a canteen at school. Gearing himself up emotionally for his visit had wiped him out and he felt ill at ease. Intimidated by the lack of privacy. The over-large mirror on the wall was bound to be two-way so the powers that be could watch their every move.

They're worried she'll try again.

He closed his eyes as if repelling the idea that she was some kind of threat.

Once left alone, she spoke first. 'You've got to get me out of here.'

Daniel bit his bottom lip, uncertain how to respond.

'You need help,' he said. 'You tried to kill me.' His voice came out matter of fact, as though he was addressing a child.

'I'm not sure what happened,' she said, faltering. 'I admit I... well, I'm not certain what I did, but—'

Daniel slowly unbuttoned his shirt and slid the linen to one side. 'This is what you did, Sophie.'

She snatched a breath and pulled back with a shudder.

'That was me?' She leant forward, peering at the scar as if it had a life of its own, then sat upright. 'You were having an affair,' she snapped.

'No. Whatever you think you found, it had nothing to do with me.' He couldn't remember how many times he'd uttered those words in the months before she attacked him. They might as well be on a recorded loop.

'The evidence speaks for itself,' she said firmly. 'You were seeing someone. Maybe you met her on one of your weekends away for work – I don't know. I refuse to say her name, but it was there on the letter. A real person. A woman you slept with. *Kept* sleeping with. I don't want to hear you deny it any more.'

Daniel folded his arms over his open shirt and shook his head.

'You're ill, darling. There *was* no letter. No lingerie I'm supposed to have bought. We looked through my text messages, my emails – there was nothing there. You were stressed, you got yourself into a state and went for me.'

Daniel cupped his hands over his eyes. The heating was on too high and he wanted to get out. Even if he *had* been having an affair, how could she not see that nearly killing him with a carving knife was far worse? How could she be getting things so out of proportion?

'I need time to sort myself out, that's true,' she said. 'My head's not right and I keep getting in a muddle. But I know what I saw. And I also need time to think seriously about our future. *My* future with Ben.'

He couldn't believe they were speaking to each other like this. Until a few months ago, Sophie had been the sweetest, gentlest person he had ever known. When she came home from work, she'd look at him in the same way people do when they spot their suitcase on an airport carousel. She'd fling her arms around him like a toddler whenever he walked into a room, kicking off her shoes to make him lift her off the floor. She'd be eager to sit close when they ate supper together, unable to speak without touching him, rattling on about her day, energised and fresh in his presence. Every day. Never anything less than innocent and loving.

Then everything changed. She started turning her back on him, avoiding him, slamming doors, yelling at him, slinging insults and abuse.

It had been like watching milk left out of the fridge slowly curdling. Over time she had thickened, hardened and eventually become offensive.

Then this. Blood. Intensive care. A psychiatric hospital. The entire situation was unthinkable.

'We can talk. We can work this out. I—' He had his tongue poised between his teeth, about to say *I love you*, but the words wouldn't come out. A hollow silence took their place.

'I need to see Ben,' she said.

'I'll bring him next time I come.'

'No. Not you. Get someone else to bring him. Not unless you stop lying to me.'

He dragged at his hair. 'I don't know what else to say to you.'

'Well, that's it, then.' Her chair shot back and tipped over with a clatter. 'If you're not going to be an adult about this, if you're going to keep on pretending the affair never happened, then I'm not going to speak to you. At all.'

With that, she swivelled on the spot, then stormed towards the door.

Chapter seven

Shareen was lying on the bed when Sophie came in. She burped, then turned towards the wall. There was a smell like bad eggs.

'I've got the squits. I shouldn't use the bog for a bit, if I were you.'

Sophie wanted to scream. She was convinced Shareen had been using her towels; they weren't wet when she'd left the room. Now they were stuffed over the radiator, emitting steam. Her hairbrush was on the window ledge, too, not at the sink where she'd put it. She didn't want to make a fuss, however, because she wasn't sure what Shareen was capable of.

'What you been up to?' Shareen demanded, opening one eye.

'Nothing.'

Sophie wanted to stamp her feet, smash her fist into the wall and hurl the chair through the window. She wanted to toss this stupid girl out of bed and into the corridor. She wanted to lock the door, reclaim her privacy, find a way to sort her head out *on her own*. But there was not a trace of energy in her body for any of it. She could barely blink without feeling exhausted. It was all she could do to turn and silently leave the room again.

'Anger management class – first floor.' It was Annie creeping up on her again. It must be Wednesday. Sophie hadn't realised another day had been and gone. She made her way to a room on the first floor. A woman with a strange accent and large feet stood at the front. Sophie looked around the circle and saw old, drawn faces on young bodies. *This can't be happening to me.*

She found an empty chair and sat staring at her hands, cupped together in her lap, and didn't say a word. She hoped it might look like she was praying.

In those moments, her head was filled with questions about her son. They batted backwards and forwards like a manic game of tennis. She wondered what he was doing; if he was playing with his Toy Story play phone; if he was wearing the new blue sailor-style trousers she'd bought him.

Who is taking care of you?

Whose neck are your little arms reaching out for?

Are you missing me?

She felt a tear stray down her cheek and quickly brushed it away.

She might be getting her days mixed up and forgetting things, but one thing was clear. Although she was being given sedatives and sleeping pills, her mind was far sharper than it was. At the beginning, none of her thoughts were moving in straight lines; they were firing off in tangents all over the place, like the silver balls inside a pinball machine.

Now, she was more in control.

Got to stay strong.

Got to keep my head together and work out what on earth has been happening to me.

And most important – I've got to get out of here.

Chapter eight

Daniel wondered if anyone could tell that today was his first attempt to pretend his life was just the same as it was before.

In many ways, he was surprised he still existed. Death had hovered like a bee outside his open window in intensive care. It had buzzed and circled around, poised to come in – then for some unknown reason, had thought better of it and flown away.

Leave the house, walk through the side streets to the Lion Gate at Kew, then through the gardens to the laboratory. That's all he had to do. He'd done it a hundred times before, but right now it felt like a new challenge he'd never previously attempted.

Since he'd been discharged from hospital, Daniel had rarely left the house. He hadn't felt strong enough to see what the outside world looked like. His mother had driven over regularly to collect Ben when what little get-up-and-go he had fizzled out – and life had passed him by.

Before he left that morning, he glanced around to see if he was leaving the place reasonably tidy. He wasn't a hoarder, nor was he messy, but he did have a tendency to put things in the wrong place. Scatterbrained, Sophie called it. She was always teasing him about it; the way things migrated from room to room.

'A comb will start off in the bedroom,' he'd overheard her say to a friend, 'then make its way via the bathroom, glove compartment of the car, to the kitchen and shed within twenty-four hours.'

He locked the front door, opened the gate and took those first steps. It was one of those mid-March days that signalled the start of spring; the sun low in the sky, taking the chill off the air. There was barely any breeze.

He was looking forward to getting back into a routine; part-time to start with, leaving Ben at the nursery first thing and picking him up mid-afternoon. He had plans to take him to the local park, the pool, the zoo – give him the time of his life. His son had suffered enough during this ridiculous debacle and it was time to put that right.

Kew was quiet when he arrived. The lake inside Victoria Gate opened out in front of him, the palm house behind it, looking like a giant glass lampshade. As he made his way to the laboratory block, thick banks of daffodils and crocuses ran alongside the path and trees were already fleshing out with green shoots and early blossoms. It felt like the promise of a new beginning.

As he entered the lab, he wondered if people would notice anything different about him. Would they spot the line of rolled flesh under his shirt? Pick up the musty disinfected smell of someone who'd spent too many days embalmed in bed sheets?

The first person he recognised was Jayne. It was a good start. She was a reserved, respectful woman who wasn't going to make a fuss. Nor would she probe him for details, then metaphorically smear his private life all over the walls of the canteen.

'Take a look at your desk,' she said with a grin. 'It's the tidiest it will ever be.'

He laughed. The department had a running joke about how absent-minded he was. They found it amusing that he could be so meticulous with his research, but so woolly-headed with everything else.

'Cup of tea?' she said.

'I do love it when you say those three magic words,' he said, as if he'd never been away.

Daniel hoped his smile conveyed his gratitude for her low-key welcome. No big hugs, no wide eyes or honey-coated platitudes.

Jayne had a fondness for black leggings and dainty Laura Ashley smocks that made him think of summer picnics. By now, she was noticeably pregnant. She carried the foetus high under her ribcage and stroked and patted the bump, unselfconsciously.

Sophie, he recalled, had been consumed by never-ending nausea during her pregnancy with Ben. It became a condition to be endured. Jayne, on the other hand, appeared to take it all completely in her stride. She seemed to envelop the unborn child, becoming one with it, carrying on as usual without any limitations or side effects.

As he flicked on his computer, waiting for the kettle to boil in the nearby alcove, he recalled how stunned they both were when Sophie found out she was expecting.

They were in the bathroom and he'd caught her expression in the mirror as he cleaned his teeth. She was sitting on the lid of the toilet holding her stomach as if something grave had happened.

'What's the matter?' he asked her reflection.

'I don't understand,' she whispered. She lifted the pregnancy stick she'd been holding out of sight.

He turned round to face her. 'It's positive?'

'This is the third test I've done. I had to be sure.'

He stared at her, ready to sweep her up and smother her in utter ecstasy. But her frown made him hesitate.

'I'm on the pill – I can't be pregnant.'

The kettle clicked off, shaking Daniel back to the present.

'No one's used it,' said Jayne, handing him a mug with a teddy bear on it, the words *I love my daddy* written on the side. 'I made sure of that.'

'Thank you,' he said, holding her gaze so she'd know he really meant it. He pressed the warm mug against his breastbone and closed his eyes briefly at the memory of Ben's first breath. Then allowed himself to relish the way his son had unexpectedly – and in an all-encompassing way – given Daniel's world new meaning.

He could practically hear Sophie crooning the words: *Ben – our most precious treasure.* Nevertheless, those words seemed to belong to a lifetime ago.

Jayne took his hand and placed it under hers over her bump. It had grown considerably since he'd last seen her. 'How long will you stay... before?'

'I'm seven months now. I'll give it another three weeks and see. I'm on a no-lifting regime and everyone's been very good about it.'

'I'm on that regime, too,' he joked, pointing to his left side, trying to look flippant.

'Martin said you'll be following up the data from the Andes trip.'

He nodded, as they wandered back to their desks. Martin, their boss, had been very understanding about his return to work, letting Daniel dictate his hours and arranging regular check-ins to see how he was getting on.

'By the way,' she said, 'just so you know, Frank finally left me.'

'What?'

'It didn't surprise me. He spent too long pretending to be interested, but he never really wanted... this.' She rubbed the bump, as if to console it.

'I'm really sorry.'

He meant it. It seemed absurd that any man would want to walk away from her. Then he realised that people's senseless behaviour shouldn't shock him anymore.

'Don't tell anyone will you? I don't want people fussing.'

'Of course not.' He felt a warm glow that came with being trusted. It made him see how much his self-esteem had been shattered by recent events.

He took a sip of tea. No one else at work knew how to make a decent strong cuppa – and she remembered he took one sugar.

'You never know how things are going to turn out, do you?' she said. The question referred to her situation, but equally applied to his. 'One minute you're pootling along a country lane admiring the view, the next you're in the fast lane on a motorway, driving the wrong way... and you don't remember how you got there.'

With that, she wandered off to her own desk.

Daniel couldn't agree more. Just seven months ago the ardour between him and his wife had burned like a cauldron. Sex, for her, was an incredible game she wanted to play over and over, where the rules shifted and the rewards got better.

'Hmm, you smell so good,' he recalled her whispering, as she buried her face into the creases in his body. She seemed to love chasing the different perfumes on his skin, as if his frame was a huge platter covered with sumptuous fruits.

Then everything collapsed. Almost overnight, she closed down and refused to let him touch her or see her naked. She withheld everything and when he asked her what was wrong, she huffed and puffed about how he *should know* and how it was *all his fault*.

Daniel found himself playing with the paperknife beside his computer and quickly let it go, as if it was scorching hot.

The rest of the morning was easy, as he lost himself in maps, figures and micro-slides of moss and lichen. Getting to Kew, it turned out, had been the hardest part.

'Okay being back?' said Jayne, as she saw him leave, just after one o'clock.

'Looks like it's a good day. A very good day,' he said.

As soon as he walked away, Daniel realised he'd never be able to make statements like that again without wondering if he'd spoken too soon.

Chapter nine

'Mrs Duke, there's someone to see you,' said Annie, looking pleased with herself.

Sophie had been waiting days for this moment. Aching to hold him. She pressed her sticky palms down her skirt and smoothed back her hair.

'Do I look all right?' she said.

'Perfect.'

A woman entered the room, holding a small boy on her hip.

'Ben! Sweetheart!' Sophie rushed over to greet him. Greta handed him over and stood back.

'Mummy, Mummy,' said Ben, burying his face in Sophie's neck. She held him in a tight embrace, then rocked and bounced him in her arms.

'Thank you, Greta. This is really kind.'

Greta smiled, while shifting her balance from one foot to the other. She didn't seem to know whether to sit, stand or leave them alone.

'I'll give you some time together,' she said, backing away towards the coffee trolley. Sophie found a chair by the window and sat down. Ben pulled something out of his pocket.

'Look, I got this,' he said. 'It's a Well card… Daddy and me did it.' There were lumpy multi-coloured flowers on the front and big letters inside which read *Get well soon, Mummy. XXX*

She swallowed the tight ball in her throat.

'I did the kisses, too.' He proudly pointed to them, as if they were the best bit. He went on to explain where he'd been going with Daddy and Granny and what he'd been doing at nursery. It wasn't long before he asked the big question.

'When are you coming home, Mummy?'

Sophie pursed her lips. 'Soon, I think darling. Soon.'

'You're not very sick,' he said, staring into her face. 'You're not in bed.'

'Mummy is sick in a… hidden kind of way. It's kind of inside.'

'Which part?' He looked at her chest and stomach, as if assessing where the problem might be.

Suddenly, Sophie could barely breathe. She felt hot and flustered, as though someone had wrapped her entire body in a tight plastic bag. She looked up in panic. Greta caught her eye and hurried over.

'I think Mummy's tired now,' she said, taking the boy in her arms. Sophie stood up, swaying, holding her forehead with one hand and clinging to Ben's arm with the other.

'No, don't take him away. I just need a break.'

Greta handed Ben to Annie then put her arm round her friend, guiding her to an armchair.

'Take some deep breaths, you'll be okay.'

Sophie tried that, only the panic didn't pass. She gripped the edge of the chair, slowly drowning.

'Listen, Sophie, I need to tell you… I'm going to Spain with Jerry for a couple of weeks, so I won't be able to bring Ben in for you. I'm really sorry.'

'Oh… don't worry,' she muttered, hearing her own words as if they came from the mouth of a normal, composed person.

All too soon their time was up.

'Say goodbye to Mummy until next time,' said Annie, trying to make his arm flap in a wave, but Ben was wriggling to get free.

'Mummy… want Mu-um-mee…' Ben reached out, his face crumpling. Sophie leant against the wing of the chair and felt the room spinning. Ben started to wail, his cries getting louder and louder. Inside her head or in the room – she couldn't tell which.

'Ben, I'm sorry, so sorry… bring him back… bring my boy back… I'm so sorry… Ben…'

Annie kept walking with him towards the exit, Greta behind her, all three of them looking back over their shoulders. Sophie pressed her hands over her ears and slid down the chair, desperate for the noise to end.

Chapter ten

It felt like a long time since he'd had a night out, though spending it with Rick wasn't his ideal choice. He didn't really consider Rick a friend, more someone he'd hung around with on and off since school. If he was honest, he probably wouldn't have had anything to do with him, if it hadn't been for a particular incident in the schoolyard when he was thirteen.

Daniel had got used to being taunted for being a 'pretty boy', but on this occasion a lad with a switchblade pulled him into a headlock behind the gym block. In the scuffle, the boy took a chunk out of Daniel's cheek with the blade. Rick barged in and saved his bacon before the maniac could take his eye out.

To be fair, it wasn't the only time Rick had stepped in to shield him from envious bullies. From that time onwards, going to school was like being fed to the lions every day. Being reserved and 'in' with the girls had a considerable downside.

Daniel patted his pockets. They were full of useless junk: chewing gum, an old plaster, staples, receipts, a button from his coat.

He tipped the handful out onto the hall table. All he needed were his house keys, wallet and phone in case there were any problems with Edith, who was looking after Ben. What else did he need? Oyster card. Sensible not to drive. He hadn't drunk alcohol since the attack and didn't know what sort of effect it might have on him. Best to play safe and go by bus, maybe get a taxi back. He felt ridiculous; as though he'd forgotten what going for a night out felt like.

He got off the bus near Hammersmith Bridge and made his way to the walkway. Even though it was chilly, it was good to take in the fresh evening air, hear the wash of the tide coming in, get a feel for the buzz of the city, now commuters had reached the end of the week. Simple things he'd missed since his life hung in the balance.

Once he reached the Thames, he turned back to look at the broad sweeping lines of the suspension bridge, repainted with its original colours of gold and sage-green after the IRA bombing in 2000. The lights sent shafts of orange into the water. He was tempted to dawdle and watch the reflections changing shape, but he didn't want to be late.

A thudding baseline reached him long before he opened the side door to the bar. Once inside, he felt like he'd fallen into a threshing machine, the boisterous throng churning him this way, then the other. He spotted chalky faces painted with the St George's cross and it dawned on him that a big match must have just finished at Twickenham.

He nearly turned round and walked out, but there was going to have to be a first time. He gritted his teeth as a surge of heat sucked him through a group of French supporters.

'Hey! You made it,' came Rick's voice from the crowd. 'What can I get you?'

Daniel smiled to himself as he recognised the hotchpotch of styles that characterised the place. Pop art images hung on seventies style wallpaper, while Bowie's Ashes to Ashes played on the sound system. Rick fitted in well here. With his winkle-picker boots and heavy metal ponytail, it was as though he was trying to relive his youth, but couldn't remember which decade he grew up in. A safety pin dangled from one ear, which would have been put to better use holding up his sagging jeans.

Daniel ordered a pint of Tangle Foot, determined it would last him the evening. They passed under domed lampshades in pink and green glass towards an empty table in the corner.

'So, how was your first day back mowing lawns?' asked Rick, bouncing up and down on the highly sprung seat. Rick knew full well that Daniel was involved in botanical research at Kew.

'Not as hard as I thought, actually. It's going to be fine.'

Rick sighed. 'Some people have it easy, man – snipping grass all day.'

Daniel laughed. Rick's sarcasm wasn't new. His ability to shift seamlessly between sharp intelligence and utter childishness had always been his trademark trait.

Rick slid a small box out of his pocket. 'Give these a try,' he said. 'One before you go to bed. Have you sleeping like a baby.'

'I can't afford to slip into a coma,' said Daniel, hesitantly. 'I've got Ben to listen out for.' He took the packet and tried to read the label, but it was too dark.

'Two will knock you out, but one will let you drift off. Or try a half to start with.' He snatched the packet back and dropped it into Daniel's pocket.

'Okay, cheers. I'm going to have to do something. I'm not getting a wink of sleep since the…'

Rick pulled a face in sympathy. He'd stopped bouncing around, but was now fiddling with a beer mat, peeling off the layers one by one. Daniel couldn't bear people who did that. It took all his willpower not to slap Rick's wrist.

'I'm thinking of moving on from Blakefield High,' Rick declared.

'Didn't you only start there last September?'

'You know me, I get bored easily. Science is blinkin' tedious. It always needs tons of bloody equipment and the little twerps keep setting fire to things.'

'So what now?'

Rick wanted to be an oceanographer when they were at secondary school, but mainly because he thought it would turn out to be one long cruise around the world. Then he wanted to be a meteorologist, but his IT skills weren't good enough. He ended up with a 2:2 at Oxford, but was easily smart enough to have got a first. He barely turned up to lectures and only went to the library once in the final term, because he had a date with one of the assistants. In contrast, Daniel only managed to come away with a 2:1 from Reading after swotting long into the night for months.

Rick took a long gulp of beer and let out an appreciative burp. Daniel saw from his open mouth that Rick was chewing gum and wondered how he could bear to let it spoil the flavour of the beer.

'Last time I saw you, you were thinking about starting an evening class in figure drawing,' said Daniel.

'Only because you get to ogle at nude models. Anyway, I changed my mind. I've decided. I want to be an actor.' Rick was now leaning forward and idly drawing a line in spilt beer on the table.

'Isn't it a bit late for that?'

'I don't see why,' he said stiffly. Rick had never been a huge fan of other people's opinions.

Daniel hid a sigh behind his next sup of ale. At this rate, one pint wasn't going to be enough, after all. Always on the verge of some 'stonking deal' guaranteed to make him rich and famous, Rick could best be described as a chancer. Never satisfied, he spent his time brewing up plans to jump on the latest bandwagon and rake in a packet. In all the time Daniel had known him – twenty years now – the winning schemes had invariably been just around the next corner. Nevertheless, Rick had refused to run out of steam.

A bunch of teenagers nearby were becoming so boisterous Daniel moved his glass away from the edge of the table just in case.

'Kids, eh?' Rick took the gum out of his mouth and rolled it into a ball, before sticking it under his seat.

'You didn't fancy bringing Donna along, tonight?' asked Daniel.

'Who?' Rick looked surprised. 'Oh, her. Haven't seen her in ages. Not my type really. I've never had the same luck with women you've always had.' Rick raised his eyebrows and made a rude gesture with his fist and crooked arm. 'Anyway, enough of that. Let's see your war wound.' He dropped his eyes to Daniel's chest with voracious enthusiasm.

Daniel reluctantly unbuttoned his shirt to get the inevitable sideshow over with.

'Jeez – she really had it in for you, mate,' he said, squinting at it. Rick always managed to overstep the mark somehow. Daniel should have been used to it by now. 'Sorry, mate. Stupid thing to say.'

'Sophie got it all wrong. I've never touched another woman since I met her.'

'Yeah. Absolutely. Still, you must have some cracking memories from Latimer High… every girl's dream, if I remember correctly. James Bond meets Poldark, eh?' Rick ruffled Daniel's thick black hair and pulled him into his shoulder. 'But not Sean Connery, more Pierce Brosnan… or even—'

'Shut up!' said Daniel, only half-joking.

With the warmth of Rick's embrace, Daniel was thrown back to thoughts of Sophie. Since meeting her, he'd left all his conquests in another dimension and only mentioned his 'former playboy' persona in a general, embarrassed kind of way. He'd convinced her of his loyalty, mainly because he was wholeheartedly convinced of it himself. Those days of one-night stands were over for good. Other women had held no attraction for him, once he had Sophie by his side.

She was his Golden Fleece, his Aladdin's cave, his flame in the darkness. And under the duvet, she was the sparkler that erupted into a thousand colours in the night sky.

Without warning, a guy backed into their table, followed by another with a shirt collar hanging off. The second man wiped his nose, smearing blood across his cuff. Daniel turned away.

'Flaming Fishbuckets – it's a punch-up,' cried Rick, gleefully, standing up.

Daniel tried to grab his arm, but Rick was already moving into the fray. Trust Rick to have brought him somewhere that could so easily erupt into volatility.

Within moments, the space in front of him turned into a landscape of legs and elbows, shoving and thrashing at each other. A shoe skidded across the floor and stopped at Daniel's feet. Then a fist swung above him and hammered into a tall man's cheekbone. Rick seamlessly embroiled himself in the scrap, cleverly dodging punches and managing to land a few random swings at no one in particular. He seemed able to bob up and down like a jack-in-a-box, weaving between the mass of bodies without getting hurt.

The frenzied activity around him seemed to be stealing all the air and Daniel could hardly breathe. He needed to get out, but his exit was blocked on both sides.

The grunt of a man as he hit the floor took Daniel straight back to the moment Sophie swung at him with the carving knife. People say that after a traumatic incident, you either remember nothing at all or everything in acute detail. With utter clarity he could still see the plaster hanging off Sophie's left heel and the poppyseed trapped between her two front teeth. Strange what the mind will pick up at a time like that, he thought. Not, *I'm about to die*, but, *she'll need floss to get rid of that black speck*.

He reared up towards the bar to see if anyone was coming to stop the brawl, but all he could see were tangles of body parts. The jukebox was playing *Another One Bites the Dust.* Someone's idea of a joke. With his heart pumping at a rate of knots and his skin breaking out in a sweat, he was going to have to wait it out on the sidelines.

Unfortunately, the man wearing a pink shirt who'd appeared to his left wasn't going to let him. He lunged at Daniel, letting out a drunken battle cry, but failed to notice there was a table in the way. It tipped over, taking the two glasses with it and the man landed face down on Daniel's lap with a snarl. Daniel wanted to push him away, but didn't want to antagonise him. His tender wound had rendered him tentative and vulnerable. He should never have come.

Behind him, Rick was grinning and lining up his foot to kick the man's backside. When the blow hit him the guy crumpled to the floor and lay there, immobile.

'Time to shift our arses, don't you reckon?' said Rick, dusting off his hands. Daniel was scrabbling to escape, acutely aware that Rick had saved his neck yet again. He ducked and dived around those who were still upright, not waiting for Rick. Desperate to get out into the fresh air before he was consumed by his first ever panic attack.

Chapter eleven

Shoving his way through the boisterous crowd, Daniel made it out of the pub door and across the pavement to the wall running beside the Thames. He thought he was going to be sick, but once he filled his lungs with the familiar salty, detergent smell of the river, he calmed himself down.

When Rick bounded outside to find him, Daniel was still shaking and he folded his arms so Rick wouldn't see.

'Same again?' said Rick, looking as though the party had only just started. 'We can drink outside.'

Daniel thought they were leaving.

'No, nothing for—'

Not waiting for a reply, Rick had already disappeared back inside.

Daniel leant over the wall and stared at the tranquil black water. The bridge, to his left, was still humming with traffic. The rhythmical clunk as tyres bounced over the expansion joints, soothing. It wasn't far from here, he recalled, that Sophie had first told him she loved him.

It was three months after they'd started seeing each other. They'd set off on a walk along the towpath from Putney and had been discussing a film, when without warning she'd dragged him into the undergrowth. Even though it was broad daylight and they were close enough to the path to be seen, she feverishly began unfastening his jeans. He put up no fight, of course. She drove him wild teasing him, playing with him, until she eased him onto his back and lowered herself down on top of him, at first gently, then with a greedy, thrusting pulse that made him cry out in ecstasy.

When they fell apart, she'd said those spellbinding words for the first time. *I love you.* Spoken with such depth and seriousness that Daniel almost wanted to cry. A month later, they were engaged.

A shout from inside the pub snapped him back to the present. Lurching out of the door came a figure which dived straight into a nearby bush to throw up. Daniel checked his watch and wished he was at home watching a tame American police drama. This was not the kind of evening he'd had in mind.

Rick eventually re-emerged with a man on either side.

'Look who I've found! This is Dave. Teaches English and Drama at the hell hole.'

Daniel had been all set to call it a night, but now it seemed rude to walk off. Five more minutes, then he'd go.

Dave raised his hand by way of greeting. He was a long way from forty, but already bore the telltale signs of middle age: a beer gut that looked like it was there to stay and shiny patches of wasteland on his temples.

The second man was introduced as Stuart, a theatre friend of Dave's, who wore a bile-green tweed jacket. Daniel noticed a stale smell of charity shops when they shook hands. Rick handed Daniel a dribbling glass and all four of them stood their pints on the wall.

Snippets of conversation suggested Stuart worked in the West End, but Daniel couldn't tell whether he was an actor or backstage and he didn't much care.

Stuart turned to Daniel. 'You known each other long?' His strong Birmingham accent made him sound like he had a permanently blocked nose.

'Buddies now for over twenty years,' cut in Rick.

Dave lit a cigarette. His forehead resembled a stretch of sand, carved into furrows by the wind. Daniel made a mental note to get back into his running as soon as his wound felt less delicate.

'Blimey…' Rick sniffed loudly. 'Makes us sound like a bloody married couple.'

Daniel tried to smile. Marriage was the last subject he wanted dragging into the conversation. He wasn't really listening to what they said next. Although aiming to smile in the right places, his mind had switched channels. All he could see was a cold house, a bewildered son and a vacant future.

That afternoon, he'd made the decision to clear away a pile of Sophie's belongings. He was fed up with being jolted whenever he came across her creams, shampoo, comb, flannel or sponge – personal items saturated with her presence. It was like touching her skin every time and gave him fleeting deceptive assurances that she'd only gone away for the weekend.

So, he'd cleared out the bathroom cabinet and shower, the dressing table and her bedside cabinet, shifting old medication, toiletries, make-up, magazines and paperwork to the filing cabinet in the cellar. He'd taken her insulin out of the fridge and added that to the pile, too. It would be past its use-by date any time soon and best left out of reach of his son's inquisitive fingers. He could always sort things out properly when he wasn't feeling so distraught.

Stuart was looking at him, saying something. He had a permanent layer of fatty sweat over his face and there was something forced about his manner, as if he was trying too hard to be liked.

When Dave suggested another round, Daniel made his farewells. An unexpected cheer from a nearby group took most of Rick's parting words with it. All Daniel heard was: '… decent night's sleep after everything you've been through.'

Dave and Stuart threw a glance at each other and several unspoken questions were left in the alcohol-sodden air, like tiny feathers slowly swinging towards the pavement.

Daniel waved and walked away, pretending he hadn't heard a thing.

He wished Rick wasn't such a bull in a china shop.

Tonight had been something of a rude awakening, but real life didn't come with built-in shock absorbers.

He was going to have to toughen up.

Chapter twelve

Sophie had been waiting by the window, her throat dry, her stomach bubbling in anticipation.

'Here we are,' announced Annie, showing Sophie's father into the dayroom. He was a broad, stocky man, wearing a thick tweed coat and a striped woollen scarf that Ben was nestling into.

Sophie hadn't been able to eat breakfast; she was too excited about seeing her son again, but it was underpinned with a daunting anxiety, sitting like a boulder in her stomach. She desperately wanted to get it right this time. To feel a deep connection with her son, to show him – and her father – what a strong and capable mother she was.

The three of them hugged. Seeing her father was more emotional than she'd thought it would be. His face was barely one shade lighter than the grey scarf around his neck. Sophie lost herself in the woody smell of his coat, reluctant to let go. Ben started to wriggle between them, so her father pulled away and handed him over.

'Hello, sweetheart,' she said, brushing her fingers through his hair and softly squeezing his cheek. 'Hi, Dad,' she said, looking up. 'Thanks for bringing him.'

Ben wanted to show her his new book, so she sat down. Her father dragged his chair closer, looking tired and taking shallow breaths.

'Not very private, is it?' he said, lowering his voice.

'You get used to it.'

He reached out and stroked Sophie's face.

'Look at you – so beautiful, even after all you've been through.'

Sophie took his hand. At last, someone was acknowledging that she, too, might be suffering.

'I don't feel very beautiful.' She lowered her eyes. 'It's been really tough, Dad. I'm so glad you're here.'

Ben tugged at her sleeve. 'Mummy read,' he demanded. Sophie opened the sturdy picture book. It was called *Good Night, Gorilla* and she could see from the first pictures that it was about the antics inside a zoo. Her father joined in as she read, pointing to the vivid illustrations of animals that accompanied the story and making animal noises. Ben laughed and giggled and insisted that Sophie start all over again once they turned the last page.

'In a minute, darling. I need to talk a little bit to Grandpa.'

Suddenly a face appeared from behind Sophie's chair. It was Shareen.

'I can read to him if you like… then you can talk to your old man.'

Sophie leaned away in horror, wrapping her arm round the boy. 'Er… I don't think so,' she said, looking up for Annie, hoping she would rescue the situation.

'I'm Shareen, by the way,' she said, extending her hand towards Sophie's father. 'I share her room.'

Hesitantly, Sophie's father took hold of her hand, a bemused look on his face. 'Vincent Barnes,' he said.

'Sorry, Shareen, but we're having a private conversation here,' said Sophie.

Ben started to fidget. 'Story, Mummy,' he wailed, digging his boots into her thighs. She winced. Her father caught her eye, sending a questioning message back.

Shareen wouldn't go away. 'I could sit right here with the boy, then you can see him,' she said. She sounded like someone on a market stall, trying to convince a customer that the cheap toy she was selling was completely safe.

Sophie wasn't sure. She didn't like the idea of Shareen, with her smelly breath and grubby sweatshirt, getting anywhere near her son.

Vincent puffed out his lips. 'We could give it a go,' he said. 'Would you like this lady to read you the story Ben, if you sit right here in front of Mummy?'

'Story,' said Ben, emphatically, as though there was no debate about the matter.

Vincent lifted up the boy with a wince and sat him on Shareen's lap. Sophie reluctantly handed over the book.

'Okay, so what is this lovely story about?' asked Shareen.

Sophie turned to her father, watching Ben out of the corner of her eye the whole time, expecting him to call out for her at any moment.

'How are you?' he asked, looking deeply into her eyes.

'Better than I was.' She could hear Ben and Shareen already engaged in an animated discussion about the animals in the zoo. 'How are *you*, Dad? When did you last see the specialist?'

He wafted his hand dismissively. 'Let's not worry about that. I'm still here, that's what counts.'

There was a point last year when he'd been given only weeks to live, but somehow he'd weathered the storm, defying all the odds. Sophie knew it wouldn't be a reprieve for long.

'Sorry, Sophie, time for your medication.' It was Annie.

She handed Sophie a small saucer with a syringe alongside two blue pills, a white one, a larger yellow one and a plastic cup of orange squash to wash them all down.

'Don't look, Dad,' Sophie instructed. She lifted her blouse, pinched a fold of flesh and expertly injected the needle into her side.

'I still get squeamish when you do that,' he said, pulling a face. 'Still twice a day?'

'Yeah, it's fine – I don't even think about it any more; it's like cleaning my teeth.' She smiled, realising it was probably the first time she'd done so since the attempt on Daniel's life.

Annie passed her a small capped bottle.

'You're like me,' he said. 'I need a nasal spray every day, now.'

'When I came here they reassessed all my medication. I've got a stronger one than I had before.'

Annie left them.

'I'm so glad you came, Dad... did I say that already?'

He smiled.

'How's Mum bearing up?'

'She's much the same. Still refusing to use a wheelchair.'

Not long after her father's cancer diagnosis, Sophie's mother was told she had MS. She was now at the stage where she was wilfully opposing anything that made her look like she'd given in. But she was fighting a losing battle. Her father couldn't pick her up any more when she fell and the doctors were warning that one day she'd hit her head or break her hip. 'They'll have to hold me down with chains,' her mother had declared when the specialist suggested the wheelchair. 'Because I'm not going in one of those bloody things while I can still breathe.'

'She's been listening to audiobooks,' said Vincent, 'now that she can't hold a novel in her hands.'

'Oh…'

Sophie blinked back tears of shame and remorse. There was so much tragedy in her parents' lives already and now she'd gone and added to it. In the last few days, the clouds in her mind had parted and the truth about what had actually taken place in her own kitchen had finally burst forth into the light. She was still in a state of shock, but she'd admitted to Dr Marshall that she did, indeed, remember stabbing her husband. Despite her earlier protestations, it *had* been her, after all.

'I'm so sorry, Dad. I did a terrible, terrible thing. I don't know how—'

'Shh…' he hummed, as if she was a child he was lulling to sleep.

There was so much left unsaid between them. Questions her father must want to ask. Surely. Poor Dad, he wouldn't know where to start. He hadn't a clue about navigating his emotional world. It made him seem like he didn't have one.

True to form, he changed the subject. 'Oh, she's written another letter, by the way.' He pulled a crumpled envelope out of his pocket. 'She was sorry she couldn't come today, but—'

'It's okay, Dad. I understand. Send her my love, won't you?'

Sophie heard a sharp cry beside her. It was Ben laughing. She turned to look at him, but he didn't look up. Totally spellbound. The story must be better than she first thought.

Ben took an interest in Shareen, running his fingers along the scars and tattoos on her forearm, exploring the rings and stud in her ears and nose. Then they were on the floor, using the empty chairs around them to play a game of hide-and-seek. Sophie asked more about her mother, letting herself relax at seeing Ben so absorbed. Before long, a bell rang to indicate visiting time was over.

'I'll ring you in the week,' said Sophie, wrapping her hands over her father's. 'Don't worry about coming back for a while.'

She couldn't bear the thought of dragging him all that way, again. Anyone could see he was in pain and not at all well.

Shareen joined them, holding Ben's hand.

'You're a natural,' Vincent said to her.

'I like kids,' she said. 'I had one once, but they took her off me. Breaks your heart, don't it?'

She shrugged and moved away towards a group of women huddled over a jigsaw.

'She seems friendly,' said Vincent. 'Looks like she's had a hard life.'

Sophie turned to watch her. Shareen had her hand on the shoulder of a woman who was known to have committed child abuse.

'I suppose so,' she said.

Once they'd gone, Sophie walked over to Shareen. She waited for her to turn round.

'Ben liked you.'

'I'm good with kids,' she replied dismissively. 'It's adults I've got problems with.'

'My father liked you, too.'

Shareen sniffed as if she hadn't heard. 'You on for a game of pool later?' she asked.

'Why not?' said Sophie.

Chapter thirteen

Daniel broke the surface of the water with a gasp. The pool hadn't worked its magic that morning. Ben was annoying the other children. Splashing wildly, he accidently kicked one boy in the face. It wasn't like Ben. The ensuing nosebleed turned the water a bright shade of pink and everyone had to get out.

Daniel had spent an awkward few minutes apologising to the boy's irate mother, then carried Ben, squealing and writhing, into the changing room.

He hadn't wanted to go into detail about Ben's difficult circumstances, but he made a mental note to get hold of some child psychology books from the library, to gen up on what to expect when toddlers are separated from their mothers. He'd have to support Ben through this. He hated the idea of him suffering as a result of Sophie's irrational behaviour.

Today's tantrum would never have happened if Ben hadn't been so self-assured in the water, although it wasn't long ago that his confidence had been severely challenged.

For Ben's third birthday, he and Sophie took him to the beach at Brighton. Ben was one of those children who was fearless around water and he had already mastered a robust doggy paddle in the shallow end at the local pool.

That day, it was windy, and bits of their picnic kept blowing away as they tried to set everything up; first the napkins, then Ben's plastic drinking cup, then the paper plates. Ben was preoccupied building sandcastles a few feet from the water's edge with a couple of older children.

They hadn't invited him, but out of the blue, Rick turned up, claiming he'd come to take a look at a second-hand car and had caught sight of them from the promenade. Daniel knew it was too much of a coincidence; he must have mentioned their plans to him at some point.

Daniel couldn't miss Sophie's look of thinly veiled horror when Rick came jauntily across the sand, all dressed up in a black dinner suit. Aside from being dressed entirely inappropriately – which wasn't unusual in the least, for Rick – he looked like he was all set to join them.

'Would you believe it, I've actually got Ben's present in the car,' he told them, 'I was going to pop round with it later on.'

A few months after he'd come back from his long stint teaching in Australia, he'd been showing up like a bad penny. There was the lecture Daniel had given at Kew at the beginning of September and up he popped at the drinks do, afterwards. Then there'd been a barbecue at Sophie's publisher a couple of weeks later. There he was again, although no one seemed quite sure who'd asked him to come.

Sophie had always made it clear how she felt about Rick, regarding him as a dysfunctional distant relative she felt obliged to put up with, because Daniel felt indebted to him. When Daniel explained his reasons for staying in touch, she made light of it. 'I can see why the lads picked on you at school,' she'd said. 'Being so quiet, studious, good-looking and cute, you were too much of a threat to the other boys!'

Sophie respected his decision and did her best to hold her tongue when Rick was an idiot and downright rude.

'Won't stay long,' he'd said, 'don't want to intrude on the "family outing".'

As things turned out, they were both shamed into overwhelming gratitude over his fluke appearance that day.

Daniel had lost the plastic cutlery and Rick said he'd head over to the beach café to get more. With Sophie chasing flighty airborne food wrappers and Daniel now searching for Ben's lemonade, no one was watching their son. It was one of those awful moments when one parent thought the other would be keeping an eye on him.

Having grown tired of building sandcastles, Ben had been desperate to float on a little boy's blow-up alligator, bobbing around on the water. When he made a fuss, an older boy helped him onto it. Ben was too young, but there was no parent on hand to intervene. He fell off straight away and within a split second got into difficulty. The shallow end of the local pool was one thing, but this was far beyond his capabilities. Ben was too inexperienced to know there were choppy waves and slippery pebbles. And the water got deep so quickly.

Daniel heard shouts and screams and looked up, but Rick was already there. By the time Daniel got to the water's edge, Rick had waded in, still in his suit and best brogues. He scooped Ben under his arm, wrestling him from the water just in time. A few seconds more and it would all have been over. Daniel and Sophie both knew if Rick hadn't acted so quickly, Ben would have drowned.

Since then, Daniel felt he owed him even more.

Ben's tug on his sleeve brought him back to the here and now.

'I'm dry, Daddy,' he said, with a whine.

'Sorry, little 'un. Let's go.'

On the way out of the changing room, Daniel caught sight of his face in one of the mirrors. He stopped to run his hands through his untamed hair, then drew in close when he spotted the half-circles, like bruises, blossoming under his eyes. He really did need a decent night's sleep. He tapped his pockets and found the sleeping tablets Rick had slipped inside when they were at the pub. Maybe tonight he'd have to try one.

Chapter fourteen

The receptionist called Daniel's name and he was shown through into Dr Marshall's office. Daniel pulled up a wooden chair. They'd spoken several times on the phone since he'd been discharged from hospital, but the psychiatrist didn't look at all how Daniel had expected. He was older, smaller, fatter than he imagined and moved stiffly as though his joints needed a thick spray of WD40.

'Your wife is showing signs of improvement – her memory is returning and she seems more lucid,' he said.

'Right – good… that's good.'

The smell of Extra Strong Mints in the room was so strong he could almost taste it.

Daniel looked down at his interlocked fingers. 'She won't see me at the moment, I'm afraid.'

Dr Marshall nodded.

'The affair was all in her head,' Daniel said, louder than he meant to. He cleared his throat. 'I just wanted to make that clear.'

'Yes, you did mention that over the phone, Mr Duke.' He peered at him over his half-moon glasses. 'The nature of your marriage isn't under scrutiny here,' he said, 'I can only comment on your wife's symptoms.'

'Sure.'

'I can't give a name to your wife's condition, Mr Duke,' he said, standing the pages of the file in front of him on end, as though he wanted to shake more information out of them. 'Not simply because labels for people with psychological disturbances are often nebulous and misleading, but because your wife's situation is rather complex.' He laid the pages flat again. 'The closest I can get is to suggest some kind of temporary emotional dysregulation. It appears that the stress of the situation at home led to a psychopathic disorder that may be resolving, now that she has been removed from that environment.' He rapped the cap of his fountain pen on the blotter on his desk. 'I did want to check something out with you, however...' Daniel lifted his head. 'Has she ever, to your knowledge, shown any signs of delusional or otherwise erratic behaviour before?'

Daniel chewed on the inside of his bottom lip – giving the question some genuine thought – and slowly shook his head.

'No. It started when she first decided I was having an affair – around September time – I wasn't, as I said. After that, she changed beyond all recognition.'

'In five months?'

'Absolutely. It was hard to see when I was in the thick of it. She'd always been easy-going and soft-hearted, but with hindsight, she turned into this brittle, defensive and angry creature during that time.'

He felt like he was talking about someone else; a delinquent neighbour or an elderly relative with Alzheimer's – not Sophie, his sparkling, creative, adoring wife.

'I know that Sophie was taking antidepressants before she was admitted, but has she ever taken recreational drugs?'

'Definitely not – she has very strong views about that sort of thing.'

The psychiatrist leant back and squeezed the flesh at the top of his nose between his forefinger and thumb.

'Hmm. Sophie's father gave me a complete history and he said the same.'

'What are you getting at?'

'How long have you been married, Mr Duke?'

'Eight years.'

'How many times have you seen your wife behave aggressively towards anyone?'

'Never. I mean, really... not once. She snaps at me, now and again. Raises her voice. But that's it. She's never raised a hand to

Ben, our son, nor has she ever looked remotely like she was going to slap or punch me.' He laughed at the absurdity of the idea. 'Normally, Sophie can't even bring herself to pull the petals off a daisy in a game of "love me, love me not".'

Dr Marshall tipped his head from side to side.

'People react abnormally under extreme stress, as I'm sure you know. It would explain the hallucinations, the fugue states, and the neurological imbalance when she first came in. But, her condition seems to be improving.' He showed Daniel the palms of his hands. 'I'm sorry I can't give you anything more concrete.'

Daniel jumped to another question that had been on his mind for days.

'What will her sentence be, do you think?'

Again, the doctor's head tipped from side to side. It was making Daniel feel like he was watching a Punch and Judy show. 'I can't really speak from a legal point of view, Mr Duke, but I don't believe we're looking at attempted murder. We've reviewed her situation and she'll be kept here for the time being. With a spur of the moment attack of this sort – grabbing a weapon that was to hand – the charge is more likely to be GBH without intent. It's known as section 20; it carries a lesser sentence than section 18, where harm is deliberately inflicted.'

'And how long is this sentence – this section 20?'

'Again, I don't want to make any sweeping judgements here, but in my experience, with GBH 20, you're looking at a maximum of five years…'

Daniel blew out a raspy breath.

Dr Marshall carried on. 'But in Sophie's case, as we're having trouble diagnosing her mental state, the situation is still inconclusive and her case won't go to court for the foreseeable future.'

Dr Marshall closed the file on his desk to indicate the discussion was over.

Daniel couldn't resist pulling up a stool beside Ben, asleep in his cot. He was lying on his side, his furry rabbit clutched against his chest. Daniel watched his eyelids flutter, listened to his breathing, taking in the vanilla smell of talcum powder.

'Thank God you're safe,' he whispered. 'Out of this terrible mess, I've still got you – the most important thing in my world.'

Ben shifted an arm above his head and let out a little whimper and Daniel left him in peace.

He was about to head downstairs when something on the landing caught his eye. There was a gap on the wall between two small paintings. He touched the bare hook and looked down, checking to see if there were any signs of glass on the carpet. Maybe a frame had fallen off the wall during the time he'd been in hospital. Except who had cleared it up? He shrugged his shoulders. It wasn't a big deal.

Chapter fifteen

D aniel's first thought when the phone rang was to ignore it, but he glanced over to check the number and decided to pick up.

'Hi, Mum.'

'Not disturbing you, am I?'

Franciska was sixty, going on forty-five. Everything about her was passionate and colourful; her richly ornate wrap-around skirts, her desire to make people feel important, her indefatigable devotion to Ben. Daniel put it down to being Hungarian. He wondered how much of it had rubbed off on him. He hoped it ran deeper than just his thick black hair.

'I got the roses – they're lovely,' she said. 'You shouldn't have bothered. I adore having Ben – you know that.' Someone significant was gunned down in the film he had on in the background, but Daniel couldn't remember if he was a good guy or a bad guy. He thumbed the volume down on the remote.

A silence hung between them. There was something else.

'Are you seeing people again, darling?' she said tentatively.

'I'm back at work. And I've been out once or twice.' That didn't seem enough for her. 'Are you worried I'm turning into a recluse?'

She didn't answer him. She was an extrovert who coped with concerns by talking, non-stop, to an array of friends or neighbours. He was the opposite, an introvert, much happier working through things either with Sophie or on his own.

Since the attack, it had become obvious that in the last few years, he'd done what a lot of men do and focused almost entirely on his family. He was 'friendly' with lots of people from university days, his work and through Sophie, but they weren't people he'd call, out of the blue, to invite over for supper, or to arrange a night out. Since getting together, all his 'nights out' had been with Sophie. All his 'nights in', with Sophie, Ben or friends who knew them as a couple. Now that he was on his own, he was in a kind of no-man's-land. He was confused and had a lot on his mind. Probably not good company.

'Why not get back in touch with Yvonne?'

Daniel yawned. Yvonne was his ex-girlfriend. Their last meeting had turned out to be highly embarrassing. He'd been to see her sing in a jazz club, and after the show, he'd gone backstage to be polite, as she'd got him the tickets for free. Sophie had flu and had stayed at home with Ben.

Yvonne offered him champagne, exuberant in post-performance euphoria, and in a moment of abandonment she'd cupped her hand over his. 'I've missed you,' she'd said. 'I never stopped loving you.' Judging by the subsequent look of horror on her face, the words had slipped out before she realised what she was saying.

He'd withdrawn his hand amidst her profuse apologies. During their relationship, it had always been clear that she was the one who had loved him more. For him there had been no real spark; too much like siblings, he'd said to her once – the sister he'd never had.

'Not sure that would be a good idea, Mum.'

'Gordon, then.' A mate from university who sent 'we must meet up' emails every year at Christmas, then never got back to Daniel when he suggested a time and place.

'We've lost touch, more or less.'

'What about Frank, your best man?'

'Moved to Edinburgh.'

'Or Sophie's friend Greta – is that her name? Or Cassandra, that other woman from Otterbornes?'

'They're not people I'd see socially, Mum. Certainly not on my own.' Having said that, getting in touch with Cassandra wasn't such a bad idea, as it happened. For no other reason, however, than to get some answers. He'd spoken to Greta already, but she hadn't thrown much light on Sophie's state of mind. He wanted to know more about his wife's last weeks at work; her behaviours, anything she might have said to help explain what happened. Maybe he'd have more luck with Cassandra.

Franciska wasn't giving up. 'Only because you haven't tried it.'

'Okay,' he said, finally able to appease her. 'I'll give Cassandra a ring, this evening.'

'Oh, good.' She sounded pleased with herself.

He'd lost his way in the film by the time the call ended and he turned it off. Heavy with weariness, he was glad to reach Cassandra's voicemail so he could leave a message, rather than be forced to engage with her.

Then he climbed the stairs to bed.

His eyes drooping, he stopped abruptly as soon as he reached the top. A clammy sense of unease slithered down his spine as something caught his eye. A tiny pile of grit. It looked like someone had shaken a pepper pot on the carpet. He looked up. Directly above was the loft hatch. He stared down at the pile again and back up at the hatch.

When did I last go up there? It must have been months ago, surely?

He couldn't be certain of the last time; his mind had been on so many other things lately. A tremor of shame sunk his spirits even further. He clearly wasn't holding things together as well as he thought. The grit must have been there for ages and he simply hadn't noticed.

Chapter sixteen

The last time he'd seen Cassandra Remington-Slade was close to three years ago. She was one of a number of Sophie's friends who'd stopped coming to the house after Ben was born. They were largely the ones who regarded motherhood as an inevitable misfortune that was best avoided for as long as possible. Any infant was nothing less than a liability. Not only an active danger to hairdos and expensive clothes, but they ruined any decent conversation. Cassandra was one such 'friend'.

Not that Daniel missed her visits. He didn't like using the word, but 'shallow' was the best way to describe her. Greta was different; she'd drop anything if Sophie needed her.

'Sophie does the same for me,' Greta had told him. 'She's a brilliant editor. The best we've ever had. She's got a gift for making people want to work their butts off for her, if that makes sense.'

He could forgive Greta's fondness for adding 'if that makes sense' to the end of virtually every sentence. He could even overlook Cassandra's pungent perfumes. But he couldn't turn a deaf ear to her obsession with calorie counting and nail polish and a conversation loop that should be marketed as a potent sedative. It revolved around Prada, fake-tanning products, the disparaging of bling and back again.

Sophie put up with it because she prided herself in office harmony.

'She has other strengths,' Sophie had said once, doing her usual trick of seeing the best in people.

Cassandra had agreed to meet Daniel after work. It was raining hard and Daniel stood under an umbrella outside Otterbornes' main door in Holborn, idly looking at the window display of new children's books they'd just released. He recognised one of the titles: *The Ogre Comes to Tea*, a book Sophie had been editing in the months before the attack. The portentous wording of the title didn't pass him by.

He checked his watch. It was ten past six and she was late. Fed up with getting soaking wet outside, he pressed the entry buzzer and was allowed through to a narrow corridor with a small desk on the right and a couple of chairs on the left. A young woman with bad acne and long greasy hair pointed to one of them and asked him to wait.

He'd only been seated a moment, when the clatter of footsteps came down the stairs and Cassandra appeared, clutching a batch of files and a mobile phone to her chest. Clumps of blonde hair, like yellow snakes, were dislodging themselves from the intricate chignon on her head and he noticed that her powdered skin was starting to crack at the corner of her mouth.

'Running late. Talk in the taxi,' she said. She pointed to the exit to indicate she wasn't stopping. He'd forgotten how she didn't bother using any more words than was necessary. The mark of someone entrenched in the world of publishing perhaps.

He couldn't help wondering how Cassandra had the time to be production manager, when, according to Sophie, her beauty regime was so time-consuming. Once she'd spent hours at the gym, the massage parlour and appointments having wraps, waxes and facials, how much time was left for putting books together?

She ran out onto the street and straight off the kerb, waving vigorously for a taxi. 'Emergency meeting. Printers,' she said.

'Thanks for seeing me,' he said. He was trying to hold his umbrella over both of them, but she kept straying into the rain whenever a cab came into view. 'I just wanted to talk to you about Sophie. You know what's happened?'

'Can't believe she… the knife… I mean,' she said, still looking out into the road. 'Is she still…?'

'In the psychiatric unit?' He nearly stumbled into a waste bin, trying to keep up with her. 'Yes, she is.'

Cassandra winced as if a pigeon had just swooped down and pooped on her head. 'Can't believe it,' she said.

A black cab pulled up and she yanked open the door and sank back into the seat. As soon as they were in the confined space, Cassandra's sickly perfume overpowered him. He slid away from her and opened the window, preferring the constant spatter of rain to the cloying air inside.

She crossed her legs and Daniel noticed the heels of her glossy red shoes must have been at least five inches high. He wondered what damage they were doing to her posture. Next, she'd be adding chiropractic to her list of regular appointments if it wasn't on there already. Her tight-fitting cream suit looked like it was made of fine silk and she wore a Liberty-print neck scarf that was starting to unravel. She looked more like she was on the way to a wedding than a business meeting.

'I wondered if she'd said anything to you. If you had any idea where she'd picked up this nonsense that I was having an affair?'

'Nonsense?' she said, recoiling.

She opened a compact and started applying scarlet lipstick. It was an exact match for her shoes.

'I certainly wasn't seeing anyone,' he said. 'I wouldn't be here asking you about it, if I was, surely?'

She rubbed her lips together and checked them in the mirror. It was stop-start traffic at this time of day and Daniel hadn't a clue where they were heading.

'Can't comment. She had photographs.'

He snapped back his chin. 'What? Which photographs?'

She shrugged.

He pressed her. 'Did you see these photographs?'

'Yes and no. Delivered to the office. Saw the envelope,' she replied, while staring down at her phone as if she was expecting a call.

'Did she open the envelope? Did you see what was inside?'

'No. Sophie opened it and was too upset. She ran out.'

'Did Sophie show *anyone* these… pictures?' He tugged at her sleeve, then let go when she froze and glared at his wet fingers.

'I don't know. She said they'd gone from her bag by the time she got home. She must have got confused. You know what kind of state she was in.'

Daniel stared blankly ahead of him.

So, once again, no one else had actually seen the 'evidence'.

'Well, if they existed at all, they weren't of me. They can't have been.'

Another figment of Sophie's crumbling imagination.

'If you say so.' She kept her eyes on her phone.

'Did she talk to you before the attack?'

'Didn't have to.'

'What do you mean?'

'She was distracted. Tearful. Jittery. That sort of thing. Very distressed. Everyone knew it was "domestic issues". Senior editor was getting hot under the collar.'

'Have you been in touch with her?'

She looked at her nails, pushing back the cuticles. Daniel was getting tired of her unwillingness to engage with him.

'Been awfully busy. Deadlines to meet.'

The taxi suddenly pulled to a halt and she got out, paid the driver and turned to go.

'Where are we?' he said, looking up, trying to find a street sign.

'Hanbury Street. E1. Got to dash.'

She was abandoning him in the middle of Spitalfields.

'Send her my love, won't you? Mwah,' she said, air-kissing as she tottered off into the rain.

He ducked into the doorway of a nearby newsagent, feeling dazed.

Not knowing where he was heading, he stepped out into the street and walked blindly into the crowds.

Chapter seventeen

Sophie was relieved to find her room empty; Shareen was probably playing pool.

As she sat on the bed, her arms wrapped around her knees, she noticed a scrap of paper sticking out from under the mat between the two beds. Sophie lifted the corner and found a small collection of magazine cuttings. Each one showed the Queen wearing an assortment of flamboyant hats at various state functions. On each one, thick black pen had been added, following the line of the Queen's mouth. Sophie shuddered. She remembered the reason Shareen was in there in the first place – you don't set fire to anything if you're in your right mind.

She stared at her roommate's pillow and felt a heartfelt sadness grip her. Shareen's life was a genuine tragedy, but it didn't mean she was a bad person. On a number of occasions, she'd used terms like 'evil things' and 'sick, unnatural things' when referring to her father's conduct. Do people ever fully recover from abuse like that? Damaged, that's what she was; this weird little collection of cuttings demonstrated that.

She slid the clippings back. In spite of the surge of sympathy that flooded her chest, she got up to wash her hands.

'I want to go home,' she said, out loud, staring into her grained reflection in the metal sheet above the sink. 'I want to be with my little boy.' She stared up at the sky through the small window reinforced with chicken wire. 'Am I really insane?' She watched the white puffy clouds slowly slide out of view. Heard no reply. If anyone was watching her they'd have no doubts that she was in exactly the right place.

She sank onto the bed, pulled the sheet over her head and tried to lose herself in Emeli Sandé on her iPod.

Chapter eighteen

After putting Ben to bed, Daniel had to open Sophie's wardrobe where she'd kept a pack of vests she'd bought for him a while back. Daniel had not looked at any of her clothes or opened any of her drawers since the incident. As the doors swung open he had to hold on to them, as though afraid of falling in and being suffocated.

It was like opening a photograph album, reminding him of the places they'd been, the life stages they'd passed through together and the different facets of Sophie he'd witnessed in the last eight years.

He spotted the long backless gown she'd worn when they first met at the Lanesborough Hotel in Knightsbridge. He'd been playing the guitar in an ensemble providing background music at a conference supper and she had been invited, with her boyfriend at the time; a diplomat, like her father.

At the end of the evening, she came over to Daniel and said she'd enjoyed his playing. The jade-green silk brought out the vibrant colour of her eyes, the dress clinging to her slim frame to the waist, then floating in delicate folds to the floor. It made her look like a Greek goddess. Through her vibrant smile, he discerned a pale trace of sadness he was instantly drawn to, the glimmer of yearning within her he felt compelled to pursue.

He was taken aback that she'd bother to approach him. He was even more astounded when she surreptitiously pressed a folded piece of paper into his sticky palm. It was her phone number. It turned out her relationship was on the rocks. Soon after, she split from the diplomat; Daniel taking his place.

A creaking floorboard under his foot brought him back to the present. He took what he needed from the wardrobe and closed the doors. Then went down to make a cup of cocoa; that's what Sophie always did for him when he had something on his mind.

He was lounging on the sofa, watching a roundup of the sport, when a sound broke through the silence from upstairs. It was barely audible. Ben must be talking in his sleep. Then he heard him laugh. Without another breath, Daniel was on his feet, bounding into Ben's room. He took a moment to adjust to the low light, but could only make out the crumpled bedclothes where Ben should have been sleeping in his cot. There was a shape at the window.

How did he climb out of his cot?

'Hey, little chap,' he said, walking slowly towards him, not sure whether Ben was sleepwalking or awake. Ben turned to him and charged into Daniel's legs, burying his face in the denim. He was giggling and dribbling.

'Ben, what's going on? You should be fast asleep, it's nearly nine o'clock.'

He squatted down, looking for clues in his face.

'Funny…' said Ben, suddenly sleepy, rubbing his eyes.

'What's funny?'

Ben laughed again and gave a tired sigh, leaning into Daniel's chest.

'Where's Mummy? I want Mummy,' said Ben.

'Mummy can't be here right now. She's sick in hospital, remember?'

Ben appeared to think about it, but didn't seem to have the energy to get upset. Daniel carried him back to the cot, noticing that the drop side was down. He lowered Ben onto the mattress, slid the side up and firmly clicked shut the childproof locking mechanism.

'Did you want a song?' he asked. 'Daddy could get his guitar.'

'Song, Daddy!'

It took two lullabies before Ben's eyelids began to flutter. Daniel stood over him to check he was asleep. In the reduced light, he swept his eyes around the room, not sure what he was looking for. There seemed nothing unusual, except for the fact that he was certain he'd locked the side of the cot earlier. He half-closed the door and went downstairs, disconcerted.

By the end of the week Daniel was aching to switch off: from work, from Sophie, from questions about the future. Since largely dismissing his mother's suggestion of getting in touch with people, he'd had a change of heart. Being with Ben was wonderful, but without an adult on hand to talk to, he was going stir-crazy. He wanted to think about something else apart from his predicament, for a change. Maybe see a film or exhibition. Anything to stop him being cooped up at home, stuck within the same four walls where the worst had happened.

He poured himself a small shot of whisky. It had been a long day. His computer had crashed at work and he'd lost several days' worth of data.

He snapped on the TV, but found himself channel hopping, unable to find anything worth watching.

Against his better judgement, he picked up the phone and rang his ex, Yvonne, but only reached her voicemail. He didn't leave a message. Then he tried Gordon, but he was on his way out to his father's birthday do. As he wondered which friend to try next, a text came in from Rick:

Fancy Chinese in Soho, tonight? Just the two of us?

Fast running out of options, he accepted and texted him back for the details.

Chapter nineteen

Having left Ben with Edith, Daniel made his way to the exit of Leicester Square Tube. He stopped by a telephone box to steel himself against the rapid Friday night tide of people. A tall black guy dressed entirely in white leather passed him, then a thin girl wearing stripy over-the-knee socks, playing ringtones to her friend. He wanted to get used to this again; get back to that feeling of being part of something vibrant and exhilarating.

He rejoined the surge of bodies and allowed himself to be jostled by elbows and handbags. After dodging impatient taxis to get over Charing Cross Road, he turned into Lisle Street. Wafts of stagnant drains and the stink of dried fish announced the gritty, edgy atmosphere that was Soho. He passed a row of shiny orange chickens hanging at the front entrance of the Cheung Kong restaurant and took the stairs down to the left.

It was hot and buzzing. He was bewildered for a moment by the mass of figures around the tables, then searched the faces for Rick. He spotted a raised arm towards the back and headed towards it.

As soon as Daniel got closer, he could tell this wasn't a meal for two. A table with six or seven people opened out before him. His heart sank. He felt like he was stepping onto a stage with an eager audience awaiting his performance. He wasn't sure if he had the reserves to spend an evening being polite to strangers. Daniel caught Rick's attention and narrowed his eyes, sending a silent *how dare you* glare. He then turned to the circle of faces tipped upwards in his direction and attempted a smile.

'Better late than never,' said Rick, smirking. 'I knew you wouldn't come if you thought there was a bunch of us, but we're not rowdy; we're arty and civilised,' he said, his reedy voice already saturated with alcohol. 'This is Mandy from work, this is her friend Sally and her brother... sorry, what was it?'

'Peter,' her brother answered. He sounded American.

'Then we've got Ralph, Diane, Ajay... and this is Jody.'

Rick pointed to an empty seat beside Jody, who was the only one to stand up to greet him. She was slim and poised, wearing navy linen trousers and an ivory silk blouse.

'Hi, everyone,' said Daniel in a blanket greeting, pulling out the vacant chair beside her.

This is awful, he thought. He should have known Rick would pull some stunt, claiming it was 'good for his recovery'.

'Someone couldn't make it, so Ajay invited me,' whispered Jody. 'I don't know anybody except him.'

'Snap. I only know Rick.'

'The guy who looks a bit tipsy?'

'That's the one.'

A menu was slotted into Daniel's hand and he ordered, choosing the first item on the list in each section to save having to think about it.

The woman was speaking again; something about being forced to do a voice-over that afternoon with a man, who, in her own words, 'had the halitosis of a hippopotamus'. He hadn't a clue what she was talking about.

'Gosh,' he said, hoping that would be sufficient.

He turned to look at her.

She went on. 'He kept doing this heavy breathing thing every time we got close to the microphone.'

Now that he saw her face properly, Daniel could understand why. Jody was gorgeous. The most striking thing about her was her hair, a coppery-red, but instead of being frizzy, it was straight and unexpectedly glossy. Tapered in a long fringe across her forehead, it brushed her cheeks in a broad curve before fanning out to the edges of her shoulders. The silky sheen made it seem as though a special spotlight was following her around. That, in combination with her smooth olive skin, meant he was finding it hard to take his eyes off her.

A waitress brought his meal over and it was only once he'd spooned several piles of it onto his plate that he realised he hadn't been given a fork. He scanned the table and discovered that everyone else was using chopsticks. This was going to be tricky. He hadn't used chopsticks in about ten years. He peeled off the paper cover and felt the chopsticks instantly turn to rubber in his fingers. This evening was going to be one *massive* embarrassment. He put the chopsticks down and took a sip of wine.

Jody hadn't stopped talking until now. She turned towards him, expectantly. Her last sentence had gone up in pitch at the end and must have been a question. Due to the chopstick dilemma, Daniel hadn't been listening. It was years since he'd had a beautiful woman at his side who wasn't Sophie – and he was completely out of practice. The schoolboy pin-up with the charm and wit for every occasion was stumped.

'Did it get better?' Daniel muttered. 'Your day, I mean… this eventful day…' He couldn't believe he was talking such rubbish.

'Not until Mr Hippo managed to split his trousers, which had obviously been made-to-measure before he'd put on three stones,' Jody added, then stalled for a moment. 'Sorry.' She rested her chopsticks on the edge of the plate. 'I don't usually make fun of the people I come across, but he was a first-rate git.'

She glanced at his plate and without a word, slipped a fork and spoon under the table onto his lap, then smiled as she refilled his wine glass.

'I'm out of practice,' she whispered, 'so I asked for these earlier.'

Daniel puffed air out of his cheeks. 'I think you've just saved my life,' he said.

She laughed and shook her head in a think-nothing-of-it kind of way.

'And you? Have you had an eventful day?'

Daniel let his shoulders sink. *Eventful day, week, month – year, actually,* he wanted to say – *and eventful doesn't begin to describe what I've been through.* But, before he could open his mouth, she leant past him and stood the salt cellar upright.

'Did I knock that over?' he asked.

'I think so.'

He couldn't cope with her question, so he grabbed instead at one of the words he'd managed to catch earlier. 'Microphone… you said microphone – do you do adverts or something?' He could very well imagine her pulling on exotic stockings or seductively lowering a flaky chocolate bar into her mouth.

'I was recording a small part in a loony kids' cartoon. I'm an actress. We're doing *The Brimstone Legacy* in the West End at the moment. Heard of it?'

Daniel wanted to say yes, but knew she'd pump him with questions about it and he'd end up looking stupid. Even more stupid. He couldn't believe how all those years of seducing girls in his teens could have left him so inept at simple conversation with a good-looking member of the opposite sex.

'I haven't. Sorry. Been a bit busy in the last few—' Daniel realised he'd been shaking soy sauce onto his rice since she'd last spoken and now his dish was flooded with it.

She pointed to it and whispered, 'That's because you wish you'd ordered soup, now, isn't it?'

He tutted, shaking his head, and she chuckled.

The business of holding a conversation was proving too much for him, so he decided to go for the easy option: 'Tell me about the play…' he said, hoping it was open-ended enough to keep her talking.

He was right. She happily stole the conversation for the next hour or so. It gave him the chance to observe her, something he felt far better equipped to do than engage in small talk. She didn't appear to be wearing any make-up; her smooth honey-beige skin didn't seem to need any and her tongue caressed each word before her sensual lips sent them, one by one, into the air. He noticed that her accent, pure Queen's English, created new words like 'valgar' and 'wanderful', but that she also had an unassuming manner that only people with genuine confidence can achieve.

When she passed the pepper grinder, her movement was graceful, almost choreographed, but without any sign of self-consciousness. All in all, Daniel was finding it hard to make her out, but he wasn't complaining.

She leant over and pressed something into his hand. 'Two tickets for *The Brimstone Legacy*. Just pass them on if you don't want to come.'

'Rick will love this,' he said, pointing to him. 'He's into acting at the moment.'

She glanced across the table. 'Bring whoever you like.'

As he pocketed the tickets his elbow sent a teaspoon spinning to the floor. He reached down to pick it up and noticed that Jody wasn't wearing any shoes. Her delicate toes were hooked over the crossbar under the table. He straightened up, convinced that he was blushing and felt cross with himself.

'Have you ever done any modelling?' she asked.

'Me?' Daniel laughed, repositioning his napkin to do something with his hands. 'No – what makes you think that?'

'You could pass for one of those guys who appear in magazines for exclusive retailers. You know, lean guys with dark rugged looks selling "quality casual" outfits.'

'You're kidding me,' he said. Not since his bachelor days had anyone been quite so forward with him.

'I'm entirely serious – and anyway, my uncle was a tailor in Piccadilly, so I should know.'

She helped herself to more rice and after she'd created a little heap on her plate, she turned, aware that he had been watching her. He saw her pupils fill out like ink blots and he cleared his throat.

'You… intriguing,' said Daniel, scrabbling around inside his brain for an appropriate description.

Chapter twenty

It wasn't until he left the train and braved the deluge that Daniel realised he'd left his umbrella at the restaurant. In spite of the subterfuge involved and the thorough soaking, he was grateful to Rick in the end. The evening had perked him up no end and the woman sitting next to him had been unexpectedly entertaining. And to be perfectly honest – very sexy.

He wondered how Jody would react if she knew he'd only recently escaped being stabbed to death. And by his own wife.

He hung his sodden jacket in the hallway, then thanked and paid Edith. Unusually for her, she was wearing a very short mini skirt, not terribly suitable for crawling around on the floor with Ben. She normally came round in dungarees or track pants.

'Very smart this evening,' he said, feeling compelled to make a comment as he'd been staring at her. 'Did you have a date before you came over?'

'Oh, no,' she said dismissively. 'Just a bit of a wardrobe shake-up.'

Edith hovered by the front door. At around five-foot ten, she was stick thin, which made her look even taller.

'Right then,' she said, 'just call me... any time.' She twirled round on the mat for no obvious reason. 'And just so you know, I don't have a boyfriend, so I'm usually free.'

She'd never said anything like that before.

He let her out. Time for bed. No need for the sleeping tablet – he was worn out.

Any other night and he might have missed it. He turned to the illuminated numbers on the alarm clock: 2.45am. He froze for a moment, wondering whether the sound he'd heard could have been the cry of a cat or late night partygoers on the street. No – it was closer than that.

He slowly folded back the duvet and crept towards Ben's room. The door was ajar and he listened without entering. There was nothing but silence. He was about to check elsewhere, when he decided to take a look all the same and stroked open the door. Ben wasn't there.

With a frantic leap across the landing he pulled the light-cord in the bathroom, but found it empty. He then shot into the spare bedroom, and that's when he heard his son's voice.

'… and baby fish as well…' As Daniel entered, Ben was standing beside the open wardrobe.

'Sweetheart?' Daniel scoured the room. 'Who are you talking to?'

Ben looked at the rug on the floor and put his fingers in his mouth. Daniel noticed a faint smell of perfume. 'Have you been opening Mummy's cupboards, Ben?' he asked, keeping all accusation out of his voice. He knew he'd left it closed.

Ben didn't reply. He stood plucking at the green giraffe sewn onto the front of his pyjama top.

'Who were you talking to, Ben?' He knelt down and held Ben so that he could make clear eye contact with him. 'Who was here?'

Ben twisted his body in a not-telling-you way.

'Are you playing games?'

Ben giggled.

'You should be in bed, young man.'

Daniel picked him up, called him a rascal and returned him to his own room. Again, he noticed that the side of the cot had slipped down. He lifted it into position and locked it shut. It seemed solid enough. He made a note to himself to check the lock properly in the morning. He needed to be more careful. Ben couldn't be allowed to climb out of his cot again like this, it was too dangerous.

He stood still and listened: only a passing car and gusts of wind whistling down the chimney. *Was Ben talking to Sophie in his sleep?* There was nothing he could do except keep an eye on him.

It was only once he was in the shower the following morning, that it struck him.

The perfume he'd smelt in the spare room – it wasn't Sophie's.

Chapter twenty-one

'Wow, that's impressive!' exclaimed Daniel.

He'd asked Edith to keep an eye on Ben while he popped out to the dentist and she'd constructed a makeshift tent in the lounge. The pair of them were hiding under a clothes horse with towels draped over the top. Edith had even decorated it with flags and fairy lights. Must have taken a lot of effort. There was a rustle from inside.

'Shh,' said Edith in a stage whisper, 'Don't let Daddy know we're here.'

There was a muffled giggle and Daniel played along until Edith finally counted down from three to one. With a flourish, she emerged and Ben popped out the other end, shouting, 'Boo!'

'He's been very good, haven't you, Ben?' she said, raising her palm and sharing a high five with him.

Ben gave them both an exaggerated nod and began playing on the carpet with his crane.

'Thanks, Edith.'

'No problem,' she said, with a wide grin.

She'd always been a first-rate childminder since she moved in next door three years ago. She tidied up after playtime and baths and never seemed to be on her mobile, like most teenagers he'd come across. Daniel had watched her with Ben on several occasions and she seemed to be the right balance of firm and fun with him. Nevertheless, she had a fragile quality that made Daniel on edge around her, in case he said something to upset her.

She followed Daniel into the kitchen to collect her payment and leant against the sink. Her straight black hair that habitually fell in clumps in no discernible style had been coiled into soft waves. She was also wearing lipstick.

Now he thought about it, since he'd returned from intensive care, she was paying more attention to her appearance.

In a businesslike fashion, he handed over the payment and led her to the door.

'Oh, before I forget.' She reached into her bag. 'I wanted to give you these.' She handed him a plastic freezer box. 'Nothing much – just some ginger biscuits,' she said, not looking at him.

Without waiting for his response, she turned and fled.

Daniel held the box reluctantly. He was going to have to be careful.

Chapter twenty-two

Rick answered the door wearing only boxer shorts and flip-flops. He was cracking open pistachio nuts with one hand while waving Daniel and Ben in with the other.

Rick rented two floors in a rundown Victorian house in Tooting. He'd moved so many times since Daniel had known him that he was hard to keep track of. He seemed to switch properties in the same way that some people traded in their cars. If he stayed anywhere for more than six months, it was an achievement. Before Tooting, Rick had lived in Brixton and before his stint in Sydney, he was in Rotherhithe; a prime example of itchy-feet syndrome.

Rick invited them into the sitting room. There was a lingering smell of mildew emanating from a damp patch by the window. In addition, a distinctive top note of fish hung in the air, the source of which he couldn't locate.

Rick treated each place he lived in as if it was someone else's squat. The carpet was threadbare and some decent furniture was swamped with torn cushions and ripped cotton throws. The ubiquitous lime-green woodchip wallpaper was a legacy from the seventies that he'd not seen fit to change and Daniel wondered why he hadn't upgraded the ancient fake coal electric fire. Apart from looking gross, it was the only form of heating in the room. It wasn't as though Rick was short of money.

Daniel removed a pile of orange peel and a tube of toothpaste and sat on the edge of the sofa. He kept Ben on his knee, jogging him in a pony ride.

'I can't believe you made me sit next to someone starring in a West End show, for goodness sake!' he said.

Rick threw a nut into the air and caught it in his mouth.

'I know people in high places, my boy,' replied Rick, tapping his forehead. 'Well, to be honest, it was Ajay who invited her.'

'She's a real live wire.'

'Lucky you – I didn't get to speak to her.' He sounded disappointed. The next nut missed its target and fell to the carpet. Rick squashed it under his foot as if it was a wasp. 'As long as she took your mind off things.'

'Thanks for your text,' said Daniel.

'I knew it was yours,' Rick said, handing him the folded umbrella. 'It was the naff Kew logo that gave it away.'

Rick gave Daniel a well-practised smirk. He'd always been a consummate smirker; his face seemed to fall naturally into that expression without him even trying. A result – no doubt – of a lifetime of scorn for other people, the world and life itself.

Rick led them into the kitchen and pulled a couple of cans of beer from the bottom shelf of the fridge.

'Jody gave me a couple of tickets for her play. *The Brimstone Legacy*. Fancy coming?'

'Never heard of it, but sure – I'm game for anything!' He cracked open a can, took a swig of beer and burped. He waved a can at Daniel.

'No, thanks, I'm driving. I just came over to get the brolly and say thanks for last night.'

'Does Ben want any juice?' Rick started pulling faces and making farmyard noises at him.

'Juice!' Ben cried in response.

'There's a fresh carton in the porch,' he said. 'Come on, let's go and find it.'

Rick left the room and Ben trotted after him.

Daniel stepped out into the hall and ran his eyes over the frames on the wall while he waited. He found himself drawn to one of Rick standing alongside his younger brother and sister. Louise had left a firm impression in his mind, but he'd forgotten about Miles. He was born nearly twenty years after Rick. Daniel wondered, not for the first time, whether he'd been a 'mistake' or whether his parents had made the deliberate decision to stave off empty nest syndrome.

It had been tragic, in the end. He remembered finding a message from Rick on his answerphone, asking him to go to the funeral, but he'd been in Italy and by the time he got back it was all over. A brain tumour had claimed him before he reached ten years of age. The boy had always seemed frail.

Rick and Ben eventually returned with a carton of orange.

'You tried those sleeping tabs, yet?' Rick asked, as they headed back to the kitchen.

Daniel nodded. 'They're helping, actually. Thank you.'

'You taken him in to see your lady wife yet?' he said, moving out of Ben's earshot.

Daniel brushed invisible fluff from his sleeve. 'She's not seeing me for the time being.'

'I can take him over there, if you like. Just pop in for half an hour or so. Keep everyone happy.'

Daniel was on the verge of giving his agreement, but his eyes slid down to the can in Rick's hand. A niggling sense of disquiet made him think again.

'That's... thanks... but Sophie's got other people she can ask.'

Rick went on, undeterred. 'And don't forget... if you need a babysitter, my sister is the best one in town.'

A mobile rang and Rick tossed aside a newspaper and a half-eaten piece of toast on the kitchen table to find it.

He pressed the phone to his bare chest and started laughing. 'Man, you've got to see this. How do people make these crazy videos?'

Rick pressed a button so Daniel could see the screen and the picture went black. 'Bloody thing – where's it gone?'

'I think you've just deleted it.' Rick had always been clueless when it came to any form of technology.

'Oh, bugger it!' Rick suddenly remembered Ben was in the room. 'Oops... sorry.'

Chapter twenty-three

As the applause after the performance of Jody's play died away, Daniel had a text from Rick inviting him to join him at a small pub behind Oxford Street. Rick had left during the interval claiming he had to make some urgent calls. Having spent most of the first half fidgeting, Daniel had the feeling he'd gone straight to the pub. *The Brimstone Legacy* clearly wasn't his cup of tea.

For a second, Daniel was torn about whether to join him. The desire, however, to take his mind off the melodrama of his own life won him over.

The tavern had a timbered front and small latticed windows, and as Daniel stooped to enter, he felt like he was stepping into the seventeenth century. It must have been built when people were discussing the aftermath of the fire of London; a time when Milton had finished *Paradise Lost* and Henry Purcell was still a child. This is the beauty of London, he thought; it's at the forefront of global economics, politics and culture, but it still has so many historical legacies embedded within it.

Edging past an old barrel by the door, he carved a path around tightly-packed groups of drinkers, looking for Rick. Fragments of conversation told him that most of the people were connected with the theatre. Cameras and phones flashed as fans snatched selfies with actors they recognised.

With no sign of Rick, he bought a drink, then spotted a familiar head of hair. Vibrant copper curls like a beacon in a black rolling sea.

'... so maybe he was the first person to make a New Year's resolution,' she explained to a group pressed in a circle around her. 'Pepys wrote in his diary at the start of 1661, "I have newly taken a solemn oath about abstaining from plays and wine..." but by mid-February he'd lapsed – just like the rest of us!' A wave of laughter followed and she gave a mock bow.

Looking up, Jody caught sight of Daniel and beckoned him into the group. She swooped him into a hug and planted kisses on both cheeks. All a bit OTT for Daniel, who felt his face blossom bright pink in response. More flashes went off and he blinked into the dazzling bursts of white.

'Hi – loved the play,' he said, aware that the surrounding figures were probably wondering who he was.

'Thank goodness it's Sunday.' She wiped her forehead and flicked her hand as if shaking off droplets of sweat. 'I've got tomorrow off and I can get those bloody lines out of my head.'

'Rick should be here somewhere,' he said. 'The guy who invited me to the meal.'

Jody stood on tiptoe turning 180 degrees. 'Ah, Rick – I couldn't remember his name.' She drew him away from the others. 'He *was* here, chatting up a chorus girl from *The Lion King* with a waist the size of a wasp.' She shrugged. 'I think he's gone. He gave me a message for you, actually. Said not to wait if he wasn't here.'

'Oh...' Daniel wasn't altogether surprised. Rick was always changing his mind and disappearing.

A couple on a window bench got up to go and Jody pulled Daniel's arm towards the opening space. She put down her wine glass on a soggy coaster and Daniel sat down beside her. It was a tight squeeze.

'Amazing place...' he said, noticing the tiny orange crisscross bricks stained with smoke above the fireplace.

'You know, when this pub was first built,' Jody said, running her fingers up and down the stem of the glass, 'the theatre was going through a "circus" phase. It was all about illusions, trapdoors, outrageous costumes, actors flying on wires – even fireworks. The legitimate Restoration drama lot condemned it – too vulgar, but it brought in the crowds – a bit like a seventeenth-century *Royal Variety Show*.'

Daniel raised his eyebrows and was grateful to sip his drink, giving him time to work out what to say next.

'I was impressed tonight,' he said. 'It's a clever script. I like the way Izzy and Frank more or less change places in the last act.' He was determined to be more articulate than when they'd first met.

'Glad you liked it. I forget after so many performances how well written it is.'

On stage, Jody was like an exaggerated version of the woman he'd met at the meal. Flamboyant, carefree and entertaining. But it would have sounded like a chat-up line if he'd said it out loud.

'How do you manage to get your voice to carry on stage for such long periods of time?' he said, instead.

'One thing you learn at drama school. As it happens, I come from a family of bellowers. My father was a bit deaf, poor love.'

'I was in a school play once and my mum said she couldn't hear a word.'

'Quite the reticent type, aren't you?' She crossed her legs and he caught sight of her shapely calves, the colour of toasted almonds. He blinked and tried to pretend to himself that he hadn't noticed. 'So tell me – which actor do you most identify with?' she asked.

'Sorry?'

Daniel was thinking about too many things at once and was finding it hard to keep up.

'You don't believe in small-talk, do you?' he said.

'Come on – answer the question. Any actor – from theatre, TV or film. Who'd be the closest to revealing the real Daniel? Think Tom Hanks in *Sleepless in Seattle* or Cary Grant in *Bringing Up Baby*.'

He gritted his teeth and tried to visualise the row of DVDs he kept by the television.

'I'd probably be... er...' He didn't want to choose someone who'd make him sound either shallow or overly glamorous. '... a simmering Anthony Hopkins?'

'Hopkins in *The Remains of the Day* or *The Silence of the Lambs*?'

He watched her raise one eyebrow. It was a trick he'd been practising since he was sixteen, but he'd never quite been able to pull it off.

'Ah!' A flush of heat swept up his face again and he brushed some invisible dust from his sleeve. 'Definitely as the restrained butler.'

'Restrained or repressed?' She leant towards him, her hands wrapped around her knees.

He put his arms up in surrender and leant back. 'I'm not sure my brain runs at the same speed as yours,' he said, laughing.

She tutted. 'Oh – you're out of practice, that's all.'

She winked at him and he realised he couldn't be happier that Rick had abandoned him.

Chapter twenty-four

'Need a pick-me-up?' Rick stood on the doorstep waving a bottle of white wine in one hand and a bottle of scotch in the other. It was a wet April evening with a fierce wind and in a bid to keep it at bay, Daniel reluctantly beckoned him inside. Nevertheless, bits of damp foliage and scraps of litter came in with him.

'Rick – it's Monday night,' said Daniel, staring at the bottles. 'Haven't you got work in the morning?'

'Easter break, thank God. Although I haven't got shot of those bloody kids for long,' said Rick, setting the bottles down on the kitchen table. 'Got a brain-numbing school trip to Paris with the little gits. Thought this might oil the wheels a bit.'

Daniel poured them both a glass of wine, making sure he tipped considerably less into his own.

'To the crap that life bestows upon us…' said Rick, waving the glass in the air, before knocking back most of it in one go.

Daniel gritted his teeth and lifted his glass. 'Cheers.'

'You eaten?' he asked.

'Yes. You should have rung.'

'I know. No juice left in the mobile.' He shook it, as if it was the phone's fault.

'I can make you some toast, if you like?'

'Make it four slices with peanut butter and you're on,' he said, sitting down, plonking his feet on the adjacent chair.

'When are you going to Paris?'

'Thursday. Two bloody days dragging them around a science museum, in a foreign language. I'd rather stick pins in my eyes. I'm sick of the little shits.'

'Bad day?' said Daniel.

'Bad *life*, mate. I don't know what I'm doing any more. The acting idea I told you about is starting to look dead in the water.'

Ah yes, the latest fad that was going to reboot his life.

'How come?'

'I can't get any auditions. No one will look at me. You need to either have experience or have been to drama school.'

It didn't sound too unreasonable to Daniel.

'Have you thought about doing a course? Going back to college?' He dropped two slices of bread into the toaster.

'I just want to get on with it. These courses make you learn frickin' poetry. You have to sing and tap dance, for effing sake. I don't want a role in *Mother Goose*...'

'What *do* you want?'

'I want to be in a decent drama on television... something like *Killing Eve* or *Poldark*. It doesn't have to be a lead role, or anything. Even *Casualty* would do.' Daniel smiled at Rick's 'realistic' grasp of the situation.

'Don't you need an equity card for that kind of thing?'

'You see? I can't win.' He leant forward, his elbows on the table, cupping his chin in his hands. He looked like a small boy who'd been told he's not good enough to be picked for the school play.

'Ah, Rick.' He put the plate down in front of him with toast cut into neat triangles. 'Sorry things aren't working out.'

'That's because life isn't satisfying, is it? Not for long.' There was a huge crunch as he took a mouthful of toast.

'I don't know. That looks pretty satisfying...' chuckled Daniel.

Rick looked up and crossed his eyes. 'There's always something that comes along to make your life shit, isn't there?' he said.

Daniel would never have shared Rick's view until recently. He shrugged and fiddled with the salt cellar, keeping his eyes on the table.

'Mum's finally sold the old house in Oxford,' said Rick, a dribble of butter glistening on his chin. 'Do you remember it?'

'No, I never went there.'

'What? Are you saying I never invited you over during all the time we were schoolmates?'

'No.' Daniel cleared his throat. 'It was down to your dad being so ill, I think. I've never met either of your parents.'

Rick let out a moan of recognition. 'Oh, that's right. Of course. Life was crap back then as well.' He rubbed his stomach. 'Anyway, Mum moved when Dad kicked the bucket and rented out the old place, but last year she decided she wanted shot of it altogether to get the money. In case she has to go into care. That's my legacy up the spout.' He sniffed. 'Louise and me had to clear the place out last summer. It was an effing nightmare; tenants had left it in a right state. Worst part was Mum kept Miles's room exactly as it was when he died – she'd had that room locked up before the tenants came in. Going back in there did my head in. Like a frickin' tomb. A nine-year-old kid. Having to pack up his train set, his Chelsea kit and Pokémon cards…'

Rick looked genuinely distraught.

'Hey, you should have said. I would have come with you.' Daniel put his hand on his shoulder.

Rick shrank back as though suddenly aware he'd revealed too much sensitivity.

'Yeah, well, you were inside your own little happy-bubble with this one.' He glanced over at Ben. 'I know you've had it tough, mate, but at least you've got him.' He glanced up at a photo beside the fridge. 'He's got your chin, don't you think? And the funny way you scrunch your nose up.'

'Has he? Do I?' said Daniel, rubbing his nose, feeling chuffed.

Rick carried on. 'He looks more like Sophie though, especially as he's got blond hair and you're dark.' He waved his finger in the air. 'You remember Dezzie Delaney from high school? His dad's got red hair and his mother is dark and he's an out and out blond. He looks more like the dog than his parents.'

From the time of Ben's birth, Daniel had searched, like most parents, he assumed, for similarities between father and son. At first he sought something of himself in Ben's physical features; his long, curling eyelashes, the dimples he had in the same place, as a kid. Then, as he grew into a toddler, Daniel couldn't see any facial similarities at all any more and had looked instead for common traits in their personalities and behaviours. Daniel had seen Ben favour his left hand at times, the same way Daniel did. Other similarities followed; he hated rice pudding, could finish a small jigsaw puzzle by the time he was two and regularly sang a melody from the radio completely in tune.

Rick brushed his crumbs onto the floor and they both turned as a howl of wind rattled the back door. Daniel turned the key in the lock and pulled down the blind.

'Things have been a bit weird around here, lately,' he said.

'I'm not surprised.'

'No, I mean… maybe I'm being forgetful or something – but it's as though there's been another presence in the house.'

'Oh man, spooky.' He fluttered his hands in the air.

'Seriously.' Daniel folded his arms. 'There have been a couple of nights when Ben's been out of his cot and I swore I'd locked the side.'

'What was he doing?'

'Well, here's the crazy bit, he seemed to be talking to someone.'

Rick snapped back his chin. 'To who?'

'I didn't actually see anyone.'

'Maybe he was pretending his mum was there.'

'I don't know. It's not just that. It looks like someone's been in the loft – there was a telltale sprinkling of grit on the floor right under the hatch. But, I haven't been up there in ages.'

'Did you check to see if anything is missing?' asked Rick, helping himself to another glass of wine.

'No, but there's nothing valuable up there. Just paperwork and junk.'

'Hadn't we better go and check?'

'There's no point, it's—'

Rick was on his feet pacing towards the hall, before Daniel could talk him out of it. Anything for a bit of drama. Daniel reluctantly pulled down the loft ladder, but before he could place his foot on the bottom rung, Rick shoved him aside. 'You're injured, mate. I'll go.'

Once his shape had disappeared, Daniel mooched up after him.

'Where's the light?'

'Above you to the right; the pull switch.'

'Ah, got it.' Rick was randomly opening boxes. 'What do you keep up here?'

'Like I said, mostly junk. Paperwork, files, books, photos. Some of Ben's old toys. You know… the usual.'

Daniel joined him, peering into dusty boxes.

'Anything missing?' Rick asked.

'Not that I can see.' He wasn't quite sure why they were up there when there wasn't anything worth pinching, anyway.

'That's weird,' he said, bending down.

'What?'

'Well, I haven't been up in ages, like I said. How did this get here?' He held up a cloth. 'It's still damp.'

The cloth smelt of bleach. He scanned the tacked panels between the beams, then cast an eye over the whole area, but could find no reason for it being there.

Minutes later they were back to the kitchen.

'Doesn't look like any break-in I've ever heard of,' said Rick, clearly disappointed. Daniel was certain nothing had been taken. 'Thief does a spot of cleaning while he's looking for the family silver?' he snorted. 'I reckon you're just a bit jumpy, mate.'

Rick had a point. Daniel watched as he helped himself to a banana from the fruit bowl. Then draped the empty peel back in the bowl, over the apples.

'Mate, you've been through a hell of a bad time lately.' Rick put his arm round him. 'You've got bad memories living with you. Maybe your mind isn't fully on the job. That's probably all it is.'

Daniel watched him chew. 'Perhaps you're right,' said Daniel, the wine acting like a net curtain, making everything seem less sharp. Nevertheless, he'd have to stop taking the sleeping tablets. He couldn't be out for the count if Ben was at risk in any way.

Rick finished his banana, polished off the wine – and started the whisky – ending the evening spread-eagled over the sofa in the lounge, fast asleep. His legs were akimbo with his dirty baseball boots inches away from a white cushion. Daniel tried to untie the laces as Rick snored, but they were both knotted. He moved the cushion instead.

Daniel put Ben to bed and when he returned, he rang for a taxi. When he heard the beep of a horn outside the house, he looped his arm under Rick's shoulder to drag him to his feet.

'Come on, sunshine, time to go.'

A sharp pain shot up the stitches in his chest and he had to prop Rick against the wall, unable to bear his weight any longer.

Rick was still asleep, his breath catching the back of his throat. Daniel was still having intermittent flashbacks and envied Rick's ability to switch off. If the attack had taken place somewhere else, perhaps it would have been easier, but he had to walk into the room where it happened every day.

Gravity got the better of Rick's head and it fell to one side, waking him up.

'Stay over if you like…' said Daniel, without enthusiasm.

'Na – got things to do – people to see. Great evening,' said Rick, stretching his mouth into a wide yawn without covering his mouth.

Daniel closed the door on him, together with the late-night chill. He stacked the dishwasher and set it running, before switching off the lights.

He stared at Ben's lime-green plastic cricket bat leaning against the front porch and, half-joking to himself, considered whether he should take it upstairs with him. Perhaps he could keep it beside his bed, just in case the intruder made another appearance. Except, chances were there was no intruder. Did he really believe someone had been getting in? To do what? What about the cloth in the loft that was still damp?

The house had been empty between the attack and his return four weeks ago, so how that had got there was a complete mystery.

He left the bat where it was. Rick was probably right. He *must* have popped into the loft at some point. It was just his memory playing tricks on him.

Chapter twenty-five

Sophie used a blunt pencil to strike through another day on the calendar above her bed, just as Shareen came out of the shower. She didn't bother to cover her body with the towel and Sophie noticed marks on her inner thigh and tattoos that were normally hidden by her clothes; a coiled serpent wrapped around her belly button, and when she turned her back, she could make out a purple butterfly with the name Kelly underneath it, at the base of her spine.

'Is Kelly your little girl?' said Sophie, looking up from a copy of *Vogue* magazine.

Shareen tipped back her head, realising where Sophie had seen the name.

'Yes. She'll be five by now.' She sat on the bed naked, towelling dry her cropped hair.

'Don't you miss her?'

'Not really. I gave her up quite soon after she was born.'

Shareen rubbed cheap cream from Poundland into the tattoos on her arms. 'I'm going to get a beetle done on my tongue when I get out.'

Sophie winced. 'Your tongue? Won't that hurt?'

'I don't mind. It's a good kind of pain.'

Sophie looked away and wondered how any kind of pain could be described as good.

'When will you get out?' she said.

Shareen dumped the towel on the bed and sat back against the wall. 'I got life, because people died in the fires, but I wasn't right in the head, so they keep reviewing my case. What about you?'

'My court case is coming up soon and Dr Marshall thinks I'm getting better.'

Shareen pulled a face. 'Getting better isn't all it's cracked up to be, darlin'. When you get better, they sentence you and if they reckon you're sane, you go to prison.'

Sophie brought her fingers to her mouth. Her once perfect nails were now chewed and tatty. No, not prison. That couldn't be right. Surely, they'd see the attack was due to some mental aberration, just one moment of madness brought on by Daniel's behaviour. Wouldn't that be mitigating circumstances? She'd get character references. Everyone would realise she'd suffered some kind of breakdown.

Her eyes travelled back to the marks on Shareen's thighs. They looked like old scars, but Shareen had said she kept a razor blade somewhere, in case she needed it. Sophie made a quick scan of the room, wondering where it was hidden.

'Yoga starts in five minutes, you coming?' said Shareen.

'Can't – I've got a group therapy session.'

Shareen pushed out her bottom lip in disappointment and Sophie realised she was probably only nineteen or twenty. So young – such a waste.

When Shareen crept into the room that evening, Sophie was already asleep. She brushed her teeth and gave her face a cursory rinse, before putting out the light. As she rested her head on the pillow, she felt a lump underneath. She flipped on the light again and ran her hand under it, pulling out a small paper bag. Inside was a folded note, with two words, *For You*, in neat handwriting. In the bottom of the bag was a small jar of Chanel No 5 body lotion. Shareen glanced over to the bundle of bedclothes, slowly rising and falling.

'Bloody hell,' she muttered, then opened the jar, sniffed it and smoothed a generous layer of the luxurious cream along her arms.

Chapter twenty-six

The Past – 5 September 2017

As he sat on the Tube, Rick pulled out the small photo he'd slipped inside his wallet that morning. The one he'd found tucked away at the bottom of a shoebox in his mother's wardrobe. It had been troubling him for days; sent him searching back through piles of useless uni notes and poring over his own snaps from way back when. All because he'd been poking around in his mother's belongings for rich pickings before she sold the house.

He checked the back again. March 30, 2002 would have been right at the end of term at Oxford Uni. Most students would have gone home, so why would there have been a party? It was a party, surely?

And why had this one been put inside a fancy frame?

He studied the scene once more. Figures were standing in pleased-to-meet-you poses with glasses in their hands. Balloons hung from the ceiling and he could pick out empty beer cans strewn on the carpet. It certainly looked like the kind of party he'd have been to.

Nothing was coming back to him.

Nor could he find himself amidst the blurred faces. Did that mean he'd taken the snap? Perhaps he'd been so blind drunk he couldn't remember anything about it. Surely he must have been there, otherwise why had the picture been kept?

There was plenty going on in the small picture. It seemed to involve a lot of water being sprayed everywhere and carpets getting soaked. And candlewax dripping down the side of someone's expensive glass cabinet. But that wasn't the whole story. There was something unnerving about the photograph that he couldn't quite put his finger on. Something important. Something that sent a tiny spiral of fear up his windpipe.

Chapter twenty-seven

The Present

Daniel sat with Ben on his lap in the kitchen. They'd got off to a good start, only it was short-lived. The *Where's Mummy?* tantrums started as soon as Daniel tried to get the Rice Krispies down him.

'Daddy's got the whole day free, so what would you like to do? Pool, swings, Granny's or stay here playing with the carpark... train set... paints?'

Ben's reaction was instant. 'Swings,' he shouted.

'Swings it is.'

Just as they were about to leave the house, the phone rang and Daniel reluctantly answered it.

'Fancy lunch at the Wig and Mitre?' said Rick.

'Sorry, mate, Ben and I are just off to the park.'

'Can't you get the girl next door to have him?'

'Not this time, mate. Ben and I have some catching up to do.'

He held the phone to his chest. The obvious option was to ask Rick to join them, but he didn't want to encourage him. Rick was increasingly finding a way back into his life and he didn't want him hanging around all the time. 'Only I'm at a loose end,' said Rick.

What harm would it do if Rick tagged along? Twice as much fun for Ben, surely. Ben seemed to like him.

'Come with us if you like. We're just going over to the Common. See you by the swings.'

Ben squealed as Daniel chased after him across the grass, imitating an angry bear. He was surprised when he looked up and saw Rick, tramping towards them so soon.

'Didn't take you long.'

'I'm Superman,' said Rick, tickling Ben in the ribs until they were both rolling on the grass. Daniel picked Ben up and tried to spin him round but had to stop, wincing with pain as the stretch tugged at the wound in his chest. He was glad to let Rick take over, otherwise he could imagine the stitches in his side peeling apart like a zip on an anorak.

For once, Daniel admired Rick's hyperactive streak. He watched them both lurch up and down on the see-saw, Ben shrieking with delight, then followed them round to the sand pit. A few minutes later he saw Ben rush over to the swings with Rick growling behind him. His son, who loved chasing and being chased even more, was thrilled by the attention.

'Rescue me,' Rick shouted, 'this boy is wearing me out!' Rick was wearing tatty jeans with tassels hanging so long at the hem that it looked as though his shoelaces were undone.

'I think you're wearing *yourself* out, but you're doing a great job,' said Daniel. He crouched down, hugged Ben to his chest and gave him a big kiss on the cheek.

'Listen, Ben,' said Rick in a pretend whisper, bending down beside them. 'Shall we run away from Daddy and see if he can find us?'

Ben whooped with excitement and Rick pulled him by the hand towards a clump of bushes. Daniel turned his back and covered his eyes. He gave them time to settle in a hidden spot and then began the charade of trying to find them.

Rick was a complete natural; he hadn't wanted to admit it before. Daniel wondered if he would ever have children of his own. The only drawback was Rick's unpredictability and reckless approach. He would have to grow up himself, first.

Daniel stood up and tried to work out which direction they had taken. There were rows of trees with undergrowth on all sides, groups of children bobbing in and out with footballs and dogs. Starting to his left, he wandered from one patch of shrubbery to the next, but he couldn't see Ben's distinctive striped yellow T-shirt. After ten minutes, he didn't have the energy to prowl around anymore, so he went back to the bench and decided to wait until they came back.

Stretching out, a wave of exhaustion swept through his muscles. He watched with half-closed eyes as figures drifted across the expanse in the distance. He sank a little lower to ease the pressure off his wound, letting the low sun's rays soothe him. It was so glaring that he closed his eyes.

A dog barked behind him, jolting him awake. He checked his watch, realised he'd dozed off for over half an hour. *Where were they?* He stood up and stared ahead of him, then turned a full three-hundred and sixty degrees. Had Rick been distracted and allowed Ben to wander off by himself? Was Rick searching for him, not daring to come back alone? He refused to let worst-case scenarios race through his mind.

Daniel patted his pockets. He'd left his phone at home. Had Rick got bored and left? He wouldn't put it past him. His palms were wet with mounting surges of panic.

Then two figures started ambling across the grass. One large, one small. They were each holding an ice cream.

'Where have you been?!' snapped Daniel.

Rick stumbled towards him, pretending to be out of breath.

'Hey, man, don't be so jittery.'

'What do you expect, going off like that?'

'Thought I was doing you a favour. You'd dozed off last time we checked.' Rick grunted and sat down. He took a big chunk out of the side of the cornet and a lump of ice cream fell onto the grass. 'Now look what you've done.'

Ben leant quietly against his father's legs. 'We did games, Daddy,' he said. 'We did a trick with coins.' He turned to Rick with excitement. 'Do the trick with the magic coins!'

'Not now, sweetheart,' said Daniel. 'You had a good time, yeah?' He patted Ben's head, hiding the rasp in his voice. A small white clump of Mr Whippy had found its way into Ben's hair.

'So, you going to shout me a beer or not?' said Rick. He pointed to the concrete building on the far side that looked like a public convenience, but was actually a café.

'A coffee, maybe,' he said.

They began making their way towards it in silence.

By the time he'd got to the till, Daniel had got a grip on himself. He set both mugs down on the picnic bench outside. Ben found a ball in the toy box in the corner, threw it on the ground and ran after it.

'He seems to be adjusting,' said Rick, flicking cubes of sugar across the table.

'All things considered he's doing pretty well. Has the odd tantrum now and then, but I'm being fairly easy on him.'

'Not like your dad did with you, eh? Pushing you to play chess at some ridiculous age, trying to get you to learn Hungarian for your mum.'

Daniel had forgotten.

Rick clicked his fingers. 'Remember the time you stole Beanie's biology essay?'

Daniel winced. 'You remember that?'

'I didn't tell on you, did I?' said Rick, slurping his drink loudly. 'Because we were mates.' Rick reached over and patted him on the shoulder. 'You're a complete fraud, Duke. Everyone thinks you're a boring old goody two shoes.'

Ben got tired of the ball and started banging the table with a plastic spade. Daniel pulled out a tractor from the jumble of toys in his rucksack. Ben liked it best when Daniel ran it over his son's chest. Rick liked it best when he revved up the wheels and sent it at speed off the edge of the table.

A little boy passed their table and Ben followed him, captivated by the spaniel playing with a rubber bone at the boy's side.

'Have you taken him to see her?' Rick asked.

'He's been with Greta and Sophie's father, but I'm still persona non grata.'

A robin hopped onto the adjacent table and tucked into a crust abandoned by a previous customer.

'Have you thought about my offer to take him? Give you a break.'

Daniel took a sip of coffee and grimaced. It was cold. He pushed the mug away and the bird took off.

'I'm not sure—'

An image came to mind of Rick dropping by for lunch at Kew a few weeks before the stabbing. He was on his way back from the funeral of his school's deputy head and had been wearing novelty socks with a matching tie. In Daniel's view, Rick hadn't done a great deal in his life to establish himself as a grown-up.

'I can put in a good word for you at the same time. Do what I do best and stand up for you.' He chuckled. 'She might see sense.'

Rick had a point. He certainly wasn't getting anywhere on his own. And Ben obviously felt comfortable with him. To be fair, while Rick could be reckless at times, *he* was the one who'd acted fast and saved his life at the beach.

'That might not be such a bad idea,' said Daniel.

Chapter twenty-eight

Sophie decided the clock in the ward lounge ought to belong in an American diner. She sat and watched the heavy minute hand jolt forward with an angry snap as she waited for visiting time. Time was strange in here: stretching out interminably in an unchanging wasteland. She took a magazine from the coffee table and flipped through it without reading a word.

In over nine weeks, the doctors and psychiatrists were yet to give a name to her condition. Dr Marshall had mentioned the phrase 'lost touch with reality' several times, but what did it mean, exactly? She'd done psychometric tests, had blood and hormone tests. She wasn't psychotic, had no symptoms of schizophrenia or paranoia. They'd taken brain scans, but there didn't seem to be any swellings, lesions or bits missing.

Was this the beginning of some mysterious mental illness? If so, it really didn't feel like it. The outburst in the kitchen felt like it had happened to someone else. The idea of wielding a knife at anyone now, least of all her husband, was utterly preposterous.

Out of the corner of her eye, she could see a woman lurking beside her. Doris had the face of a thirty-year-old, but shuffled around like someone far older. Wearing a pinafore and tatty slippers, a bunched up yellow rag hung out of her pocket. She looked like she was about to start dusting. Instead, without saying a word, she reached forward and ran her grubby fingers through Sophie's hair. It wasn't the first time one of the other patients had wanted to touch her. If Sophie had learnt anything in here, it was patience; she wanted, more than anything, to push Doris away. She had to squeeze her fists and force herself not to scream: *I'm not some doll on display for you to play with whenever you feel like it!*

It wasn't Doris's fault. And more to the point, Sophie couldn't risk the consequences if she reacted. It wouldn't help her cause one bit. *Violent streak.* She could hear the psychiatrists drawing their own conclusions about her. Instead, Sophie ducked out of the way, beckoning Annie to come to her rescue.

'Come away, Doris, leave the pretty lady alone.'

Doris muttered something incomprehensible as she was guided towards the television set and Sophie was left dabbing at her hair with a tissue when Rick walked in holding Ben's hand.

She hurried towards them. 'Thanks for bringing him,' she said, gazing only at her son.

'Any time,' he said.

Ben climbed straight onto Sophie's lap as soon as she sat down and she breathed in the smell of him, soothed by his familiar warmth against her belly.

'How's it going?' Rick asked, looking shiftily from one patient to the next, as though expecting one of them to charge at him with a flaming lance.

She hissed her response. 'These people in here... honestly, they are seriously out of it.' She glanced over at Doris, who was now tearing pages from a *Radio Times* into long strips.

'I can see that. I brought some books and magazines. I had to leave them at the front desk. Not sure why. Maybe to check I haven't slipped in a nail file or something.' He winked.

'Thanks,' she said, ignoring his attempt at levity. Sophie would never have agreed to see Rick had he not brought Ben. He was merely a conduit to her son.

Ben was wrapping her hair around his fingers and watching it uncurl, but within minutes had fallen fast asleep in her arms.

'So, how's Daniel?' she whispered.

'Moping. Not good, Sophie. Stuck at home the whole time.'

'Seriously?'

'Yeah, he's hardly been out.'

'Really?'

Rick shook his head. 'Pretty much. There was a feeble night out with the lads a while back, that's all. Oh, and he dragged me to a West End show.' He did the shifty thing again with his eyes. He looked like he was going to say more, but changed his mind.

'Come on, spit it out. What else has he been up to?'

'Nothing much, I'm sure. Honestly. He came to a meal in Soho. Theatre people. Nothing special.'

'So... having a great time, then.'

If Rick was trying to reassure her that Daniel was miserable as sin without her, he was making a lousy job of it.

'No! He's in a bad way, Sophie. He frickin' misses you.' Her eyes darted up to see if anyone had heard. 'He doesn't know what came over you.'

'Rabid jealousy. That's what came over me. He was cheating all right, but even so. How the hell I could attack him like that is completely beyond me. We should have worked through it, like sensible adults.'

He thumbed his eyebrow. 'Dan wants you well again. He wants you back. That's all I know.'

There was an awkward silence.

'His laddish days are over. You know that,' he went on. 'He's a reformed man; he was as soon as he met you.'

'Is he? Leopards have spots, Rick, and you can't wipe them out or paint over them for long.'

He shrugged.

Sophie folded her arms. There was something about the whole conversation that made her think Rick had been trying just a little too hard to convince her.

Sophie watched Ben sleep. She'd had her heart set on reading him a story, playing a game, chatting about nursery, but their time was fast running out.

'Hasn't he been sleeping properly?' she asked.

Rick shook his head, turning up his nose. 'Dan said he gets up in the night. Cries. Misses you... you know.'

She sighed. Ben was suffering as much as anyone in this situation. It was so unfair.

Rick idly began dismantling pieces from a jigsaw on a nearby table. He dropped one abruptly.

'Urgh… frickin' sticky,' he said, wiping his fingers on his jeans in disgust.

A patient who'd recently joined the unit launched to her feet and cried out, 'If anyone dies on this bus, I'm getting off…'

Then, just as abruptly, sat down again.

'What the f—' Rick exclaimed. 'This place is a total loony b—' He cleared his throat. 'A total nightmare.'

His outburst woke Ben, and startled by the unfamiliar surroundings, he began to cry. Annie called time on the visiting hour and reluctantly, Sophie handed her son over and watched them leave.

Chapter twenty-nine

Daniel was too restless to go to bed. He dragged the empty trunk out of the cellar and bumped it, stair by stair, up to the bedroom. As he unfastened it, a smell of musty hymn books engulfed him.

It made him think of funerals and he had to remind himself that Sophie wasn't dead.

But *something* was dead.

They couldn't go back in time. It was impossible for what had happened to be removed without trace. Even if Sophie came back declaring her love for him, full of remorse, how could he possibly sit in the kitchen with his back to her and not wonder what she held in her hand?

The trunk wasn't quite empty; a single green ribbon lay forgotten in the corner. He was convinced it was the same one Sophie had worn with the backless dress, the first time they'd met under the chandeliers at the Lanesborough Hotel. It seemed a hundred years ago and it unsettled him. There was no room for nostalgia at a time like this.

His mission was to drag all Sophie's clothes off the hangers in the wardrobes, clear all her drawers and cupboards and lay everything to rest out of sight. They could join the other items in the loft or the cellar.

He wound the ribbon around his fingers, then left it on the dressing table and shook his head. None of this should have happened. All based on incriminating items and photographs no one had seen, but her. All figments of her imagination. None of it real.

He shut the trunk and sat on it, unable to bring himself to disturb any of Sophie's clothes. If he left them exactly as they were it would keep the dream alive. If he bundled them away, she might never be coming back.

He left the room in a daze and crept past Ben's room to brush his teeth. Toothpaste in hand, a sudden chill swirled into the bathroom making him shiver uncontrollably. How could he ever trust her with Ben, again? His dazzling, tender-hearted, murderous wife.

He rubbed his bare arms. No, the air around him really was colder than a few moments ago. He looked up, but the window was closed. He must have left another one open.

Once on the landing, traffic from the road roared and a passing motorbike sounded like it was heading straight for the lounge, downstairs.

He couldn't have left a window open down there – he hadn't opened one. He hooked his neck over the banister and stared into the charcoal shadows beneath. Then snatched a breath.

The front door was open. At ten o'clock at night.

He scuttled down the stairs. With the lime-green cricket bat primed above his shoulder, he hurried outside along the short path in his slippers.

A male figure walked swiftly into the distance, one way. A woman hurried into the night, the other. No one else.

He shut the door and flipped on the light. There was no way he'd left the front door not only unlocked, but wide open. *No way.*

Ben!

He charged up the stairs, still holding the bat and flung his son's door open. Ben was there, fast asleep. Daniel stared at his blanket, watching his little body rise and fall, just to be absolutely sure.

Going back down to the hall, he came to a halt on the threshold of the lounge, to listen. Not a sound. From anywhere. He ducked behind the sofa, jiggled the long curtains and moved on to the kitchen. Nothing out of place, nothing out of the ordinary.

As he approached the cellar door, he could see from the white line under the door that the light was still on. He'd switched it off, earlier. He was a hundred per cent certain, because he'd used his elbow to avoid letting go of the trunk.

Someone had *definitely* been in the house.

With his mobile in his hand primed to call 999, he gingerly drew open the cellar door. Again, he stopped to listen, but could hear only the hammering of his own heartbeat.

He crept down the steps for a closer look; tossed open the flaps of various large boxes, checked for any signs of disturbance. Nothing was out of place.

He approached the filing cabinet in the corner and checked the drawers. Firmly locked. As they should be, even though it was only stuffed with old bank statements, various personal papers belonging to Sophie and her old medication and toiletries – the ones he'd moved from upstairs. He didn't know why he'd still hung onto them, just like he didn't know why he'd kept most of the junk down there.

He stepped over a spare car battery, the vacuum cleaner, toolbox and all the usual bits and bobs he really should go through properly one of these days.

Still holding the phone, he returned to the front door. His fingers were trembling so much, it took him three goes to get the key in the lock. For one terrifying moment, he thought someone had fitted a new one while he'd been upstairs cleaning his teeth. They hadn't, of course, but the idea of changing the locks was a mighty fine one.

There wasn't enough to go on to alert the police. A sceptic might even insist that all the odd incidents were down to him losing the plot: the missing picture on the landing, Ben out of his cot apparently talking to someone. Then there was the grit under the loft hatch, the white spirit, the damp cloth, the open front door – they could all be put down to absent-mindedness.

There had been no signs of forced entry, so who had a key? His mother – who else? Edith, next door. She was showing signs of having a bit of a crush on him, but surely she'd have no reason to creep about the place in the early hours. Then there was Sophie's own key – had she given it to someone?

He wondered if, over time, every item in his house was gradually going to open, move or disappear. Whoever it was, he'd had enough.

He was going to put a stop to these shenanigans once and for all.

Chapter thirty

Annie was beyond the point of exhaustion. She had pins and needles in her legs and she was starting to feel nauseous with fatigue. She'd done a double shift and wanted to get home.

She took a sly look at her watch, then handed Sophie a glass of water as she waited for her to swallow her tablets.

Sophie pulled a face as they went down.

'He cheated on me, you know. Daniel is so convincing and such a good liar.'

Annie nodded, but didn't respond. It wasn't her job to argue or make her see sense.

'If he'd just admitted it – it would never have happened.'

'That's all over now,' Annie said, hoping to close the matter so she could get off home without any histrionics.

'Look – new pictures. They're date-stamped last week.'

'Where did you get these from?'

'Melody on reception gave me them this morning. Someone left them here, but there was no note or anything. Just these polaroids.'

Annie was on the verge of whipping them out of her hand. 'I don't think you should have had these. Were they signed off by the psychiatrist?'

She'd have to up her game; too many double shifts were making her sloppy. These must have slipped through the net.

Sophie let her hold one of the square shots. A stunning woman was in the throes of holding a man's face and kissing him. Very intimate. It certainly looked like the husband who'd come in to visit her.

'It's a different woman from the last pictures. Can you believe it?' whispered Sophie. 'A redhead this time. He's all over her.'

'Do you recognise the place?'

'No. It looks like a pub or a party somewhere.'

Thoroughly animated, Annie flicked to another picture. 'Yeah, it's a pub, see the bar in the background?'

'Can you read what it says on the blackboard behind the barman?' Sophie asked her.

'Looks like… Thorndale… Thorndike Tavern.'

She shrugged, her face blank. 'Can you look it up for me on your phone when you go off-duty? I just want to know where it is.'

'I'll have to check with the psychiatrist on duty, first. I don't want this to upset you.'

Most women in the ward weren't the sort she'd normally feel a scrap of admiration towards, but Sophie Duke was different. She had class and dignity. She was worth going that extra mile for.

Annie handed back the picture and was quiet for a moment. A batch of shots such as this looked, to her, like the work of a private detective. Perhaps Sophie had failed to tell her something.

'Did you get someone to do this?' she asked. 'Did you pay someone to follow your husband?'

'Me?' Sophie laughed. 'Absolutely not! I'd got all the evidence I needed weeks ago.'

Annie was curious and more than a little mystified. Someone had gone to a lot of trouble, not only to take these shots, but also to get them to Sophie. Annie knew it wasn't her role to make judgements, but she couldn't help feeling that perhaps Sophie hadn't been so delusional after all.

'Does your husband know you've got these?' Annie asked.

'No.' Sophie dropped her head and let the photograph fall to the floor. 'It's all a bit late now, isn't it?' Annie saw the light go out of her eyes. It was replaced by a hopeless stare.

'I want it all to be over…' Sophie whispered. 'I can't do this…'

Annie put a hand on her arm, in the way she'd reassure a friend, not a patient. 'Why not go to your room – have a lie down?'

'My life's a mess. I don't want to be here any more…'

'Come on.' She bundled the photos back into the envelope then walked with Sophie to her room where she left her sitting on the bed, staring into space, the envelope on her knees.

Annie went straight to the office to stick a 'yellow flag' at the top of Sophie's file. A 'yellow flag' was the code for suicide watch; it meant the staff would be monitoring her closely over the next few days.

Shame, thought Annie, as she pulled on her coat, ready to leave. Hope she doesn't go and do anything stupid. Looks like Sophie Duke might just have a case for mitigating circumstances.

Chapter thirty-one

Dear Daniel,

It's taken me some time to see I did a terrible thing and for that, I am truly sorry. I was wrong. I shouldn't have attacked you. I still can't explain what took hold of me, but it should never have happened.

Nevertheless, I am seriously looking at my options for the future.

I believed you before we married when you said your one-night stands were all in the past and that you'd be faithful to me. I was stupid to be taken in.

I've made a decision.

I want a divorce.

I understand it's on hold until they decide I'm sufficiently 'compos mentis' to know what I'm doing. But, I know already this is what I want.

I've seen more photos of you getting up close and personal with someone else, this time! Who's the woman with the red hair? One of the nurses here copied them for me and managed to trace the place where you met, on her phone, so I know the pictures were taken at the Thorndike Tavern, in Oxford Street.

Don't bother to deny it. It's plain to see you're back to your old ways, after all your empty promises.

Once I'm out of here, Ben and I will be moving on.

I can't bear to see you.

Sophie.

Daniel picked up the photocopied sheets she'd included that had floated to the floor as he read. Sitting on the bed, with Ben only feet away along the landing, he was thrown into utter panic.

Someone had taken pictures of him and Jody and sent them to Sophie. Only these really were genuine photos this time, but only up to a point. Their meeting was entirely innocent; the hugs and air-kisses just the hallmarks of the overblown greetings actors give each other all the time. There was nothing in it. Nevertheless, the shots had been taken at such strategic moments that it looked like he and Jody were all over each other. Damn!

He glanced at the letter again and this time the word 'divorce' flashed out at him. Her plans were not only to leave him, but to take Ben, too. It was all going to be over.

How the hell had it got this far?!

He hunched over, snatching shallow breaths. No, it wasn't how things were going to be. She was obviously not yet in her right mind. Everything could still work out. Once she was moved to prison, he'd get her to see sense. He'd explain the photographs. He'd be able to do that. She'd have lots of time to think and realise how good the two of them were together, how brilliant they were as a family. Then, once her sentence was out of the way she'd be coming back home.

His breathing slowed down, but his lungs seemed to be full of something sour. He couldn't get to the scene in his mind where she walked through the door and into his arms without feeling that sharp pain in his side.

The legacy of her actions he might be able to forgive, but he would never be able to forget.

He couldn't imagine Sophie in prison. Two things that should never go together. Like wet fingers and plug sockets or children's pockets and fireworks. For a moment a wash of compassion swirled around his chest. He couldn't imagine a worse punishment for her. Not just losing her freedom, but her dignity and self-esteem crushed in one go.

But others were being punished too, not least Ben who was being robbed of a mother and having to adjust to an entirely different future. That was the worst outcome.

Before then, they had the trial and the sentence to cope with. One step at a time.

He kept hearing the words of an old OMD song in his head: *The future is unfolding, but it's not what you had planned.* And the question kept eating away at him: do you still love her?

In many ways the answer was easy. The Sophie he'd married; the woman who'd seen beyond his good looks and reached into the very core of him with understanding and acceptance. Yes, absolutely. Just being in the same room with her used to make him feel taller, brighter, warmer, more alive.

But the other Sophie? The one she'd become in the last nine months? He didn't want to answer that.

The pertinent question was which one was the *real* Sophie? And he didn't want to answer that either.

He reached for the green ribbon he'd left on the dressing table and brought it to his lips. He searched for her perfume on it, but there was nothing of Sophie left. He stuffed it down the back of a drawer and slammed it shut.

Chapter thirty-two

When Daniel got home from nursery a text came in from Jody. She wondered if he was free to meet that Friday after the show.

His first impulse was to accept. Then, the more he thought about it, the more it felt like a 'date' and it didn't seem appropriate. What if someone took more pictures of them together? Of course, the damage had already been done, but he was going to have to be incredibly careful not to make matters worse.

He began chopping leeks for tea, but was running entirely on autopilot. He was still reeling after Sophie's letter. Someone had done a magnificent job of planting seeds of destruction in her already wayward mind. Who was it? Who had taken photos and delivered a select few that were deliberately misleading to his wife?

The nurses said she had no access to a mobile phone or social media and the only visitors she'd had were Vincent, Rick and Greta. As far as he knew. Perhaps someone else was going in?

He put down the knife, wiped his hands on the tea towel and picked up his phone. Seconds later he was being put through to a nurse on Sophie's ward, but the call got him absolutely nowhere.

No, they couldn't give him a list of everyone who had visited his wife.

No, they didn't know who had left photographs for her.

And, finally. 'Yes, you're right, Mr Duke, anyone could have dropped by with an envelope.'

Sunday morning lie-ins weren't what they used to be. Dragged from sleep at some ungodly hour, Daniel had been subjected to the clanging of a toy drum – kindly bought by people who clearly didn't have children – for the past twenty minutes.

Even though the locks had been changed, he was too worried about someone emerging through the walls, like Harry Potter on platform 9¾, that he hadn't allowed himself another sleeping tablet. As a result, he'd counted sheep – several hundred in fact – for hours, without dropping off.

At 4.05am precisely he'd made a decision. He couldn't merely rely on new locks, he was going to get an alarm fitted.

When the doorbell rang between drumbeats and squeals, Daniel was relieved to find Rick standing there, waiting to take his son to the hospital for a second visit.

Daniel had subsequently flopped back into bed and had only just showered, when they returned. They went into the kitchen, where Daniel had started washing up. Rick sat at the table with Ben on his knee, holding his favourite new book.

'He's moved on from *Good Night, Gorilla*,' said Rick. 'He's into *Shark in the Park*, now.'

Daniel nodded with a smile. 'He's been looking through the portholes – it's a clever book.'

He turned round, wiping a glass.

'Did Sophie mention any incriminating photos when you went to see her?'

Rick looked confused. 'The ones that didn't exist, you mean?'

'No. There are real ones. Shots of me with theatre people. That woman I sat next to in Soho, to be precise.'

He shook his head. 'Sophie didn't mention anything about photos. I stuck up for you, though. I told her you'd grown out of the hanky-panky since you got married. That you'd only got eyes for your wife. I laid it on good and proper. Honestly.'

'Someone took those shots and made sure she got to see them.'

Rick scrunched up his face and put Ben down on the floor. 'Who would do a thing like that?'

Daniel pressed his hand into his forehead. 'Exactly. Deliberately made it look like something was going on between us.' He leant against the sink. 'Sophie wants to end our marriage.'

'Shit…' Ricks eyes were bulging so wide he looked like a cartoon character.

'Nothing will happen until there's confirmation she's capable of making sensible decisions.' He turned and watched the frothy water slip down the plughole. 'It's the last thing I want, but the problem is I've got Ben to think of. I need to make sure he's always going to be safe when—'

'You're absolutely right.' Rick sounded horror stricken. 'You'll never be able to forget what she did. She'll always be a liability.'

Chapter thirty-three

She was sitting on a bench, her bare legs outstretched and her face tipped up towards the sunshine with her eyes closed. Daniel, holding Ben in his arms, stood in front of her, casting a shadow over her body. Daniel wondered how long it would take before she noticed her private patch of sunlight had been stolen. She opened her eyes.

'Hi,' she said, sleepily.

Daniel lowered Ben down in front of her.

'Thanks for taking the time to see me... us.'

'No problem. This must be Ben,' she said, sliding along the seat to make room for them both.

'Say hello to Jody,' said Daniel.

Ben uttered a polite greeting, then clambered up onto the bench beside her.

'This is a bit awkward,' he said, 'I wanted to see you... to ask you something.'

'I'm good with awkward,' she said, unperturbed. 'Fire away.'

'Someone took photos of us when we met after your show.'

She blinked fast, confusion claiming her features.

He went on. 'You and I. At the tavern near Oxford Street.'

'Oh. The Thorndike.'

'Someone took a picture that made it look like you and I were—' He glanced down at Ben swinging his legs, watching the pigeons on the path. 'There were shots that could have been misconstrued. You don't know who took them, do you?'

'Sorry, no idea. There are always people hanging around the theatre snatching selfies and... well, you know... paparazzi and all that. I don't pay much attention any more.'

He shrugged. 'I thought I'd ask.'

She seemed genuinely concerned. 'Has it caused trouble of some sort?'

'You could say that. I won't go into it now.'

'Oh… I'm sorry.'

Ben prodded the white paper bag on Daniel's lap. 'Can we do the secret, Daddy?' he said, growing impatient.

'Well now, what have you got there?' she asked on cue, pretending to peer into the bag.

'You'll have to wait and see,' replied Daniel, taking a flask out of his rucksack. He began pouring coffee into two plastic cups and as he did so, she pointed to the bag and whispered something in Ben's ear.

'Muffins!' Ben said gleefully, clapping his hands.

Daniel rolled his eyes and handed her a steaming cup.

'Ben! You weren't supposed to tell!' He tousled Ben's hair and nudged his cheek with his knuckle. Ben grabbed the bag and handed it to Jody, watching her every move.

'Ben don't snatch.'

His son ignored him, having eyes only for Jody.

She unrolled the top of the bag in slow motion, then handed a muffin to Ben and Daniel, taking the last one for herself. 'Talking of secrets,' she said, 'this place has tons of hidden history. Did you know?'

Daniel looked up. The square, tucked behind St Paul's Church in Covent Garden, had figures spilling into every corner like a painting by Lowry. He'd only ever known it as a sanctuary for the Londoners who knew it was there.

'I'm sure you'll tell me if I ask nicely.'

He took out a carton for Ben and pricked the top with a straw. Ben crawled onto his thighs slurping the chocolate milk.

'The first ever *Punch and Judy* show was performed here. Pepys wrote about it in his diary.' She waved vaguely towards the red-brick façade of the church. 'It's called The Actor's Church because of all the memorials... Vivien Leigh, Charlie Chaplin, Noel Coward.'

'You're wasted on such a small audience,' he said.

'Small, but appreciative.' She narrowed her eyes. 'These are fabulous.' Her cheeks puffed out with cake.

She carried on with her patter, her voice soothing, making him feel safe. She was wearing an amber-coloured silk dress and as she spoke, one thin strap slipped off her shoulder. Daniel noticed freckles of different sizes, like a night sky crowded with stars, scattered over her chest and upper back. He wasn't sure whether he found it attractive or not.

'Good week?' he asked, when she drew to a close.

'Actually, it's been a bit rough.' She finished the mouthful and set the broken muffin down on her lap. She spoke by his ear so Ben couldn't hear. 'One of the backstage crew was killed. Hit by a guy on a motorbike.' She stared at the ground.

'Oh, God. How awful. Did you know him well?'

'Only for drinks after shows. It still shakes you up.'

'We take things for granted, don't we?' said Daniel. 'We're used to building on yesterday to make today. We think everything is set in stone.'

'You're right,' she said. 'Even the most obvious, everyday, rock-solid certainties can simply fall apart.'

You can say that again, thought Daniel.

Ben spoke, suddenly pointing upwards. 'Blue sky, Daddy,' he said.

'Yes, that's right. It's blue. Very good.' He turned to Jody. 'They must be doing colours at nursery. Although, he did say the sky was green the other day.'

She laughed.

Daniel looked up and watched the cherry blossom from the overhanging tree cascade to the ground in the breeze. It gathered on the flagstones like tumbles of confetti. As the petals were crushed beneath people's feet, he found himself thinking about his wedding. How different everything could have been, if Sophie's obsession had never taken hold.

Ben was pulling at his sleeve and Daniel realised Jody was saying something.

'… when I found out about Corinne, it nearly killed me.'

'Sorry, Jody. Miles away.'

'I was saying, you know, about things coming at you out of left field.'

'Corinne?'

'My younger sister. Yeah, Corinne wasn't my dad's daughter. She was really my half-sister.'

As she spoke, a hard-boiled egg slipped out of Daniel's fingers onto the ground. It rolled into a dip between the flagstones and before he could retrieve it, it disappeared under the sole of someone's trainer.

'You had no idea?'

'Mother spent the night with the vet – can you believe it?' Jody guided the loose strap back onto her shoulder and absently stroked her neck. 'Suddenly a foreign element crept into my relationship with my sister whether I liked it or not – half of someone I thought I knew became a complete stranger to me. I only found out a few years ago.'

'How did you deal with it?' He brushed the crumbs from the muffin to the ground and two pigeons instantly appeared, challenging each other for the pickings.

'I believe in moving on, I suppose. I can't bear wallowing. I had a massive showdown with both Mum and Corinne, and we had a cooling off period. I hated the fact that they'd kept a spectacular secret from me for so many years.' She screwed up the paper bag and tossed it into the bin by the seat. 'We're fine now.'

Jody sighed, indicating that she had closed that chapter.

'Listen, I've got to go in a minute and I haven't asked about you,' she said.

'Don't worry. I'm glad to talk about something else… for a change.'

'That bad, huh?'

He didn't reply.

She patted his knee, then checked her watch. 'This has been lovely.' She slipped her sandals back on and picked up her handbag. 'Don't forget, if you need to talk and there's no one else around, don't hesitate.' She did a little curtsy in front of Ben. 'Very pleased to meet you, little man.'

They parted at the corner of Henrietta Street, the three of them waving until her floating shape melted into the crowds.

Chapter thirty-four

The phone rang beside Daniel's pillow. He moaned as he stretched out his hand.

'I'm so sorry, Daniel,' cried the voice. Daniel could hear a police siren in the background and the thudding of what sounded like heavy boots on bare floorboards. 'I know it's really late. I got back from the theatre tonight and the place has been burgled.'

The red digits on his bedside clock showed, 2.07am. Friday night, or Saturday morning to be precise.

'Jody?' he said, pushing himself up onto his elbow. Daniel didn't recognise her voice until she'd mentioned the theatre. 'Are the police there?'

He was trying to work out why she was calling him and not one of her plethora of other friends.

'Yes – they're here now. I'm so sorry to wake you. I shouldn't have rung. I tried a few other friends, but—'

'Don't be silly. I'd come over, only I've got Ben...'

'Of course. It was stupid to ring. I'm so sorry.'

'Look, I'll be over as soon as I can tomorrow. Ben's going to a birthday party and I'm not at work.'

He rang off and lay for a moment, his arms folded behind his head. He pictured her when they last met, the light filtering through her dress. He shook the picture from his mind. It felt wrong to hold an image of Jody in his head and savour it. He turned over and went back to sleep.

Chapter thirty-five

On Saturday morning, Daniel found the house in Hampstead, but it looked so upmarket that he had to refer to his scrap of paper to check he'd got the right place.

The elegant three-storey property, possibly Regency, was painted with white stucco and looked as if it belonged to a rich banker. The path was chequered with black and white tiles like an elongated chessboard. He climbed the steps that led to the porch, or perhaps it should be 'portico', as it was grand enough to have columns either side, with two bay trees in aluminium tubs. The brass doorbell was one of those bell-pushes he'd come across at National Trust properties – the ones that were usually accompanied by a sign pointing to the servants' entrance round the back.

He took a deep breath and wiped the top of his shoes on the back of his jeans. Jody answered sooner than he expected and nearly caught him at it.

'Enter if you dare,' she said, grim-faced.

Daniel went in and began stepping over upturned furniture in the hall. Lying in between three-legged chairs was smashed glass, torn books and broken china. It looked like the place had been completely trashed.

'What a mess. I'm so sorry,' he said.

Jody was holding a dustpan and brush and as though realising how ineffectual they were, she propped them carefully against the skirting board and put her hands on her hips. He could tell she'd been crying. Instinctively, he went towards her and briefly wrapped his arms around her.

'I'm sorry, I didn't drag you here to weep on your shoulder.'

'Don't worry about it,' he said, drawing away awkwardly.

'I'm sorry I rang you in the middle of the night. No one else was around.'

'No problem.'

She picked up the hose of the vacuum and tugged the appliance behind her like a disobedient dog, shifting it out of the way.

They waded through the mess to the kitchen. He couldn't see one item that wasn't broken in some way. A lifetime of accumulated belongings deliberately destroyed. It was an exact visual representation of the way his own life felt at that moment.

'*Everything's* been turned over...'

He spotted the kettle, apparently intact. 'Can I make you a drink or something?'

'Not sure my stomach could cope with any food, but a coffee would be nice.'

Daniel took in the scene around him – it was like a shipwreck without any water.

'Do you have an alarm?' he asked.

'We do, but it kept going off for no reason, so I had to switch it off.'

He made a mental note to make sure the alarm he got installed was top of the range.

'What's weird is I can't think of anything that's gone missing,' she said. 'It was one of the first questions the police asked me. It seems like nothing's been taken, they've just smashed it all up. Who would do that?'

'Maybe they were looking for something,' he suggested.

Jody shrugged. 'Looking for what? What state secrets have I got hidden in my closet?!'

'You live here alone?' he asked.

'Not usually. My older sister Nikki was staying with a friend last night. Her mobile was switched off. She's on her way back, now.' She pointed to the back of the kitchen, her arm shaking. 'Someone got in through the French windows.'

Glass crunched under their shoes as she led him to the jagged hole alongside the door handle. 'I've got someone coming to board all this up.'

Outside, old steps edged with moss led down to an area paved with narrow bricks, with a bird bath at the centre. The courtyard reminded him of a corner in an overgrown cemetery and he felt a chill on his bare arms.

They waited for the kettle to boil.

'An impressive place you've got here,' he said.

'Well, it was,' she said, exasperation in her voice. 'How about you? Where do you live?'

'East Sheen. A small terraced house.'

'Nice area. I have an aunt who lives in Putney.'

They sat at the kitchen table to drink the coffee.

'I'm going to clear up in shifts,' she said. 'Nikki's bringing a couple of friends and two mates from the theatre will be here at lunchtime.'

'I'll give you a hand now,' he said, getting to his feet. 'Where do you want to start?'

She flapped a hand at him. 'I've been clearing up since the police left,' she said. 'I need a break.' She propped her bare legs onto the chair beside him.

They both took a sip of coffee.

'Thanks for coming,' she said. 'Might help take my mind off all this.' She glanced down at the gold band on his wedding finger. 'I know you've got a terrific little boy, so are you married, divorced?'

Her directness was going to take a bit of getting used to. He decided to come clean and gave her an honest résumé of the past few months.

Her mouth fell open with unmitigated horror. 'Oh my God, how are you coping?'

'I don't know, really. To be honest, I think I'm still in shock.'

'Is that why you were asking me about the photos someone took at the tavern?'

'Yeah. Someone sent them to my wife in hospital.'

She whipped round to stare at him. 'Really? That's disgusting.'

'They were innocent pictures, as you know, but now she's even more convinced I'm cheating on her. She wants a divorce.'

Jody looked genuinely aghast. 'Oh, Daniel. I'm so sorry.'

'I'm still trying to get my head around it. Between September and February my wife became a different person. She turned into a... a monster. Bitter, cold, aggressive – not like my Sophie at all.'

He couldn't believe how easily the words slipped out in her presence. To a virtual stranger.

'If you ever want to talk about it, any of it, I'm a good listener.' She lingered over the words, her eyes trained on his.

'Thanks,' he said, scratching his nose even though there was no itch. 'I think you've got enough of your own problems to deal with.'

She sighed.

'Look,' he said. 'you can't stay here. Have you and your sister got somewhere else to go tonight?'

She shrugged. 'We can book into a hotel for a couple of nights, until we get this place cleaned up.'

'Why don't you both come and spend at least one night at mine. I've got plenty of space.'

'That's very kind Daniel, but we can't impose.'

'It wouldn't be – seriously.'

'I don't want to make things difficult for you... you know, after those snaps that were taken.'

'It would be both of you, and, to be honest, I'd enjoy the company.'

Chapter thirty-six

About of chicken pox had put paid to the party Ben had been invited to that afternoon, so when Rick suggested a few hours of child-centred fun at his place, Daniel was reluctant to turn it down.

'I've got balloons, sausages on sticks and party hats,' Rick explained. 'You never know when they're going to come in handy.'

Knowing Ben had been bursting to make balloon animals and play jolly games, it seemed a shame to waste the chance.

Rick had indeed pulled out all the stops. He started with party tricks and wowed them with his detachable thumb, then magically mended a broken piece of string.

'You've been practising,' said Daniel, trying to work out how the button he'd had his eyes glued to had ended up under the wrong egg cup. But he wasn't joining in as much as he wanted to. Pain around his wound, no doubt due to helping Jody clear up that morning, was niggling him. So, he bowed out as they started a game of Twister in the sitting room. It had the pair of them bending and crawling between each other's arms and legs – too much for him. Ben was in fits of giggles and Rick was in his element, throwing himself into it.

Daniel left them to it and went along the hall to the loo.

'Let's play a trick on Daddy when he comes back,' he heard Rick call out in a stage-whisper.

Here we go again.

Rick had always been fond of silly pranks. As Daniel flushed the loo, he recalled the time on a friend's stag night when Rick had blagged his way into his hotel room and propped a blow-up doll on the toilet. There was also the time he used his sister's keys to get into her car, wound down the driver's window and left chunks of a broken glass shelf on her seat, before running inside to raise the 'false' alarm. That was mean. Luckily, Louise had a sense of humour.

On his way back from the toilet, Daniel could hear the pair of them sniggering conspiratorially. Rick was a good sport, he could give him that. He was bound to have had far better things to do with his Saturday.

'Quick! Daddy will be back in a minute. Tuck that apron around it, so he won't see.'

Daniel took that as a cue to loiter, so he retraced his steps and wandered into the box room Rick used as a study. He'd rarely had a reason to go in there before, but it was just as cluttered as everywhere else. In the midst of cardboard boxes full of school chemistry apparatus and piles of textbooks, the heavy kneehole desk arose like an island. On it were scattered files with labels such as 'Exams – June' and 'Coursework Results, Year 12'. A closed laptop nestled in the middle.

He climbed over the detritus and took refuge in the large leather chair. It was scuffed and ripped in places, but moulded to Rick's shape and rather comfortable. To begin with. As he leant back, it lurched to the side then slowly sank down giving out a loud hissing sound. Typical. There didn't appear to be many items in Rick's flat that hadn't fallen off the back of a lorry – perhaps literally.

Daniel interlaced his fingers across his stomach and stretched out his legs for maximum stability.

In doing so, his foot hit something under the desk, knocking it over. He got down on his hands and knees to check what he'd disturbed and, clawing his way to the back, found a stack of papers, held together with string.

He pulled them out into the light and read the covering sheet:

Piecemeal – A play by Richard Fox

Daniel smothered a tiny snigger to himself under his hand. Rick hadn't mentioned this! He'd written a play, for goodness sake. Why had he kept it secret?

He unknotted the string and slid out the top page in order to read the opening, but found instead several sheets of handwritten notes. The first was not in Rick's handwriting and appeared to be feedback on the masterpiece:

Lead female needs a stronger story arc... Jack is too much of a caricature... Tabitha's final lie comes too soon, I thought we said it would be in the last act?

The section at the bottom caught his eye. Scrawled in Rick's handwriting was an address in Hampstead he recognised, and underneath it, an email address and mobile number. Reaching into his back pocket, he pulled out his phone and searched through his recent incoming callers – and there it was. Jody's number.

His mind was buzzing with questions as he straightened up. Jody implied she barely knew Rick. Had Jody read his play and given him a critique? When, exactly had they been in touch?

He considered having a peak on Rick's laptop. Looking for what, he wasn't sure, but he was certain Rick would have some obscure and ludicrous password and he couldn't afford to hang around typing one attempt after another. Instead, he pulled out the drawer in the centre of the desk. He had no idea why; his hand seemed to find the handle of its own accord. Part of him was appalled for snooping like this, but the other part was sick to death of the odd, unexplained events that had been percolating into his life.

He came across a muddle of crumpled notes, loose staples, paper clips and a hole punch buried in a mound of small white circles. Just junk. Seeing something squashed at the back, he pulled the drawer further out and gripped several crumpled cards. He flattened the first one out. It was a photograph: Daniel was coming out of a shop with his arm round Sophie's shoulder.

When was this taken? He recognised the street.

A dog barked outside Rick's window, making him jump. He'd already spent ages away from the others, so he stuck his head out of the door to see if they were looking for him. He heard Rick make a roaring sound, followed by Ben squealing with laughter.

Daniel retreated and flipped straight on to the next photo. He was too intrigued with what he'd found to leave just yet.

The next picture had been digitally altered, because what had been the newsagents, was now a grand hotel. In the next print, the figure of a woman he didn't recognise had been put in Sophie's place. The result was Daniel, clear as day, coming out of a hotel with his arm around another woman.

But there were more.

Shots of him alongside the same woman, walking hand in hand across Hyde Park. One of him cupping the stranger's face in his hands on a platform beside a train, another on the beach in Brighton in a passionate embrace. Each one was familiar, but where Sophie had once stood – an impostor had taken her place.

They were so cleverly done that he couldn't help but admire the finished product. Except this couldn't be Rick's handiwork; he was useless at anything the least bit geeky, like this. Yet, these were seamless; the figures looked like a genuine couple. There were several more in the pile showing different stages in the process that were less convincing.

He swore out loud and stuffed the pictures down the back of his trousers. Then he put them back, realising it would be a dead giveaway if Rick discovered they were missing. Instead, Daniel hurriedly took close-up pictures of each one on his phone, then pushed them to the back of the drawer.

He sank down into the chair for a moment, his body suddenly too heavy to do anything else. His eyelids batted against his cheek furiously as he tried to take in what he'd just seen. Why the hell would Rick be holding on to pictures that made it look like Daniel was seeing someone else?

Rick's call made him launch to his feet.

'Hey, Dan, where've you got to?'

He'd spent far too long in there. With a foul taste in his mouth, he bolted out of the study and rejoined the pair still giggling in the sitting room.

Chapter thirty-seven

Before the doorbell rang, Daniel had completely forgotten he'd invited Jody and Nikki to stay over. Cases and bags started piling up in the hallway.

'Sorry, I know it's only for a day or so, but we were loath to leave anything behind!' said Jody. 'You okay?'

He stood still, looking blank before responding. 'Yeah – sorry, come in.' He was still feeling shell-shocked from his discovery in Rick's study.

A figure at the gate paid for the taxi and joined them inside.

'Meet Nikki,' Jody declared. 'She's only back in London for a couple of days.'

Daniel saw in her an older, frumpier version of Jody. She was probably in her mid-forties and had the same shade of hair as Jody, but it was cut into a short unkempt bob.

'Where are you off to?' he asked.

'I'm seeing friends in Bruges, then spending a couple of weeks in the south of France. My contract has just ended, so I'm making the most of it before the next one.' She was wearing black dungarees which made her look as if she had no waistline, and heavy Dr Martens boots.

He caught himself returning to Jody's familiar face and for a moment wished he was behind a two-way mirror, so that he could spend time comparing the two of them without being seen.

'I know you've probably eaten, but we're both starving,' said Jody. 'We've been clearing up all day. Any chance we can get a takeaway?'

Since his discovery, he hadn't given food a thought. 'Italian? Indian? Chinese? You choose.' Their presence had instantly sent his mood in an upward trajectory.

'Surprise us,' said Jody, as she brought out a bottle of wine from a carrier bag.

Daniel lit a couple of candles and carried them to the kitchen table.

'I'm sorry to be a nuisance, but have you got any painkillers?' Nikki asked, rubbing her forehead. 'The fumes from the cleaning fluid have given me one hell of a headache.'

Her accent was edged with an American twang, nothing like the pure Brit cut-glass tone of Jody's.

Daniel went upstairs to the bathroom cabinet, but stopped short as soon as he reached the mirrored door. It was ajar by a fraction of an inch and when he checked inside, the lock was broken.

'No, no, no,' he moaned, under his breath.

Did this happen before or after he had the locks changed? It was always locked for safety reasons, even though it was well out of Ben's reach.

He scoured the contents. Nothing seemed to be missing and once again, there was no conclusive evidence he could show the police. He hadn't opened the cabinet in a long while; the lock could have been broken accidentally weeks ago.

'What's going on?' he said out loud.

'You okay?' asked Jody, who had appeared out of the blue and was leaning against the doorframe, holding their bags.

'Oh, nothing,' he said, with a snuffled laugh. 'I couldn't find the tablets, but here they are.'

The Lebanese takeaway was laced with sizzling spices; just what he needed. The chilli scorched his tongue and made its way down his throat, matching the fierce rage already burning inside him over Rick's betrayal.

There was no question that's what it was; in some way, he was party to those faked pictures.

What Daniel didn't understand was what it was all for. Were the photos part of some sneaky plan to discredit Daniel, so he could worm his way into Sophie's affections? Did Rick fancy her? Is that what this was about?

He forced his mind back to the last time the three of them had been together. It would have been January when Rick had turned up at a book launch at Otterbornes, helping himself to canapés and free champagne. Sophie thought Daniel had invited him – and he thought she had. It was only afterwards that they twigged neither of them had requested the pleasure of his company.

He was searching his memory for other occasions. A time when he'd walked into a room to find an incongruous silence, meaningful glances or too much space between the two of them. Had there ever been any unusual behaviour? Any flirting? He'd never had reason to question it before, but no matter how many scenes flashed into his head he could find nothing.

Sophie had always made it clear she wasn't the least bit keen on Rick as a human being. She did her utmost to avoid him and was always complaining about how crude and uncouth he was whenever he showed up. Either that was true – or she'd been giving an Oscar-winning performance all these years.

What was Rick playing at?

And why hadn't Jody mentioned her contact with Rick over his play?

Nikki began clearing the plates when Ben's voice at the kitchen door took them all by surprise.

'Daddy – need a story,' he said, standing barefoot, swinging on the door handle. He was wearing pyjamas with a bemused cat on them and the word *Catastrophe* written underneath. Daniel thought it summed up his own week rather nicely. He beckoned him in and propped him on his knee.

'Sorry, sweetheart, did we wake you up?'

Jody opened the cupboard behind the ironing board and pulled out an apron to start the washing up.

'Can the nice lady read me a story?' asked Ben, pointing to Jody.

'Go on,' said Nikki, taking the rubber gloves out of Jody's hands. 'I'll do these.'

Daniel offered to take over instead, but Nikki was insistent. So he followed Jody upstairs, carrying Ben. He settled Ben in his cot and handed Jody a couple of books. When he left the room, he hung around just outside, unable to resist eavesdropping.

'Miranda woke to a purple sky so she knew it must be Tuesday,' she said. 'The sky on the planet Arzon is a different colour every day. Did you know that, Ben?'

'Yes!' came a triumphant reply.

The story didn't sound familiar. Daniel held his breath, not wanting to disturb them and slowly peeped around the door. Ben was entranced, staring up at Jody's face as she knelt beside the cot, but there was no book in her hand.

He crept downstairs in awe.

'He's dropped off – sweet little chap,' said Jody when she rejoined them soon after. Nikki had been telling him about her latest job in America, producing commercials for a high-profile TV station. She was open and friendly like Jody, but if Jody could be likened to a crimson peony, Nikki was a white lupin. Perky, but understated.

'You're a miracle worker,' said Daniel. 'Getting Ben to settle since…' He stopped when he saw Jody's knowing nod. 'It's set us back months in his development.' Jody slipped off her shoes and sank back into the sofa with a sigh.

'I'm shattered – I'm going to turn in,' said Nikki.

Jody spoke before Daniel had the chance. 'You know which room we're in?'

Nikki nodded and left the two of them together. Daniel and Jody both waited in silence until her footsteps melted away.

'Just now, reading to Ben – is that a story you know off by heart?'

She did the lifting one eyebrow thing again and a ping went off, like an electric shock inside his chest. 'You were listening!' she cried. 'No, that's drama school for you. We did a lot of improvising. I loved it. Making things up as you go along – I'm good at that.'

'Very impressive.' He refilled her glass with wine. 'How long have you been acting professionally?'

'About twelve years now. It's a weird job. People tend to put you on a pedestal. I've not done anything noble or of any real value, yet I get followed around and bombarded on social media. All because I pretend to be someone else for a living.'

He decided to try something.

'Ever written any plays? Helped aspiring scriptwriters?'

She hesitated, her eyes narrowing slightly. 'I'm not into writing, myself. Too much like hard work.' She twisted a lock of hair into a tight spiral, then let it go. 'I've had a go at directing, though. I certainly plan to do more of that.'

The script he'd found at Rick's; he didn't actually know for certain if the handwritten notes on it were hers.

Jody stifled a yawn. 'Sorry, it's been a long day.'

'You're right.' He got up and stretched. 'Time to get some sleep.'

As he lay in bed, listening to the sounds within the house, he found himself mulling over the possibility that Rick could be the intruder who'd been snooping around his house in the dead of night. The more he considered it, the more likely it seemed. It was the sort of underhand behaviour that smacked of Rick. Why hadn't he thought of it before?

Perhaps Sophie had given him her key for some reason, although now the locks had been changed that little trick wouldn't be working any more.

Daniel turned over to face the empty pillow beside him, wrestling with one final question. The broken lock on the bathroom cabinet, the grit under the loft hatch, the light on in the cellar. What the hell had Rick been looking for?

Chapter thirty-eight

Annie, the nurse, showed him through to the far corner of the dayroom where Sophie was already seated.

'Thank you for agreeing to see me,' he said.

'This better be good.'

Sophie sounded formal, as though welcoming him to a job interview. Between Sophie now and the Sophie he'd married, lay a huge divide. A plunging, black chasm he didn't understand and had no desire to peer into.

Daniel took a seat beside her. Annie stood beside them, her hands clasped in front of her and her legs spread apart, like a sentry.

'I think you'll want to take a look at these.'

Daniel laid out the pictures he'd printed from his phone in front of her on the coffee table. He'd spent an hour and a half at reception, trying to get the right person to understand how imperative it was that Sophie got to see them. In the end, the duty psychiatrist would only let Daniel show them to her if Annie was glued to his hip. 'In case it upsets her,' she'd said.

He gave Annie a hard stare in the hope that she might back off a little, but she didn't shift an inch.

Daniel put the first picture in Sophie's hand. 'Look, this is us. Me, holding you close with my arm around you, leaving Desmond's newsagents in Highgate. We were on our way to one of those guided walks at the cemetery. You remember?'

'Yes. Yes, I do.' Her eyes narrowed. 'What is this for, Daniel? To remind me how in love we once were – before you cheated on me?'

'Now, look at this one. Spot the difference?'

For a surreal moment, Daniel felt like a detective, slapping crime scene shots before a suspect and demanding answers. This shot showed the same pose, but with the altered backdrop – the hotel – and the woman he'd never met in the space beside Daniel. Sophie gasped and a shudder gripped her shoulders.

'This is one of the pictures sent to my office!' she cried.

'You've seen it before?'

She scrabbled through the pile on the table. 'Yes – all of these. They're the same photos. You remember? The ones that had disappeared from my bag by the time I'd got home from work.' She gritted her teeth. 'You didn't believe me!'

It's true. He hadn't believed her. With nothing concrete to show him all along, he'd concluded that everything about the so-called affair was inside her head.

Annie peered over at the pictures, then looked away nonchalantly when Daniel caught her at it.

'Well. They're very clever,' he said, 'but they're not real. They've been digitally altered.'

'These are fake?' she cried. 'This isn't… these aren't how it was?' She lifted each photo close to her face, then compared them with others that looked similar, but which had various alterations. He watched the realisation twist her features with each image.

'Oh, my God… I see what you mean.'

Out of the corner of his eye, he could see Annie shuffling closer, but she kept quiet.

'They look completely genuine until you see them altogether,' said Daniel. 'Then, we finally get to the originals. Look, this is you! In every one of them.'

Sophie pressed her hand over her mouth. 'These are me! These were *our* pictures.' She stared at them, shaking her head the entire time. 'I believed them, of course I did. It fitted with everything else I found.'

Daniel took stock. These must have been the photos sent to her office, just as she said. They must have triggered some kind of mental breakdown where she started imagining other 'evidence' to support her assumption.

Sophie's face clouded over. 'Where did you find these?'

'Rick made the mistake of leaving them around,' he said.

'Rick?!' Sophie swallowed with a loud gulp.

'I found them in his flat.'

Annie's jaw fell open. She looked as though she'd been swept into an episode of EastEnders.

Sophie froze with her mouth half-open and she blinked hard. *'He* must have been the one who left them for me at Otterbornes,' she whispered haltingly.

She sat back, staring into space. 'Were the others fake, too? The ones with you and that redhead? At the Thorndike Tavern?' She flicked through the pile looking for them.

He'd been expecting that question.

He cleared his throat. 'Ah... no... they were real pictures, but they were taken completely out of context.'

Annie straightened up, folding her arms. Sophie turned up her nose as if she was being fed rotten meat.

'Honestly, they were completely innocent,' he insisted. 'A few pats on the back after a performance I'd been to, because that's what theatre people do.'

She shook her head, unconvinced.

'But it must have been Rick who took them,' he went on, desperate to plead his case. 'He was *there* in the Tavern. He asked me to meet him that night.' He flapped his hand around aimlessly. 'He's been trying to make it look like I've been with other women.'

'Why?' Sophie's voice sliced through his protestations.

'I don't know. To reinforce what you thought was going on? To add fuel to the flames?'

'But why would he?'

'I don't know! To destroy our marriage?'

She dropped her head into her hands.

'Maybe he's in love with you,' he said. 'Perhaps he wants you for himself?'

She let out a loud guffaw. 'You're joking. He's an idiot. I've only put up with him coming in to see me because he brought Ben.'

'So, you and he—?'

'Daniel!' Her dismissal was reassuringly absolute. 'What has he said?' She was indignant now.

'Nothing. Not a thing. He doesn't know I came across these photos. I wanted to see you first. I was completely thrown. There's something else…'

He explained about the intruder, about changing the locks.

'He must have stolen a key,' he concluded. 'Or had one copied. If you think about it, he's been turning up to our house a lot since last summer.'

Her gaze went back to the photographs. 'Are you absolutely sure it was Rick? He's useless with this kind of thing, isn't he? Remember when I asked him to crop a screenshot of a paperback Otterbornes were publishing. He didn't have a clue. He wouldn't know the first thing about photoshopping images, like these.'

'I know! That's one of the weird things about this.'

'And why use hard copies when he could have sent images online. It's a bit old-fashioned, don't you think?'

Daniel had considered that, too. 'I reckon Rick didn't know how to email them without giving away his own details as the sender.'

'How to post them anonymously, you mean?'

'Far too sophisticated for Rick, I'd say. And the ones delivered to the reception here were probably left by him too. He would know you wouldn't have access to your mobile phone in here.'

She toyed with her lip. 'He has been a bit strange when he's brought Ben in here to see me.'

'In what way?'

'When he talked about you it was as though he was playacting. On the surface he was defending you – saying you were gloomy without me, stuck indoors the whole time – then he "accidentally" let it slip you'd actually been out quite a bit. Like he was doing the opposite and actually maligning you.'

Daniel thought about it. 'Hmm… he was pretty keen to bring Ben in to see you. Perhaps that's why. He wasn't "helping out" at all, he was using it as a chance to turn you against me. To drive a wedge between us.'

Sophie was silent, but her eyes continued to dart around the room. 'I don't believe this… this is… I mean – it's incredible.'

'Yes. It explains a lot.'

She bit her lip, her eyes unfocused, no doubt still piecing things together in her mind.

'Are you going to confront him?' she asked.

He returned to the question he'd been chewing over for the past twenty-four hours.

'No,' he said, nipping his lips together. 'Not yet. If I force a showdown, I won't be able to watch what he's up to. If he thinks I have no inkling—'

'But this is all lies…' she threw a glance at the pictures, strewn on the table. 'Can't we tell the police?'

'There's no crime. He hasn't broken the law,' he said with a sigh. 'People create fake pictures all the time. To wind people up, to make themselves look important, successful. And we have no proof it's him.'

'It might *not* be him,' she interjected. 'Perhaps he was looking after the photos for someone else.'

'Hmm…' He shrugged.

'So, you're not going to do *anything*?'

'It seems crazy to carry on as normal, but I think it's best to hang fire. I don't want to do anything rash. I need to find out what the hell he's up to. To observe. Be patient.'

'Better the devil you know?'

He gripped her hand. 'Yes!'

At last, they were on the same page.

Chapter thirty-nine

It came to him in the middle of the night.

It was the day Daniel had the home alarm system installed, and as the engineer set up sensors and connected wires, it led him to reflect. Sophie always said he switched on his super-meticulous brain when he went to Kew and switched it off the moment he walked through the door at home. From now on, he was going to have to change that. He'd need to tune in to sharp-brain mode every hour of the day if he was going to work out what was going on.

With that in mind, just before he turned in, he'd made a list of the unnerving events that had taken place at his house after the stabbing. He'd then tried to add dates to each one.

He couldn't remember exactly when he noticed the framed picture was missing on the landing or discovered the grit under the loft hatch. But none of those dates mattered, because they only pinpointed when he'd *noticed* those irregularities. It didn't mean they'd happened then.

He'd also noted the couple of occasions when the side of the cot had been lowered and Ben had been pottering around in the dead of night. The second time was definitely after the evening meal in Soho. Edith had put Ben to bed and Daniel had checked he was asleep when he came home. Everything was as it should have been. The cot could only have been tampered with during the night.

The only other incident he could pin down to an exact date was when he found the front door wide open and the light on in the cellar. That was definitely April 12.

What had shaken him out of his sleep was that final date.

Rick hadn't been in London on April 12. It was during the Easter holidays and he'd been moaning about being forced to lead a school trip to Paris.

Nevertheless, Daniel didn't just take Rick's word for it. He opened his laptop and looked up the Facebook page for Rick's school. On that precise date, a photo had been posted of a bunch of teenagers standing by the Cité des Sciences et de l'Industrie. Rick was there, all right, at the back. Several comments had been left on the page by pupils making fun of his deerstalker hat.

Daniel spent the rest of the night in a spin.

If Rick *wasn't* the intruder sneaking around the place, who was?

Chapter forty

When the curtain fell for the final time, there was the usual rush of actors retreating to their dressing rooms as the stage crew checked their clipboards and began rearranging props. Jody was exhausted and wanted nothing more than to shed her costume and get home. She gave her face three half-hearted wipes with a wad of moist cotton wool and flung her wig and outfit on the rack.

'Sorry, Gina, I haven't the energy to hang them up.'

'Don't worry, girl,' said her dresser. 'Go on, clear off home, I'll sort this lot out.'

'Gina, you're the world's best wardrobe manager and I'm going to take you out for dinner one of these days,' said Jody, blowing her a kiss as she ducked out of the door. Two steps down the corridor she heard Gina calling after her.

'I want that in writing!'

Jody fled from the smell of greasepaint and stale sweat out onto the street. It got too hot and claustrophobic in the theatre; the lights, the heavy costumes, the tight backstage squeeze. She filled her lungs with sweet London night air and managed to flag down a black cab straight away.

Twenty minutes later, she paid the driver and opened the gate to her house. As she walked up the path and before she reached the front steps, she had the distinct impression she wasn't alone. It was hard to explain; something intuitive.

She looked about her, peering into the dark bushes to the left of the path, but saw nothing. She put her jumpiness down to the recent break-in. Surely it was a one-off incident. Burglars don't return to the scene of the crime, do they? Except it hadn't been a straightforward burglary; neither she nor Nikki had discovered anything missing.

She was standing on the top step, unzipping her bag, when she heard a branch snap behind her. She turned again, telling herself not to be stupid. It was probably just the neighbour's cat.

She was about to pull out her keys when, out of nowhere, a gloved hand clamped over her mouth and she was shoved into the front door. The figure pushed a fist into her spine, as the other hand kept her mouth covered. She was finding it hard to breathe; the thick woollen glove pressing over her nose, blocking her airways.

She struggled, but her elbow was being yanked right up towards her shoulder and the pain was excruciating. She yelped, but the sound was muffled by the glove.

Why was her front door so far from the road? Even so, surely with the light on over the porch, someone would see her, realise she was in trouble, come to her aid. She was about to use her stiletto heel to stamp on one of the feet behind her, but what if he – she was certain it was a man – had a knife? What if he tugged her head back and smashed it through the glass panel in the door?

If only Nikki had still been here. Jody could have manoeuvred her weight so she fell against the doorbell to raise the alarm. But Nikki had already gone to the airport.

Forcing his knuckles into her spine, the man said two words: 'Open up'.

'Okay, okay,' she said, through the glove, nodding her head.

With one arm loose and her whole body shaking, she fumbled in her bag for her house keys. Her fingers found the keyring, but she made a snap decision. No way was she letting this creature inside her house. There was just one thing she could try.

She let the keys fall to the ground. When her abductor looked down, she put her foot over the keys. She knew she was taking a risk as she reached for the small canister right at the bottom of her bag. She gripped her fingers around it and took in a sharp breath before pointing it over her shoulder and firmly pressing down the top. Instantly, a piercing squeal took the attacker by surprise and Jody managed to shake herself loose. The ear-splitting noise seemed to temporarily paralyse him, so she grabbed the keys, kicked off her shoes and scrambled down the steps towards the gate.

She ran straight out into the narrow road, clutching her bag, waving and screaming as cars approached from both sides. *Make as much commotion as possible!* The street was suddenly alive with screeching tyres and tooting horns; the alarm in her hand still giving out a high-pitched wail. One car swerved, but didn't stop, and she could hear herself whimpering, 'help me, help me' as a second car began to slow down and the driver wound down his window.

'I'm being mugged!' she cried and pressed herself up against the car.

The driver got out. He was short and overweight, with thick eyebrows and a T-shirt with the words "Pete's Diner" emblazoned on it.

'Okay, love – you all right?'

'He grabbed me…'

Jody looked up towards her front door. The man had gone. There was no sign of him. There was no indication that anything had happened apart from the continuing screech of the rape alarm. She didn't know how to switch it off.

She strained to see both ways along the street and could see no one, except a woman strolling towards them with a small dog.

Chapter forty-one

The Past – 12 September 2017

Rick lifted the shoebox out of the bottom drawer of his desk and took off the lid. Then he stuffed the photograph he'd been carrying around in his wallet all week at the bottom. He'd made no headway whatsoever in working out why it was significant. But there was definitely something disturbing about it. Nevertheless, seeing it every time he reached for his credit card was just annoying him now.

Apart from the rather nifty discovery of his grandfather's vintage pocket watch wrapped in tissue paper, there had been nothing in the box but a batch of old family snaps. A trip down memory lane.

He'd already flicked through the timeworn pictures; some of his parents after their wedding; several at the seaside and more that looked like they were taken in Egypt or Morocco. They didn't mean much to him.

This time, as he lingered over the rest, he felt himself unexpectedly dewy-eyed. A picture of Louise – around ten years old – doing a handstand with her skirt falling down over her head, and several of Miles in the garden when he was about seven. Rick stood that snap against his mug and sighed. He missed him. He'd been about twenty when Miles was born, an age when the idea of a baby brother coming along was about as exciting as finding out there was a sequel to *Bambi*.

But once he'd got past the nappy stage, Miles had turned out to be a cute little chap. He was wide-eyed and enthralled by Rick's magic tricks and sleight of hand. Mile's favourites were when Rick made things disappear. Like the time he made all the coins in his mother's biscuit tin vanish. Or the time Rick cast a magic spell at bedtime. By morning all the gnomes in the neighbours' front garden had gone. Miles thought that one was great.

Rick pulled out another photo and leant it against the computer screen. The camera had captured Mile's quirky half-grin and Rick realised that over time he'd let it slip from his memory.

All he could remember were the hushed voices when Miles was lying in hospital, his bleached-out face barely distinguishable from the cotton sheets; the rain at the funeral and the half-sized coffin. And Whitney singing 'I will always love you', as the little box parted the curtains. He didn't even make it to the age of ten. That was by far the cruellest trick life could ever play on them.

Rick was about to put the lid back on the box, when he spotted that blasted picture again. Dog-eared and slightly out of focus, it had worked its way to the top of the stack. Last week, it had stood out from all the rest because it was in a frame. A silver one, as if it was special. He'd taken it out to look at it more closely, but this time he went one step further and held up a magnifying glass.

Aha – what do we have here?

He took it to the light of the window to be sure, but he was right; it was definitely Daniel and a group of others at a party.

He'd turned it over to see the date again: *30 March, 2002.* He and Daniel would have been nineteen.

It was definitely Oxford; he recognised several other faces as fellow students. Why had Daniel made the trip over from Reading University that day?

Suddenly he twigged: it must have been the annual boat race. Scenes of dark blue bodies hitting the water under Chiswick Bridge flooded his mind. Daniel must have come over for the race and Oxford had won that year. As good an excuse as any for a party.

Still, the party itself rang no bells for him whatsoever.

He sat back and tried to remember what it was like being nineteen. Second year of university. Oxford came with ready-made friends and its own neat structure. It was a gift. Late nights, lie-ins, a few lectures thrown in if he could be bothered. You didn't have to think about anything. Not like real life, where you had to make choices and face the consequences.

Something about the picture felt strange, but he couldn't for the life of him work out what it was. He leant back in the lopsided typists' chair he'd pinched from the school skip and tapped the glossy paper with his nail. He tried to put names to the faces: Stanley Meredith – a brainy twat who annoyed the hell out of him. And that girl who couldn't keep her legs together… what was her name? Nancy something. Bet Daniel had his hands all over her. Other faces were too blurred to make out, even with the magnifying glass.

He tutted and slapped the picture back in the box.

Then it hit him.

What the f—

He leant forward, doubling over as the realisation grabbed at his belly like an invisible animal trying to rip open his flesh. Why had it taken him so long to work it out? It was obvious.

This was going to blow everything sky-high.

Chapter forty-two

The Present

Jody was standing where he'd left her in the spare bedroom, still wearing her coat. She was clutching a warm towel to her chest like it was a missing child returned safely home.

'I'm sorry to turn up without any warning, like this,' she said, for the third time. 'Once I'd given my statement to the police, I couldn't go back to the house on my own.'

'I'm glad you did. You're safe, now.' He peeled off the handbag she still had slung over her shoulder and led her into the bathroom. 'Come on, you said you wanted a bath – I'll get the water running.'

Although Daniel was horrified to hear what had happened, it was almost a blessing to deal with someone else's crisis for a change. With the trial coming up and Sophie's future in the balance, it was refreshingly therapeutic to focus on Jody's misfortune.

'That would be divine.' She dropped down onto the edge of the bath and kicked off her boots, as the water gushed and steam curled around the room.

Daniel turned off the taps and silently closed the door behind him, leaving her to it.

Once she'd dried off, she told and retold him the story of her ordeal, sitting with her bare feet curled underneath her on the single bed and wrapped in one of Sophie's fluffy dressing gowns. 'I thought he was going to kill me… I should have been better prepared… I'm so glad I still had the rape alarm in my bag… I was so scared…'

Daniel sat beside her and allowed her to lean against him. Other than listen and offer her sanctuary, he didn't know what else he could do.

Eventually, she burned herself out with the endless monologue. Her breathing deepened and when he looked down, her eyes had closed. He carefully guided her head towards the pillow and reached for the duvet. She was still clad in the bulky dressing gown and when he tried to cover her, she opened her eyes.

'Please don't leave me.'

For a split second, Daniel imagined the possibility of another scene altogether playing out in his mind. He swallowed hard and forced the images away.

'I'll only be in the next room,' he replied, taking his hands away from the bed and edging backwards as though she was a primed hand grenade.

The following morning, Daniel left a cup of tea beside Jody's curled-up shape and left her to wake. He'd already phoned Kew to say he'd be late.

'*I* want to say hello,' Ben said, trying to get into the room.

Daniel kept his hand on the door handle. 'No, Ben. We mustn't wake her up.' He put his finger to his lips. 'It's time to go. We're going to be late.'

She must have heard them and called out. On hearing the voice Ben bounded in, a rucksack shaped like a bumblebee on his back with his name on it.

'Sorry about that,' said Daniel. 'Someone was keen to see you before nursery.'

'Are you still crying?' asked Ben, who'd caught a fleeting glimpse of her when the doorbell had woken the pair of them after midnight.

'I'm much better now, thank you. Look – dry eyes,' she replied. She turned to Daniel. 'Sorry about last night. I was in a bit of a state.'

Ben sat on the bed and she stroked his hair.

'Are you staying again tonight?' Ben asked. 'Then we can have a story.'

'Not now, young man,' Daniel intervened, 'Jody has had a nasty shock and she needs lots of rest.' He ushered him out of the room and held up ten fingers twice to let her know how long he'd be.

By the time he returned from the nursery, Jody was fully dressed and sitting hunched over a mug of coffee in the kitchen.

'I'm starting to get really worried now,' she said, her head propped up in her hands. 'A break-in and now this, in a matter of days?'

'This guy who threatened you – did you see him at all? Notice anything that could identify him?'

'No, he was behind me. He came from nowhere. He wanted me to open the door, so he could get in.' She shivered and gripped the mug.

'A crazy fan from the theatre, maybe?'

She shrugged.

'Old or young?'

'He had a deep voice,' she said, 'I'd say it wasn't a teenager, but…'

'What do the police think?'

'They can't do much.' She shrugged. 'They did tell me something, though. Useful for another time – heaven forbid.'

Daniel gave her an inquiring look.

'If you're in trouble and call 999 and stay silent, the police won't respond to the call, but if you dial 999 and cough or punch in 55, they'll be on their way. It's meant for times when it's dangerous to be heard calling the police.'

'A bit late now,' he retorted. 'What else did they say?'

'They're going to send a patrol car round more often to keep an eye on the house, but it's not very reassuring, to be honest.'

'No, I'm sure.' He dropped his car keys on the table and sat down. 'It wasn't a random mugging? He didn't want your purse?'

'No – he was already in the front garden. Waiting. He wasn't interested in my bag. He wanted to get into the house. He wanted something inside. It *must* be linked to the break-in.'

'What about your sister?'

'She's in France. I haven't told her yet.'

'Maybe she should come back.'

'Long trip – for what?'

Daniel drummed his fingers on the table, unable to offer her an answer.

Chapter forty-three

Rick was late. As he came within sight of the stage door, he spotted Stuart leaning against the wall with a cigarette, reading *The Sun*. Stuart crushed the cigarette under his baseball boot and folded the newspaper.

'About time. Where's the best place to go?' asked Stuart, picking up a couple of carrier bags full of shopping. 'Have you got it?'

'Let's go to Vince's café. And yes, I've got it.' Rick tapped the pocket of his jacket.

Vince showed them to a small private room at the back and brought through cappuccinos and a doughnut each. The room smelt of blocked drains and was crammed with tins of soup, beans and stacks of toilet paper.

Stuart took a mouthful of doughnut, scattering sugar down his used-to-be white shirt. Rick couldn't help noticing how much strain the buttons were under.

'Here we are,' said Rick, brushing away the granules from the table. Stuart snatched the wad of tissue paper and unwrapped the gold item with greasy fingers.

'It's in good condition,' asserted Rick.

Stuart turned the pocket watch over in his hands, then walked over to the barred window to hold it up to the light. Stuart wasn't just a propmaker at the theatre; for the last three years he'd been making a nice little earner on the side selling jewellery, paintings and various not-so-antique antiques.

'You've done your homework?' Stuart asked him.

'Just needs you to engrave the magic words inside the lid: "Count Aspen, April 1914".

'And he was definitely on the Lusitania?'

'Duh!' exclaimed Rick. 'I've traced the records.'

'Well, once I've finished with it, no one will be able to doubt it's the real thing,' said Stuart, using two oily fingers directly on the lens to push up his glasses. Rick wondered how he could possibly see out of them at all, never mind carry out such intricate work.

Stuart opened the back to look at the mechanism.

'It's not working,' Rick told him.

'Good. It shouldn't be after all this time. It doesn't have any water damage so we'll need to make out it was in a waterproof container of some sort.'

'Sure – just make it look authentic for Hank.'

'I'll disguise the serial number,' said Stuart. 'It'll look like genuine wear and tear. I think he should fall for it.' He gave Rick a sugar-coated grin. 'Hank was never the sharpest tool in the cupboard anyway.'

'It's "in the box".'

'What box?' Stuart was searching on the table for something he thought he'd missed.

Rick sighed. 'I think you'll find it's "the sharpest tool in the…" never mind.'

Stuart rewrapped the tissue around the watch and slipped it into his inside pocket. He took another mouthful of doughnut and allowed the jam to ooze onto his fingers. 'Count Aspen, right?' He stabbed at the sugary remains on the plate.

Rick nodded impatiently. He was keen to get to the important bit. 'How much will we get for it?'

Stuart hesitated.

'Come on – it cost me five hundred quid,' Rick protested.

Rick took a swig of coffee. It cost no such thing, of course, but he was damned if he was going to hand it over for nothing. Stuart didn't need to know it had been lying forgotten in the shoebox in his mother's wardrobe for years. If she hadn't decided to sell the house in September, he'd never have come across it. Even so, he'd given the watch little thought for months, having become obsessed with the other significant item in said box.

'Don't forget Hank gets his cut,' Stuart reminded him. 'Once I take off the fee for the magnificent job I'm going to do forging an accompanying letter and producing phoney photographs to prove provenance, you should be getting in the region of fifteen hundred for your trouble.'

'Is that all?'

'Do you want me to do this or not?'

A bead of spittle dribbled onto Stuart's chin. Rick turned away and dropped his own doughnut back onto the plate without taking a bite.

'We won't know for certain until Hank gives it pride of place in his gallery. I'll let you know once I've done the inscription and faked the paperwork.'

'Sounds good. Pleased to do business with you, again.' Rick couldn't bring himself to look at Stuart's sticky face. 'You up for other deals, if they come my way?'

'Definitely.' Stuart raised his tacky hand for a high five, but Rick pretended he needed to tie his shoelace at the last second to avoid any contact. Then he opened the door to the clatter of dishes and smell of bacon from the main café area.

Stuart bent down for his bags of shopping. 'Let's go for a drink sometime,' he called out as Rick strode ahead of him.

'Sure,' said Rick, without turning round.

Rick passed the till and was out of the place before Stuart had a chance to realise he'd been left with the bill.

Chapter forty-four

Sophie was sitting on the bed listening to her iPod while Shareen was doing her usual trick of pretending to speak to her, silently moving her mouth and forcing her to pull out the earphones.

'I said, have you got any Lily Allen on there?'

'Sorry, no.'

'I'm bored,' grumbled Shareen, kicking at the edge of the rug on the floor.

'No one playing pool?'

'I'm sick of pool.'

'What about a jigsaw in the dayroom?'

'Nah. There are always pieces missing. Doris eats them, silly cow.' Shareen began picking the skin around her nails and tugging bits off with her teeth. 'You been in the witness box yet?'

'No. Should be today.'

'Wanna talk about it? I can take you through what happens – the rough guide to getting the jury in the palm of your hand. Done it plenty of times myself.'

Sophie's stomach couldn't cope with a discussion about what lay ahead. 'It's okay, thanks.'

Shareen sighed and stared at Sophie's magazine on the end of the bed. 'You finished with that?'

Sophie handed it over. 'Keep it.'

There was a photograph of a B-list celebrity cradling her newborn child on the front. Sophie found she couldn't drag her eyes away from it. 'It makes you think about what's really important in life, doesn't it, being in here?' she muttered. She leant back and reached under her pillow, pulling out a photograph of

Ben. She cradled it in her hands, fighting a flood of imminent tears. But it was like trying to hold back the Aswan Dam with net curtains. They spilled onto her cheek no matter how much she willed them not to.

Shareen slid off her own bed and sat alongside without touching her. 'Ah, but you'll get to be with him soon, girl.'

'No, I won't,' she whimpered. 'I'm going to end up in prison.'

Shareen shook her head vigorously. 'No way. The judge will see sense. You're not the murdering type. They'll let you off. They've got to. You had a bad day, that's all. They'll see you got deluded with stress or something. It was one moment. They'll see that's not what you're really like. They've got to.'

Sophie let out a loud, shuddering sob as she clutched Ben's picture. For the first time since the day she discovered Daniel's infidelity the tears weren't for herself – they were for Ben.

'You hoping to go back and play happy families with that bloke of yours?'

'Yes. No,' she whimpered, 'I don't know.'

Over time, Sophie had gradually let Shareen know the sketchy details that had led to her being sectioned. Under normal circumstances, telling someone such as Shareen her innermost thoughts would have been unthinkable, but these weren't normal circumstances. Besides, it hadn't been as awkward or shameful as Sophie had expected. Shareen had never pried and there were times when Sophie found her down-to-earth approach easier to bear than Greta's non-stop deflecting chatter and her father's pitiful sympathy.

'But some lowlife faked those photos to make it look like your husband was screwing someone else.'

'Yeah, but there's still the other proof I found around the house. And this new redhead he's been seeing.'

'You ain't letting him off the hook, then?'

'I don't know what to think. I can't seem to work it out. Was I just delusional? Am I still unstable, is that why it doesn't make any sense? Thing is, I feel so normal now. The mushy feeling in my head has completely gone.'

'You certainly don't seem off your rocker to me, sugar. In fact, put you alongside most of the other nutters in here and you stand out a mile.'

Shareen gave her a teary smile.

'I suppose I should take that as a compliment.'

'Don't give up, darlin'. You'll be all right. Some funny stuff's going on for sure, but it'll all come out in the end.'

'Will it?'

Overcome with renewed panic, Sophie buried her face in Shareen's torn T-shirt and felt an arm wrap around her. They stayed liked that, locked together, for what felt like a long, long time.

Chapter forty-five

The storm that had been brewing all day finally cracked open the sky with a tumultuous deluge as Daniel drove back from the last day of the trial.

He pulled up outside his house just in time to see a text come in on his phone. Jayne had given birth to a little boy and both were doing well.

The joy and relief he should have felt barely touched him, but he faked a jubilant tone and sent a cheery message in return. Regardless of the disaster that was his own life, he couldn't let her down.

His phone buzzed again as he was getting out into the downpour.

'How did it go?' came his mother's anxious voice. 'How is she? What was the verdict?'

Franciska had been turning up at court regularly until today, when she'd slipped in the garden after breakfast and twisted her ankle.

Daniel didn't have the energy to bolt for the front door, so he slumped back into the driver's seat.

'Guilty,' he croaked, finding the word loathsome to get his tongue round.

'What? No!'

'I can't believe it either. We all thought she'd get diminished responsibility, but it looks like that didn't hold enough water.'

She sounded horrified. 'Why not?'

'The barristers think the jury were swayed by the fact that she had no history of mental illness and had showed no ongoing signs of instability.'

'What did the judge say?'

'That the jury decided she was overcome with rage and lost control.'

Daniel felt through his shirt to the thin fold of scar tissue and reran the chilling events of that ill-fated afternoon in February. At this moment, however, the attempt on his life was looking like the least of his concerns. All in all, the nightmare was just beginning.

Franciska snatched a breath. 'But what about the psychiatrists?'

'They concluded that she was acting out of character, but essentially of sound mind. The problem is Sophie seemed completely normal during the trial. You mentioned it yourself, so poised and composed. It weighed against her.'

She sighed heavily. 'So, what happens now?'

Daniel felt his mouth go dry. 'With the support of Dr Marshall's reports and my own statement, the sentence has been dropped to two years.'

'Two years...'

He simply gave his mother the facts. He didn't want to dwell on the impact of it right now. Until he'd worked through it for himself, he couldn't possibly put into words how he felt to anyone.

'She's been taken to Glenbrook women's prison in Sutton. Her lawyer did his best to convince us all afterwards that she'll be released early. It could have been a lot worse. Everyone says.'

There was a silence. A cyclist shot past the car sending spray onto his window.

'I'm really sorry. That's dreadful. Poor Ben. I can't...' Franciska's voice was high-pitched, strained. Just like Vincent's voice had been when they'd discussed the outcome in the foyer of the court. Greta and Cassandra were there too, standing with their mouths open, unable to take it in, together with numerous other friends and family. Rick, thankfully, hadn't shown up.

Franciska tailed off, just as everyone else had done, unable to finish whatever she was trying to say.

Daniel blew hot breath on the window beside him and watched the glass turn cloudy.

If only you knew the half of it.

Chapter forty-six

'Whoever it was who introduced matinee performances,' cried Jody, kicking off the tight peep-toe shoes, 'it certainly wasn't an actor!'

They were fifties' originals, designed for someone with feet at least one size smaller. She sat at her cluttered dressing table and rubbed her toes.

'Why do actors sweat so much?' Gina asked, holding up a blouse stained around the collar with make-up.

'It's grease-paint, not sweat,' rebuked Jody, talking to her reflection in the mirror. 'And anyhow, we work like Trojans under bright lights, that's why.'

'Sounds like a cushy number to me. You should try ironing outfits all day. No standing ovations in that job and it's just as hot.'

'Poor Gina. One day, you'll be plucked backstage by some budding director and Hollywood will realise what they've been missing.'

'Ha bloody ha.' Gina stopped combing Jody's hair. 'Seriously, for a moment. We'd better get a move on.' She glanced up at the clock. 'Steve has arranged a few drinks and nibbles backstage as a kind of tribute to Mark.'

'Oh, of course.' Jody got to her feet. 'Did the police find out who ran him down?'

'No one's said anything. A busy street in the heart of the city – you'd think someone saw something, wouldn't you?'

Jody was less unconvinced. 'It's really hard to identify motorbike riders, especially in their helmets. You have to get the licence number. You can't even tell if it's a man or a woman half the time.'

Crew and actors were already forming small groups in the gaps between gantries and stepladders. Steve, the stage manager, was directing people to a trestle table with drinks, and Nola – one of the wardrobe assistants – was handing round bowls of crisps and snacks. Nobody was saying much.

Jody put her glass down and leant against a large black trunk, taking a moment to watch the faces of those who'd become her professional family during the past few months. She wondered how many would be on her Christmas card list in two years' time. The theatre was strange, like that. Strangers thrown together into intense relationships within the sweaty buzz, fear and elation of performance. In a few months the show would finish and everyone would go their own ways.

A voice from behind made Jody jump.

'I didn't expect to see you here,' she said.

'We wanted to pay our respects,' said Rick. He was accompanied by a man dressed all in black. 'You know Stuart?'

She nodded vaguely. 'A prop maker, aren't you?' she said.

'He and I go back a bit,' said Rick with a smirk.

Stuart offered his hand and bowed in a ridiculous fashion, giving Jody an insipid grin. His grip was not only limp, but damp.

'Did you know Mark?' she asked him.

'Not really, but it's all rather dramatic, isn't it?' responded Stuart. 'Hit and run, everyone's saying.'

Stuart was not only dressed like an undertaker, but clearly possessed an unhealthy interest in the dead. Besides which, he had too many teeth for the size of his mouth.

Jody discreetly wiped her hand on her jeans and looked over his shoulder, searching for the first opportunity to escape to an alternative group. Thankfully, they were joined by one of the lighting crew, who wanted to ask Stuart about a job he was working on. Jody slipped away, but was closely followed by Rick. He cornered her.

'Old Danny-boy is not so squeaky clean, you know,' he said. Jody hated the cynicism in his face, as if he knew something she didn't and wouldn't hesitate to use it against her.

'Sorry?' She tried to move away, but he blocked her path. Rick began to speak, but was interrupted by the director clapping his hands and asking for quiet. There followed a short speech after which they all raised their glasses to give Mark a final toast.

'You like mysteries, don't you?' whispered Rick, once the formalities were over. 'Well, here's one.' He leant towards her in a conspiratorial fashion. 'Go to the cemetery at Barnes Bridge and find the gravestones on the left of the chapel of rest. There's one there that'll give you something to think about.' He tapped the side of his nose.

'Don't be ridiculous.' She backed away from his foul-smelling breath. He'd obviously had several drinks before he'd arrived. 'What makes you think I'm going to set off on some stupid wild goose chase?'

'Because you're intrigued; because you want to know if Mr Daniel Duke has skeletons in his closet and...' He dipped his finger in his glass and sucked it dry, 'because I've seen the way you look at him.'

She sucked her teeth, shaking her head, impatiently.

'You've fallen for him, haven't you? Hook, line and sinker...' he added.

Rick's weatherman smile switched on and instantly faded at the edges. She hated it. He clinked his glass against hers before she could turn away.

Chapter forty-seven

It took Jody longer than she thought to drive over to Barnes Village. She left the car by the pond, with its draping willows and white picket fence, and set off across the grass. A couple of Canadian geese waddled behind her, hoping for scraps.

It was a balmy May morning; the sun already toasting her neck as she took in the smell of hot bread wafting through the open door of a local baker. An idyllic rural scene, more remarkable for being on the fringes of the hectic city.

The Thames opened out before her and she passed under the wrought-iron railway bridge, gazing at the glistening water as it curved away into the distance. On the way over, she'd wondered what she was going to find, but now she was here, she couldn't help drawing the conclusion that it was simply Rick taunting her with a silly game.

Why had she wasted her time?

Because she was intrigued. Because she was nosy and found it hard to ignore it when someone dangled an enigmatic insinuation in front of her nose. And Rick had been right; because she *had* taken a fancy to Daniel – a very big fancy.

She took a turning to the left and, checking the app on her phone, cut through side streets until she reached the gates of the burial ground. The scene looked deserted. Sombre and still.

She followed a narrow path that led her towards the small chapel. Rick had said something about looking at the gravestones to the left of it, but she realised now that she didn't know from which direction he would have assumed she'd approach the chapel from. If there really *is* something to find I could be here some time, she thought, bringing her hands to her hips and surveying the expanse of headstones.

She decided to find the main entrance to the chapel and begin searching to the left from that position. There were rows of grey stones, interspersed by larger tombs and plinths and she started reading the ones nearest the path, though she still had no idea what she was looking for. Rick had implied that whatever she found would show Daniel had something to be ashamed of. How would she know if any of these old graves had any significance? Would it have Daniel's surname, Duke, on it?

Most of the stones nearest to the chapel showed dates at the end of the nineteenth century: children, wives, husbands, mothers and fathers. Surely, a grave from as far back as the 1890s was too remote to have any relevance. She moved on and the further away she went, the more recent the dates became. 1920s, 1930s. She decided to skirt the whole section and start again, working inwards from the outside path.

The ones at the edge were from the twenty-first century and included recent mounds of earth covered in cascades of cards and dying flowers, the headstones having not yet been laid. Moving from one to the next, Jody scanned the names, but was becoming increasingly angry with herself for giving Rick's stupid accusation the time of day. The idea of abandoning the search and returning to the village for a much-needed cup of coffee was becoming far more compelling.

Suddenly a dog appeared, snuffling in the grass at her feet. She looked up and the distant owner, an elderly man with a walking stick, called the terrier's name.

'Sorry if he frightened you,' he shouted. Jody waved her arms to indicate that no harm had been done.

For a moment she watched the dog as he moved from one stone to the next, sniffing and wagging his tail with complete disregard for the calls of his owner. The dog then cocked his leg and Jody moved away, her eyes temporarily resting on a nearby stone. A shiver charged up to her throat. She stopped and read the stone again, then as the terrier scuttled away, she took out her phone to take a picture.

The stone was carved with the words: 'In loving memory of Miles Charles Fox, beloved son and brother, who died 19th March 2011, aged nine years. May you sleep with the angels'.

Rick's family name was Fox, wasn't it?

This must be the one she was supposed to find. She presumed it must be Rick's younger brother, but she was perplexed by what his passing could possibly have to do with Daniel. Was Rick trying to suggest that Daniel harmed the boy? Was Daniel responsible for his death?

She straightened up and walked back to the gate. Did she need to be concerned about this? Of the two men, Daniel seemed by far the more trustworthy.

Suddenly she wished she hadn't come. She'd given in to her own inquisitive nature and now felt duped. Worse than that, she felt two-faced, especially given how supportive Daniel had been recently.

And guilty.

Really guilty about something she'd done – but she couldn't bring herself to think about that now.

The sun was giving her a headache and she decided to skip the coffee and head back. As she turned onto the main road, several rowing boats glided towards her along the river, but the tranquil scene passed her by. She was distracted by too many unanswered questions, the first and most important being, *What on earth am I going to do next?*

Chapter forty-eight

Daniel left his desk at one o'clock on the dot so he wouldn't be late. Since Jayne lived in Kew and wanted to avoid any crowds, she'd suggested a quiet spot in the gardens, so he didn't have far to go. She'd suggested their 'usual spot' – the Syon House end of the main lake.

He found her on a bench close to the water. Ducking under a branch of a deodar cedar, he stepped onto the spongy bark chippings to join her.

'Hey, you,' she said with a dreamy smile. 'We're watching the swans.'

He put a selection of sandwiches and deli delights down next to her, before realising the newborn baby was suckling at her breast. He squeezed her shoulder in lieu of the big hug he'd planned on giving her and she looked up at him with warmth.

Her cheeks were rose pink and she didn't look the least bit exhausted. In fact, she had an aura of serenity about her, fresh and relaxed in black capri pants and a bright cerise tunic.

'I'm afraid Robbie couldn't wait for lunch.' She stroked the top of the boy's head as if motherhood was her natural state. 'He'll say hello in a minute.'

Daniel sat down with a chuckle, but it was short-lived. Seeing Jayne like this, enchanted by her baby boy, brought back tender memories of Sophie with Ben days after he came into the world. It churned his stomach.

'You okay?' she said, reaching out for his hand.

'Just brings it all back, you know? Those first weeks. The way this little bundle turns your world upside down and brings a sense of desperate love with it.' He sniffed. 'Sorry, that sounded a bit melodramatic.'

'No. I know exactly what you mean. Life will never be the same again. I can see that. It's like realising the rest of your life has been in black and white and suddenly there's this thing called "colour". It's a new kind of love to me.'

As usual, her unruly blonde ringlets were tied back into a ponytail. She once described her hair like the wiry stuffing in old mattresses and, unfortunately, her description was pretty much spot on.

One of the swans ducked its head into the water, then slowly stretched out its wings.

'They have wings like angels, don't you think?' she said. 'Pure white and elegant.'

He nodded, watching it. 'Their call always reminds me of those paper party-blowers.'

'You spend too much time around kids,' she said, glancing down at the bundle in her arms and laughing.

'I miss you at work,' he said. 'It's pretty dreary without you.'

'No one to make you a proper cup of tea?'

He shrugged. 'That too.'

'And the trial? Is it over now?'

He leaned back into a more comfortable position and gave her all the details.

'How are you coping?'

'Sophie wants a divorce. I'm not ready for that. Everything has happened so fast. I can't get my head around it.'

'She doesn't mean it, surely?'

He gave her a wry smile. 'After what she did to me, anything is possible.'

The baby stretched his arm in the air and squirmed, so she moved him over to her other breast.

'You look so at ease with him. Like he's your tenth child, or something.'

She smiled, taking her eyes straight back to the baby.

'Any news from Frank?' he asked. 'Has he seen sense yet?'

'I don't think there's any chance of that. He hasn't been to see Robbie. I think that says all I need to know about his intentions with this little one.'

'Are you okay with that?'

'I'd rather be on my own than with someone who doesn't want to be there,' she said.

He let the words sink in. 'You're right,' he replied with conviction.

'In any case, I'm not alone, am I? There's a new man in my life and he's not going anywhere.'

Daniel squeezed her hand again, too emotional for words. He couldn't agree with her more. Ben was his number one priority now. Father and son would forge ahead and have a terrific future together, no matter what happened.

Chapter forty-nine

'**B**loody kids', Rick shouted out loud, as he slammed the front door. It was gone midnight, but he was still ranting to himself.

He kicked off his trainers. Felsham and Wiley were going to have to watch their step, because he wasn't bloody well having another day like this one.

Rick dropped his rucksack in the hall and poured himself a large whisky, even though he'd already got through several at the pub. *No one blows out the windows in my lab and gets away with it.*

At three o'clock everything had been ticking along as normal. Kids were being unruly and insolent, but nothing worse than usual. By three fifteen, a cocktail of green goo and broken glass erupted all over the place and Rick had been forced to abandon the class and stay behind to clear it up. Where was the effing caretaker for God's sake? Wasn't that *his* job?

Poor Jonny Piper looked like he'd lost an eyebrow. He said something about Felsham making a 'Multi-dimensional Implodertron out of liquid nitrogen and jelly-babies'.

Bloody lunatics.

And all the flak would fall back on him. *Should have been more vigilant, Mr Fox. Why weren't you supervising, Mr Fox? A case of incompetence, Mr Bloody Fox! Nah. Nah. Nah.*

Then he'd have to face the head and it wouldn't be pretty. He knew for definite now: teaching wasn't for him.

Chapter fifty

He scrubbed his arms with a flannel at the kitchen sink, still grubby from the afternoon's events, and took his tumbler into the study.

The deputy head had told him to write a report of the incident and have it on his desk first thing. He should have got home earlier.

As Rick waited for the computer to load up, he noticed his printer was out of paper. Reaching into the bottom drawer of his desk, he had to pull out the shoebox to get to the stack of A4 sheets he'd pinched from school.

That bloody box of photos again; he should stick it someplace where he'd never have to come across it. It was too painful.

But it was too late.

That picture. He had to take another look at it even though it made him want to throw up.

He sank back into the rickety typists' chair and stared in horror at the fuzzy images. Definitely Dan, looking smug.

The truth had come to him in a flash on that day in September last year. He'd recognised the neat handwriting and had known for certain that it wasn't his. That's when he'd realised that the photograph itself didn't belong to him.

At first glance it looked like there had been nothing remarkable about the party. Just a bunch of students getting plastered at the end of term. But there *had been* something remarkable about it – something mind-blowingly significant about the picture.

With the same descending horror, he relived the moment when it had hit him; the crippling pain in his gut when it had all made sense. When it had all become clear.

One simple phone call and he'd been a hundred per cent certain.

The plan he'd put into place as a result was coming along just fine. Daniel didn't have a clue what he was being punished for, so each new turn of the screw brought delicious fresh damage. Delectable to watch from the sidelines. If Daniel thought he'd suffered enough, he'd need to think again.

The game was only just beginning.

Danny-boy – get ready to pay for this one, big time!

Chapter fifty-one

Sophie sat on the tarmac, leaning against the wire fence in the corner of the enclosure, holding her face up to the sun. She'd only just closed her eyes when the prison guard called out to say time was up. They were only allowed thirty minutes a day in the fresh air.

She followed the others back inside. As the new addition to the cell, she'd been allocated the bottom bunk. That meant she had to put up with Tanya above her, who, overweight and lax when it came to personal hygiene, tossed and turned all night, often calling out expletives in her sleep. Not forgetting the never-ending cough that sounded like someone trying to start a car with a dead battery.

Tanya sneaked around the place looking furtive. Sophie half-expected to climb into bed and find a huge spider between the sheets or get the blame for hiding something in the cell and lose all 'privileges' as a consequence.

Sophie knew it was pointless, but she found herself looking for Shareen. In the cafeteria, the corridors, the gym. She knew she wasn't there, but with each new dawn, she lived the hope again.

The search for a friendly face wasn't the only thing she did that was futile. Between hours spent watching Jeremy Kyle or packing plumbing parts, she kept listening for hurried footsteps rushing towards her cell; the ones that were going to lead to the announcement that there had been a terrible mistake and she was going home.

It meant she spent barren stretches of time sitting on the bed, waiting. And waiting – for those footsteps. But she knew even as the minutes turned into hours that it was never going to happen. For the simple fact that the courts hadn't got it wrong.

She'd stabbed Daniel.

There could never be any doubt about that.

Chapter fifty-two

'This is a great idea,' said Daniel, 'Ben's never been on a big boat like this before.'

Jody had rung him on the off-chance, she'd said, because the weather was so good.

Daniel hadn't been in touch since she'd turned up at his house after the mugging. He'd sent a polite text a few days later to check she was fine, but hadn't taken it further. To be honest, he'd felt a bit awkward after their last encounter. Seeing her barely dressed, straight out of the bath, had stirred up feelings he shouldn't have been having. Jody was a commanding, powerful woman, yet she'd allowed him to witness her extreme vulnerability and it had disconcerted him. He'd also sensed the brewing of a different kind of energy between them that was nothing to do with being friends.

Once they'd boarded, Ben charged ahead and grabbed a spot at the front to bag the best view. Daniel lifted him up so he could watch the bow cutting through the water.

They passed under the bold white Portland stone of Kingston Bridge and Daniel encouraged Ben to make 'coo-ee' echoes in the shadows.

As Daniel felt his hair tossed back by the breeze, he glanced around to find Jody staring at him. He turned away, pretending to be engrossed in the rushing water. He'd thought having Ben as the focus of their meeting meant there'd be no room for self-consciousness, but he'd made an error of judgement on that point.

He cleared his throat.

'A king used to live at Hampton Court,' he said, addressing Ben. 'It's a big palace and is going to have swords and armour…'

He went on to paint a vibrant picture in words that made Ben's mouth fall open.

'And ice creams?' Ben asked, when he'd finished.

Jody laughed, her hair trailing across her face, almost covering her eyes and getting caught on her full lips. Daniel very nearly leant forward to stroke it to one side, but Ben reached out and tugged at it first.

'Gently!' said Daniel, sending his eyes skywards by way of apology. Nevertheless, he was grateful Ben had broken the uncomfortable moment.

The pleasure boat slowed down and eased into the bank with gentle thumps. Daniel guided Ben's eyes towards a man throwing a loop of rope around the mooring bollard and they watched as he expertly coiled it around, before allowing the passengers onto the gangway.

Ben was enthralled by the palace. Daniel wondered if the other visitors assumed they were two adoring parents, as they both watched him gaze up dumbfounded at the thrones and cavernous fireplaces with their huge copper cooking pots.

Once the tour had ended, they wandered over to the gift shop. Jody asked Ben which part of the tour he'd liked best.

'The big pie on the table!' he announced. 'But Daddy said it was pretend!' He then declared he was hungry.

'Okay, little chap – time for our picnic.' Daniel led the way out of the swirling main gates to a patch of grass on the riverbank.

Ben began munching through a tuna sandwich and crisps while Jody browsed through a brochure with photographs of the palace grounds that Daniel had bought for his mother. Daniel took his sandals off and helped himself to a cube of cheese, but he didn't have an appetite. He spotted more than one passers-by glancing at them with a half-smile. The three of them probably looked like the perfect little family.

Jody sat cross-legged, her flimsy summery skirt barely covering her knees. Occasionally their bare arms brushed together and each time Daniel felt a tiny electric shock flutter inside him. He cursed himself. How could he allow himself to feel the least bit entranced by this woman, when his wife had just been flung behind bars?

A stiff silence hung between them and he wondered what on earth they would have talked about if Ben had not been with them. Unaware, his son squeezed between the two of them and plonked himself down to drink his juice.

Jody looked up, lost in thought, at a boy standing in front of them at the water's edge. He was wearing shorts and looked about ten years old.

'Seen Rick lately?' she asked dreamily.

'No,' he said, without elaborating.

'Did you know his family?' She propped her sunglasses on top of her head and turned her face up towards the dazzling rays.

'A bit. I knew his sister, Louise; she's a couple of years younger than Rick. She's something of a free spirit.' Daniel leant back in the grass with his arms folded under his head. 'I never knew his parents; we didn't go to his house. It was all a bit difficult at home, because his father had stomach cancer, so we usually met at mine or in town. There was a younger brother too, he came along a lot later, but I only saw him once or twice.'

'Do you remember his name?'

He pushed himself up onto his elbows. 'What is this... twenty questions?'

'I'm being curious – sorry. Naturally nosy. Change the subject if you like.'

'It was Miles.' Daniel reached for the sun cream and began stroking it into Ben's arms. 'I remember him saying "I'm Miles from Oxford" and I said, "Yeah, but what's your *name*?"'

He chuckled, but was aware it carried a suggestion of melancholy. Jody twirled a blade of grass around her finger.

'Rick said he died.'

'Yeah. Six or seven years ago. A brain tumour, I think.' Jody appeared to scrutinise his face. 'Why are you so interested?' he added.

'No reason. Sorry.'

'Curiosity killed the cat!' he said, and piled a handful of plucked grass on top of her head. Both he and Ben started to laugh. Playfully, Jody flicked the blades away with a shake of her head.

'Another sandwich?' he suggested, taking one, then pushing the plastic box towards her.

'Just one more.'

He glanced at his watch, having lost all track of time. 'I think we'll need to get the next boat back. I'm supposed to be finishing a report for Kew and I must arrange a childminder for later this week.'

Ben got up and they watched him chase a handful of long-suffering ducks on the water's edge.

'Poor Ben,' she said. 'Must be so hard on him without his mum.' She let her eyes rest on his. 'And on you, too.'

'I don't recommend it.'

He couldn't face the rest of his sandwich and dropped it back into the box.

'I'm going to ask you a tough question now,' she said, without looking at him.

'Here we go...' Daniel was getting used to her let's-not-beat-about-the-bush approach. He braced himself. 'Go on, then.'

'Why did you cheat on your wife?'

Daniel took a deep, laboured breath.

'I told you – I didn't.' He screwed the cling film from the sandwich into a tight ball.

'But—'

'I didn't. I was set-up. Someone put the idea into Sophie's head and she started seeing things in her imagination. I didn't do a thing.'

At the sound of his raised voice, a couple walking by gave him a stare.

'How did someone put the idea into her head, exactly?' asked Jody. 'Sorry – I'm being very nosy again.'

'Someone sent digitally altered photos to Sophie's office back in September. That's how it all started. Then her disturbed mind ran away with her and did the rest.'

She snatched a breath. 'Why would someone do something like that?'

'I have no idea. Someone who doesn't like me? Someone who wanted to see my marriage break up?' He got to his feet. 'They've done a pretty fine job.'

'Do you know who it was?'

He slapped the blades of grass on his jeans. 'Yes – I think I do.'

Ben came racing back to them and there was no chance to say more. He insisted they swing him between them as they made their way over to the landing stage. Once underway, Jody said she'd stay onboard to central London, leaving them at their starting point in Richmond.

As they pulled into their stop, she grabbed Daniel's arm.

'We can't talk now,' she said urgently, glancing down at Ben, 'but can you call me when you get a good moment? It's important.'

Chapter fifty-three

It was lying on the mat. Daniel spotted it as soon as he opened his front door. He picked it up and looked at the scene: Oxford University. He turned the postcard over but there was no handwriting on the back, just his address printed on a label that had been stuck on.

There was nothing else; no greeting, no signature – but it was a London postmark.

Daniel frowned, then flipped over to the photograph. It didn't look like a recent picture. Apart from being the place he grew up in, what did Oxford have to do with anything?

Except it was the university Rick went to when Daniel had gone to Reading. Was this some kind of senseless obscure message from him?

Daniel tossed it onto the side table in the hallway. As if he didn't have enough to worry about. Thankfully his son wasn't there to witness his downturn in mood after their exciting trip to the palace. Ben was next door with Edith. He'd been yearning to play with her new puppy for days and she'd popped round after they got back to ask if now was a good time.

Heading into the kitchen, Daniel found a note Edith had left on the fridge:

It must be difficult now you're on your own, so I thought I could cook some evening meals for you and Ben. I could bring something in or use your kitchen – whatever's best. I make a mean tandoori chicken and Dad says my lemon meringue is to die for! Any time. Just let me know. E. XX

Tricky. He'd need to make sure he kept his boundaries crystal clear with her from now on. It wouldn't be the first time during his married life that a nineteen-year-old had taken a shine to him.

The place smelt stale, like something was rotten, so he opened the back door to let some air in, then sat on the outside step.

He remembered Jody's parting words and the anxious look on her face. What was so important? Why all the questions about Rick's family?

He rang her number, but it was engaged. He gazed up at the shifting puffs of clouds instead, but found himself picturing Jody in his mind's eye. The way her bright hazel eyes and delicate eyebrows were in a dance of their own, making her face constantly animated. The way she licked pineapple juice from her fingers, not realising how seductive she looked.

He found himself making comparisons between Jody and his wife. They both had a natural glowing beauty and a way of making other people feel important. It struck him that Sophie was softer, more refined. She was utterly feminine, with no coarseness, whereas Jody was louder, brusque and rough around the edges.

Jody and Ben had seemed to hit it off straight away; he was completely at ease with her. In turn, when she'd been at the house, she seemed relaxed and laid-back, as though she belonged there.

He reflected on the various stages in their short, but intense, history. Meeting her at Rick's meal in Soho, seeing her on stage, the break-in, then the mugging, then sailing down the Thames on the boat. He had to admit, had he not been married, had he never met Sophie, he might *possibly* have been tempted by Jody's sophisticated allure and refreshingly honest approach.

Absently, he flicked through the five or six text messages they'd exchanged since they'd met.

Then he shot to his feet, a bitter taste flooding into his mouth.

His fingers trembling, he tried her mobile again.

This time she answered.

'I need to see you!' he said, before she could utter so much as a 'Hello'.

Chapter fifty-four

'I'm glad you came over,' she said, as she answered the door.

He hung back on the step. 'Before you say anything else, I have a question for you.'

He forced the door open and stepped inside. 'How did you know where I lived? That first time after your break-in?'

Jody fiddled with the handle, not looking at him.

It had only occurred to him when he was looking through his texts. 'I never actually gave you my home address, did I? I never sent it to you. I never wrote it down for you.' He jabbed his hands into his hips. 'You already *knew* where I lived.'

'Yes. I knew,' she said, under her breath.

He gritted his teeth, but before he could grill her any further, she jumped in with a question of her own, throwing him off guard.

'Who sent your wife the faked photos you mentioned?'

'What?'

'Who sent them?'

'I'm pretty sure it was Rick. Richard Fox. I found mock-ups at his flat.'

Her face appeared stricken with pain and she retreated along the hall.

'I saw your details on a play he'd written. You said you'd never met Rick.'

She backed away again, as far as the newel post.

'Did you know him?' he persisted.

'Yes. I knew him more than I let on.'

'Why? Why lie about it?'

'Promise me you won't let this spoil everything. I know how this must look, but—'

He folded his arms. 'No, I can't promise anything! My life has been blown apart. I don't know what the hell is going on!'

Packed with black plastic bags and boxes, the hall was too narrow for them to stand without touching. He backed onto the front mat and pointed to the door at the far end. She led the way.

Once they were in the kitchen, Jody sat at the table, but Daniel remained standing.

'I knew where you lived, because I'd been there before... more than once.' Her voice melted away. He could feel his head tilt to one side the way animals do when they hear a sound they don't understand.

She raised her voice. 'I've been getting in.'

He sank down onto the wooden chair, as if he'd been kicked in the stomach.

'What the hell...'

With dizzy recognition, he pictured Jody tying his apron around her waist after their takeaway, that first night at his place. She'd gone straight to it in the cupboard behind the ironing board without asking. How did she know it was there? *Because she'd been in his house before...*

She went on. 'Rick gave me your address. He'd had your house key copied. He claimed you'd been having an affair.'

Something irrepressible was bubbling to the surface inside Daniel's head and he wasn't sure how to handle it. He got up and began pacing about, unable to keep still.

He thrust his hands into his hips. 'You were prowling around, in the middle of the night?'

He flashed back to the times when he'd been convinced someone else was there, the times Ben had been out of bed, sounding like he was talking to someone.

'I'm really sorry,' she said, evenly. 'Why don't you scream at me or something?'

He turned away from her, holding his forehead. 'My son could have been terrorised out of his mind!'

She picked up the salt cellar and twirled it around in her hand. 'He was really sweet, actually. He didn't seem to—'

'I could have hit you over the head with a cricket bat…' It almost sounded comical and Daniel was angry it might appear he was making light of it.

He slammed his fist into the table leg. 'You unlocked the cot so he could get out. I thought it was my fault.' He shuddered with disbelief. 'Thought I was unfit to be a father, negligent – but it was *you!*'

The perfume he'd recognised in the spare room – of course… He laughed at the absurdity of it.

She set the salt cellar down as though afraid it might get broken.

'What were you doing there?' he said, his voice trembling.

'It was for Rick. He asked me to snoop around.'

Daniel shot up abruptly, the chair making a screech across the floor like a wounded animal. 'For Rick? Snoop around for what?' He remembered the grit under the loft hatch, the light on in the cellar.

'It doesn't matter now. I didn't find anything.'

His brain was in overdrive. 'But why would you do such a thing? You had no grudge against me,' he said, almost in tears. 'You didn't even know me.' He turned his head from side to side as though searching for an answer somewhere in the kitchen.

'I didn't have much choice. Rick forced me into it.'

'What do you mean?'

Her head dropped. 'He found out my sister and I had lied to police.'

He folded his arms, waited for her to explain.

'Nikki and I hired a car to get up to Birmingham for a charity performance one night in January. Nikki was driving. To cut a long story short, we were involved in a crash and people were injured.' She rubbed her forehead, hiding her eyes behind her hand. 'I didn't realise Nikki had been drinking before we set off. She panicked when the police arrived.' Jody dropped her arm. 'I told the police I was driving. I took the rap. We were stupid.'

'I see. So, Rick found out about your little secret?'

She nodded, looking sheepish. 'We'd gone up in convoy with other people from the theatre. Rick said Stuart's dashcam clearly showed Nikki in the driving seat just before the accident. He told Stuart not to mention it for the time being, but that at any time he could spill the beans. Rick told me he'd mark it up as a debt to be repaid in the future.'

Daniel shook his head in despair. 'And not long after, he called in his debt?'

'Exactly.' She raised her voice. 'Rick made you sound like a nasty piece of work. I can't bear it when people cheat. My stepsister, you remember? Mum cheated on Dad with the vet all those years ago… it makes my blood boil.' She contorted her lips as though tasting something unpleasant.

'I *didn't* cheat on my wife!' he yelled. 'I *told* you.'

She shuddered at his words. 'I know that now. You said the photos were fake and I believe you. Rick was totally convincing and he made it hard for me to refuse. I'm sorry.'

'I trusted you. I *helped* you.'

'I've made a terrible mistake. I'm telling you the truth, Daniel. And I'm gutted about what I've done. I'm so sorry.'

He leant on the table for support, both arms outstretched. 'I thought we were becoming friends. And it was all a con to get inside my house.'

He was still having trouble taking it all in.

'I didn't know you were going to turn out to be such a… a wonderful guy.' She stared at the floor. 'I didn't do any harm. In fact, I was quite helpful. I cleared away a dead mouse I came across in the loft.'

Ah – that explained the damp cloth he'd found up there. 'With bleach?'

'Yeah. Just to clear away any germs. It wasn't very nice.'

'Is that it?' He did nothing to keep the exasperation from his voice.

She looked sheepish. 'I'm afraid I did break a photograph on the landing. It was dark, the lights were off, I caught it with my rucksack. I cleared up all the glass.'

Right. The gap on the wall. Pieces of the puzzle were gradually drifting into recognisable shapes inside his mind.

'Unbelievable,' he growled. 'But, the middle of the night? I mean… why didn't you snoop around when the place was empty? Why take the risk when we were there?'

She sighed dramatically. 'Oh, that's my weird body clock. Ever since I've worked in the theatre, evenings are my time for getting my brain into gear. After performances I'm totally wired up, bursting with energy. Sleep is the last thing on my mind. Rick said you were both out all morning, but I'm sluggish until lunchtime. I make mistakes. It had to be after a show.'

'I see,' he said, shaking his head in dismay.

'I feel terrible about it,' she said, staring up at him, chewing at her bottom lip. 'Rick is clever. He's devious.'

He straightened up. 'Well – that's probably the only thing we actually agree on.'

And with that, he stormed out.

Getting home was a blur. He flung the back door open again and plonked himself down on the bottom step. He could hear Ben giggling and the new puppy yapping as they played just feet away, over the brick wall.

Thank God Edith was still keeping him entertained. He couldn't have coped in the role of 'happy and jolly daddy' with all this grubby underhand treachery flying around.

Rick! Not only had he been behind the photos designed to frame him, but he'd bullied Jody into prowling around his house. For what? It didn't make sense.

He ran his finger between two slabs of concrete and scooped out a chunk of moss. He held it up, staring at the spongy mass of spores rising like tiny green snowdrops. Brushing the fragile tips, he watched them spring back. Nature was resilient, but what about him? His entire life was broken. Each ongoing step was precarious, like walking barefoot on cut glass.

Was there anyone left to trust?

His wife had tried to kill him... because his so-called mate had done his utmost to make it look like Daniel was cheating on her. And now, this fresh-faced, sensitive woman who had come into his life from left field, had turned out to be part of some foul, convoluted scheme of Rick's.

He squashed the piece of moss back into the crevice, damaging the spores.

How dare she! Inveigle her way under his skin, abusing his trust. Sneaking into his house like a common thief. What a complete idiot he'd been! He'd opened himself up to her and this was the crap he'd got back in return.

And Rick? He'd inexplicably turned into a devious enemy – for no reason at all. He'd wanted Jody to snoop around for something, but what had he got that Rick could possibly want to pinch? It didn't make sense.

He launched to his feet and aimed a kick at the plant pot standing on the edge of the step. It made a feeble clunk as it hit the flagstones and failed to break. So he swung at it again with all his might and it flew across the backyard into the fence and shattered into tiny pieces.

A worm left behind from under the pot fell onto the dry flagstone and began bucking from side to side. Daniel resisted the urge to splat it to death under the heel of his shoe, but he didn't rescue it.

How many other deceptions in my life are waiting to crawl to the surface?

He let the worm writhe in the heat.

Chapter fifty-five

Rick answered the door wearing wellington boots, holding a scythe. Tiny spikes of grass were stuck to beads of sweat on his forehead. Daniel hadn't noticed until now how tightly stretched the skin across Rick's face seemed to be. It was as if there was barely sufficient flesh to cover his bones and it made him look like he could have come from another planet.

'Oh, it's you,' Rick said nonchalantly. 'Come in. I'm having a go at the lawn, but I've got one hell of a headache...'

'I know about Jody,' said Daniel.

Rick didn't falter. He carried on through the living room and out of the French windows into the garden.

Daniel followed him, unable to avoid the trail of Rick's saveloy-smelling sweat left permeating the air.

'All I could find was this.' Rick held up the curved instrument. 'I think someone has stolen the lawnmower.' A small corner of the knee-high jungle that used to be a lawn had been roughly hacked down. There was a long way to go. 'I feel like crap, so I'm giving up.'

They came to a stop by some tomato plants that were growing beside the French windows. They were looking the worse for wear. It was no act of nature – the stems where the tomatoes had been forming, like tiny green marbles, had been severed with clean strokes.

'Someone's hacked them off,' said Rick.

Daniel found himself thinking it couldn't have happened to a nicer guy.

He'd been rehearsing what to say on the way over, but now, whatever he could say would never be enough.

He turned to Rick and swung a fist into his face. Rick dropped the scythe and staggered backwards.

'What the…?' shouted Rick, clutching his nose.

Daniel hit him again and Rick's flailing body sank back into the tall grass, making the sound of a tree being felled. Blood began to ooze through Rick's fingers and into his mouth.

'At least now we don't have to pretend any more,' said Daniel.

Rick rolled onto his side in the foetal position, spitting blood into the grass.

'Don't you have anything to say for yourself?' demanded Daniel. He hid his fist, which was now smarting, behind his back.

'Not really… I've got a hangover. I don't have the energy.'

'You gave Sophie faked photographs. You tried to make it look like I was having an affair.' Daniel thought he heard Rick snigger. 'Do you fancy her, is that it? Did you do this so you could step into my shoes?'

Rick snorted. 'No way. She's too stuck up for me.'

'Then why?'

'You don't know, do you? You really don't know.'

Blood continued to dribble from his nose and Rick smeared it with his fingers and then used the front of his T-shirt.

'Tell me! What is this ridiculous farce all about?'

'You're going to have to work out the rest for yourself. That's all I'm going to say.'

'You tore my marriage apart, you broke up my son's home and my wife is serving a sentence for GBH… and that's all you've got to say for yourself? That I have to *work it out* – like it's some ludicrous contest?'

Rick managed a smug grin. 'Yup – that's about the long and short of it.'

Daniel snatched the scythe. Rick instantly got to his feet and shuffled towards the nearest undergrowth. He crouched between a holly bush and the fence like a five-year-old playing a reluctant game of hide-and-seek.

Daniel swung the scythe in his hand, getting a feel for the weight of it.

'If you kill me you'll never know why I had to do it,' said Rick, defiance behind every word.

'You blackmailed Jody into sneaking around my house.'

'Yeah, she was up for it at first. Went a bit flaky towards the end.' Rick stayed where he was, cradling his nose. He didn't look like he had the strength to stand upright just yet.

'Why? What did you hope she'd find?' Daniel continued.

'That would be telling, wouldn't it?'

Rick pulled a holly leaf off the bush and examined it. 'You've got quite a bit of working out to do, old boy, haven't you?'

Rick sounded for a horrible moment like he might be gaining the upper hand.

Daniel considered the cowering figure and took one step towards him. Rick flinched and backed deeper into the hedge.

'It's all just a game to you, Rick, isn't it? Just one long ridiculous fucking game.'

'I like to think so.'

Daniel glared at the pathetic figure squatting behind the holly bush and made himself stop and think. His immediate impulse was to lash out at him with the scythe, but he was too acutely aware, following Sophie's outburst, of the consequences. That was the difference between him and Rick – Daniel cared about the damage he might cause people and Rick didn't give it a second's thought.

Daniel wiped a trickle of sweat from his forehead and turned away.

Sensing victory, Rick popped his head out of the bush with a gleeful smile like a jack-in-the-box. Nevertheless, he kept his distance, stripping a leaf.

'So what're you going to do, now?' Rick asked. Again, the five-year-old making a childish pact over something meaningless.

Daniel had switched off from Rick's pathetic banter and was concerned about something else. Something Jody had mentioned. He flung the tool in a high sweeping arc to the back of the garden and decided Rick wasn't worth the bother. There was something else he needed to do that was far more important.

Chapter fifty-six

Franciska was clipping stems of vibrant blue delphiniums when he and Ben arrived. She left the flowers in tap water in the washing-up bowl and carried freshly-made lemonade out to a cast iron table on the back patio. It was one of those days that felt like it was beyond spring, yet not quite summer.

'A jumper for Ben,' she said, lifting up the baggy woollen shape on the patio table. 'Only, I've gone wrong somewhere.' She let it roll into a heap and poured Ben a glass of lemonade, then turned to Daniel. 'Coffee for you?'

'No. I don't want anything.'

'Has something happened?' She scrutinised his face.

'Yes.'

'Sounds ominous,' she said, shifting newspapers so they could sit on the double swing seat.

Daniel turned to Ben who was drawing his finger through the icy condensation on the outside of the jug. He watched him push down a cluster of ice cubes that were bobbing on the surface of the lemonade. As he tried to lift one out, it ducked away from his fingers.

'Too hot, Daddy,' he said and drew away from the table.

'I think you mean too cold,' said Daniel cheerlessly.

Ben found a spot under the yellow parasol that was stabbed into the grass, flapping in the faint breeze. He pulled a racing car out of his pocket, sat down and started making 'brum-brum' noises.

Franciska and Daniel set the swing in motion simultaneously with their feet.

'Give me a minute,' he said, lifting his face up to the pale sky. His hands were shaking.

He took a breath. 'A woman I met recently told me she discovered her sister was actually her *half*-sister. Her mother slept once with the local vet. Turned out she'd kept it secret for years.'

Franciska looked at him as though she was expecting some kind of punchline.

'Things have been so surreal lately. So many certainties have gone up in smoke. I needed to know.'

'Needed to know what?'

Finally, he said it. 'I've taken a paternity test.'

'You've what?' She flung herself forward, grabbing hold of the metal frame of the swing as if she was falling through the air.

It was such a simple process to request a check. To ask for a yes or no that would have unimaginable ramifications for his identity, his future, his entire world. The best result or the worst result, like flipping a penny. A fifty-fifty chance.

Within a few days he'd know the truth.

Chapter fifty-seven

The shopping mall was full of screaming kids and equally raucous mothers trying to keep them in check. Rick was nearly run down by two pushchairs as he made his way to the centre of the ground floor. The seating area had been cordoned off with mock ranch fencing wrapped with plastic ivy to make it look like the place had class. Stylish it wasn't. Cheap it was.

He found a table and a waitress, with the words 'Hot and Steamy' ironed onto her apron stood over him. He hoped it referred to the drinks, because it certainly wasn't referring to the woman who wore it. He checked his watch and ordered two cups of tea. They arrived in plastic cups just as Stuart turned up. Behind his right lens was a whopping black eye.

'You been messing around with someone else's girl?' asked Rick.

Stuart avoided his stare. 'Nah. Walked into a wall.'

Considering the usual filthy state of Stuart's glasses, it wasn't so unbelievable. 'This wall have big knuckles, eh?'

'This for me?' Stuart turned up his nose and pulled out a white plastic chair. 'Is this what you meant when you said you were treating me to afternoon tea?'

'Got another business opportunity for you,' said Rick, ignoring the snub.

Stuart watched as Rick drew something on a scrap of paper before turning it round and pushing it towards him. It soaked up old drips of coffee as it slid across the table.

Stuart tried to whistle, but instead sent spittle over the drinks.

'You planning on robbing a bank or something?'

'Not exactly.'

Stuart studied the diagram. 'Aluminium?'

'Yes.'

'Two, the same, right?

'That would be the idea.'

Stuart looked like he was waiting for Rick to tell him more, but it wasn't forthcoming.

'Just keep your mouth shut about this, all right?' Rick stretched out his legs. 'More tea?'

'And one of those Chelsea buns,' said Stuart.

Rick waved his arm and the same waitress came back. She huffed a loud breath and pulled the pencil out from behind her ear. When she'd gone Rick asked him how long the job would take.

Stuart absently stroked the edge of his bruise. 'Dunno, it depends on getting the right materials and I'll need a workshop.'

'So, what are we saying?'

'A week, two weeks max.'

Rick considered it.

'A week tops – no longer.'

'You planning on leaving the country if this bank job goes wrong?'

'It's not a bank job. And no, I'm not leaving the country. If I can help it.'

Stuart screwed up his eyes, no doubt speculating on the secret Rick had up his sleeve.

'I haven't seen a penny from our last job yet,' said Rick.

'Yeah. Well, it's only just gone into Hank's antiques place on Portobello Road.'

'Any hiccups getting it to look authentic?'

'Tricky job. Took longer than expected.'

'Mmm…' Of course it did. He was bound to say that, thought Rick, toying with a toothpick. 'A cut up front would be a nice gesture. If you've made a decent enough job of it, that watch should be snapped up in no time.'

'How about the coat off my back?' Stuart snorted. 'You want that too?'

He was beginning to rise above his station. Rick decided it was time to put him back in his place.

'That won't be necessary. Just don't forget who owes who in the long run here, will you?'

The smug smile on Stuart's face faded. Just as well Rick had a hold over him. Ever since the day Stuart misjudged how long it would take him to get over a wall carrying a framed oil painting. It wouldn't be every day Stuart came across someone willing to give him a solid alibi, just when the police were breathing down his neck.

'Our business is done here,' said Rick.

'Wait. We haven't fixed a price.'

'Hundred and fifty quid, all in.'

'Hundred and fifty each.'

'Deal.'

Rick knew it was going to be money well spent. Although he'd never let on to anyone, in his current situation the cliché, 'beggars can't be choosers' fitted him like a glove.

Chapter fifty-eight

Franciska was already at the front door. She must have been waiting at the window for his car.

'You've brought Ben?' she said, sending up her eyebrows in bewilderment as Daniel unclipped the car seat. She stared at Daniel's face as though trying to read if there was some sort of message in Ben's presence.

'Edith was busy,' Daniel said lightly.

She led them through to the garden. There were no newspapers on the double swing this time; she was ready for him.

Franciska fussed over her grandson, getting him settled on the grass with a drink of juice and a carton of fat crayons.

'Edith's got a new puppy called Bradford,' said Ben.

'That's wonderful sweetheart, why don't you draw him?' she replied. 'Then you can tell me all about him later.'

Daniel swayed gently on the swing waiting for her to join him.

It was warm, but the sky was blighted by a crowd of dark clouds to the east. It could stay bright or disintegrate into a storm; it was hard to tell which way it was going to go.

There was never going to be an easy way to say it, so he decided to get it over with.

'Mum... Ben isn't my son,' he said, without looking at her.

For a moment his mother didn't react. Daniel dug the heels of his shoes into the soil and the swing stopped abruptly, leaving two crescent-shaped dents in the turf. He turned to her and watched as she pressed her fingers over her mouth.

'But he *must* be...'

'I've had the results. We don't have the same DNA.'

He noticed the heavy clouds had crept closer.

'They can't be right,' she croaked, the shock having stolen her voice. Daniel caught her looking at his eyes, from one to the other, trying to gauge his emotional state.

'There's no mistake.'

'Oh, my God…' she said, turning to look at Ben, as if checking he was still there. 'I can't…' She halted and cleared her throat. 'There must have been a mix-up at the lab,' she said, squeezing her hands into fists.

'I did it twice. It's conclusive.'

She let out two hoarse gasps, then sank back into a dazed silence. He gave her time to let it sink in; he was in no hurry to speak again. Words seemed useless at a time like this.

Suddenly she came to life again. 'And Sophie has the nerve to accuse *you*!'

'She's really been full of surprises, hasn't she?'

Franciska bowed her head. 'What are you going to do?'

He took hold of her hand. 'You're the only one I can trust, Mum.' He stared across the garden at the tidy beds of deep purple rhododendrons offset with cleverly placed spires of delphiniums. Everything in her life was neat, orderly and predictable.

'I'm going to have to see Sophie again,' he continued, 'have it out with her. She said she wants a divorce, anyway.'

He narrowed his eyes as another thought struck him.

'If she knew Ben wasn't mine, why didn't she fling it in my face a long time ago? During one of her hateful outbursts towards me. Why didn't she ever mention it?' He rolled his tongue over his top teeth. 'I can't work out what she's playing at. *She* was the one who was cheating, so why try to turn the tables on me? Why not just admit that Ben is someone else's child and take off with the guy?'

Franciska shifted her gaze to Ben, who had given up on drawing the dog and had started digging a hole in the lawn with a toy car instead. She went over to him.

'Don't do that, darling. Come here and see what I've got for you.'

She led him inside and they returned with a plastic bag full of toys. 'Let's tip them out and see what you want to play with.'

Ben busied himself plucking out various items and bringing each one over to show Daniel.

She joined Daniel again on the swing seat. 'I can't believe he's not your boy,' she whispered, sounding baffled. She tipped her head on one side following her grandson's every move, as though seeing him for the first time.

Ben was absorbed in a world where dinosaurs met fire trucks on the grass.

'What made you think he—?' she went on. 'What made you question it? You never gave any indication when Ben was born that you thought Sophie had been seeing someone else.'

'Well, that's because I never doubted her. Ever. It's just with such odd things happening lately, I wanted certainty. Reassurance.' He laughed. 'I didn't expect this. I really didn't.'

She shook her head.

'There's something else,' he said.

He told her about the photographs he'd taken to Sophie's unit.

'Rick wanted to make it look like I was having an affair. He's hiding something from me. Now this.'

She gulped nervously. 'Are they connected, do you think?'

'I've thought about it long and hard, but I don't see how. Not directly. Sophie can't bear him. Well… she *says* she can't. And Rick said she's too stuck up for him.'

Although, so many lies and deceptions had been flying around lately it was hard to tell truth from fiction.

'You've got to have it out with him!' she exclaimed. 'And her!'

There was a rumble of thunder. Desperation seeped into his words. 'I'm totally out of my depth.'

She took a sharp intake of breath. 'Oh, Daniel…' He looked into Franciska's eyes and saw the same pain he'd witnessed when his father died. He wondered at what point emotional torment became too intolerable to bear.

She squeezed his hand. 'Sweetheart, if there's anything I can do…' He'd forgotten to take into account her unwavering resilience and determination. He hoped it ran in the family.

They both looked up, expecting the tiny patter of raindrops to follow. They waited, but the grey clouds dispersed and no rain fell. Daniel was disappointed. A raging storm would have matched his mood.

Ben came to sit between them and, soon after, fell fast asleep; his head nestling against Daniel's hip.

He stroked the boy's hair. 'I need to know who the father is.'

'Do what you have to do,' she said ominously.

The phone rang and she jogged inside.

Daniel continued to stroke Ben's curly blond locks, careful not to wake him. Until the day the test results arrived, he had taken up all the space in Ben's life as his father, never doubting his position. Nothing had changed within him or between the two of them and yet now, somehow, *everything* had changed.

'We've done everything together,' he whispered, 'you and I. I heard your very first words. You watched your first firework display from my shoulders. I held you the day you stamped that staple into your thumb. And I will take you to your first day at school, be there when you graduate and be proud of you on your wedding day.' He stared ahead of him, unseeing. 'But I am *not your father*'. Warm tears rolled down his face and he could only let them go.

Franciska faltered as she crossed the lawn towards them, then turned and went back inside.

Daniel watched the boy's abdomen rise and fall, saw his eyelids flicker with the images of innocent dreams. All the aspects of himself; the physical characteristics, the personality traits that he thought he'd seen in Ben as he grew from month to month, had been one thing and one thing alone. Wishful thinking.

As Daniel drove away, Franciska bobbed down to car-level and mouthed, 'I love you'. Daniel raised his arm out of the window in a silent salute.

On the drive home, he replayed the moment when he'd read the letter from the online DNA service. He'd tried to fool himself into thinking they'd sent it to the wrong person; that they'd got his details mixed up with someone else. He'd phoned the service and insisted on speaking to the test supervisor. Then he'd done the test again.

But, there was no mistake. It was all there in black and white. Innocent patterns of bars across a screen, like Morse code.

But the code wasn't spelling out *his* name. Instead, it spelt out the name of a stranger; a nameless person who had slept in Sophie's bed and who was Ben's biological father.

He didn't know how he was going to carry on after this. Only a few months ago, he'd had a devoted wife, been a loving husband and a doting father – and now his whole world had come crumbling down.

How was he going to take one breath after another, take one step after the next in a situation that was broken to the core?

All he could feel was bitter disappointment and rage with Sophie, with Rick for sparking the whole thing off, with the stranger who had come between them, with the world for letting this happen. A scorching savage rage that had a mind of its own. For the first time in his life, he understood how someone could snatch whatever was to hand and launch it at another person. To hit them, shoot them, stab them.

Is this how Sophie felt when she attacked me?

He pulled into a space in front of the house with a fierce jolt. Ben woke up and started to wail. Daniel held him in his arms and they both cried as they made their way to the front door.

As soon as Daniel left, Franciska staggered into the lounge and collapsed onto the sofa. Ben was her only grandchild and he couldn't, *absolutely couldn't*, be taken away from her.

She lifted her head towards the large portrait above the fireplace. To the photograph of dear Tom, who had never known him. Dear Tom, who through his genetic links was living again inside Ben, filling part of the gaping hole left by his absence – or so she had always believed.

She got up and paced into the hall and back again. A burning fury inflamed all her limbs and she didn't know what to do with it. Divorce was bad enough – all the legal wrangling about who would have Ben. But what happened when Sophie had served her sentence and made a claim for Ben, making it clear he wasn't Daniel's son? What then? She might never see him again.

She stormed out into the back garden towards the pile of logs she'd meant to ask Daniel to chop for the fire. She barged into the shed and pulled out a rusty axe from the cobwebs in the corner. Rolling up her sleeves, she took a deep breath before swinging the heavy axe down onto the chunks of wood, one by one, muttering obscenities with every breath.

It began to rain but she didn't stop. She slashed and hacked until all that was left was a mound of splintered chunks on the edge of the lawn, like a funeral pyre.

Chapter fifty-nine

Daniel found the visitors' car park of Sutton's Glenbrook Prison after a fraught journey on the A23. The prison had been built recently, with pale orange brick and two lines of silver birch saplings edging the drive. If he hadn't known better, he'd have thought it was a new ice rink.

After signing in, he was taken to a room that smelt of sour mattresses and stale deodorant with top notes of disinfectant. There were rows of yellow formica tables and red bendy plastic chairs. Dismal. It reminded him of the unemployment office where he used to wait for Rick, who insisted on signing on in the months before he went to university. Unlike Daniel, who'd got himself a temporary job.

Sophie was sitting on the edge of the seat, her head down and her hands folded in her lap as if she was waiting for pallbearers to arrive. The room was filled with couples leaning across the tables towards one another, desperate to claim some level of intimacy.

Sophie's skin appeared yellow-grey. Daniel hoped it was due to the fluorescent lighting, but her delicately honed cheekbones certainly appeared angular and protruding. As he dodged around chairs to get to her, he felt a boulder fall in his abdomen and he knew his feelings for her had changed. He felt pity for her, but it was a distant and hollow commiseration, no longer rooted in love.

'You didn't bring Ben?'

'It didn't seem right today. Edith has him.'

Daniel sat back in his chair and sighed. 'I wanted to tell you in person that I'm agreeing to a divorce,' he said.

'Oh...' She hooked a loose strand of stringy hair behind her ears, looking disconcerted.

Isn't that what you wanted?

He couldn't be bothered to say it out loud.

'But I'll fight for custody of Ben,' he added. That was the important part. He braced himself for retaliation, convinced he was about to hear the announcement he'd been dreading: that Ben wasn't his own son anyway.

'Okay,' she said, hunching over without any defiance.

Nothing.

Her compliance threw him. Surely, now was the time to declare the truth about Ben. To push that knife in, the one she'd failed to kill him with – just a little further to make him really squirm in agony.

But no.

Daniel was confused. He returned to the same question he'd had when he spoke to his mother. During the months before the stabbing, in her most vehement accusations, why hadn't she thrown Ben's paternity at him? Didn't she know that would be the ultimate means of hurting him? She could have told him it was tit for tat. He was playing the field now, but she'd had an affair a few years earlier. Why hadn't she used it then? Or now?

'I need to say something and I need you to be honest with me in return.' His voice was grave and slow, like the tone he'd used to give the eulogy at his father's funeral.

She looked at him with concern. 'Is Ben okay? What's happened?'

'He's fine.' A fleeting inner warning made him hold back from mentioning Ben just yet.

'I know you had an affair with someone,' he said. 'After we were married.'

'What are you talking about?!' Her response was instant; her voice like a crisp bell cutting through the hushed exchanges of those around them. '*I'm* the one who was faithful. Every. Single. Day!' Her face twisted with disdain.

She was so utterly adamant, it threw him off balance.

'You're trying to tell me you never slept with anyone? Not once?'

She visibly shivered, her mouth open in disbelief.

'No way! Where did you get that stupid idea from?'

Something made him hold on to what he knew; made him wary of saying more.

'How can you ask me that,' she went on, 'after everything we've gone through?'

Her tone softened. 'I've been thinking about those fake photographs. Have you seen Rick? Have you confronted him about it?'

'He admitted everything. He wants to punish me for something.'

Her face contorted as though finding something stuck in her throat. 'Punish you for what?'

'He refuses to tell me. I have no idea what I'm meant to have done.'

'So you accuse *me* of having an affair? How is that related?'

He didn't want to come out with the truth. Not yet. He was still testing the waters and didn't trust her. 'I… it crossed my mind.'

'Rick's stupid trick made everything worse, but it wasn't just the pictures…' She avoided his eyes.

'So you say,' he said with a sigh. He didn't want to go through it all again.

'But, I have been thinking,' she said. 'My medication has been adjusted and I'm feeling almost back to normal again. I was irrational, completely distraught before, but now…' He let her grab his arm, but he kept it rigid against his body. 'I thought, perhaps we might…'

'Might what?'

'See if we can make peace between us, perhaps even start again. Not just for us, but for Ben.'

He shook himself free from her. 'Too much damage has been done,' he said, his mind flashing back to the unambiguous letter from the DNA clinic. Maybe in her deluded state, she really believed she'd never slept with anyone else. But, the facts were there.

'I don't think we can come back from this,' he concluded.

A frown quivered between her eyebrows. 'But we have Ben, we are a family. We have to try.'

He hadn't expected this. Not at all. Only recently she'd wanted a divorce and now she was taking a U-turn. She really was deranged! So much for her mental state improving. It looked to him like she needed a rigorous reassessment.

She reached over the table to grasp his hand, but he pulled away. Her pleading only made him want to get it over with.

'I'm sorry…' Daniel got up and held up a palm to make the prison officer aware he was leaving. 'I'm ready to sign the divorce papers,' he said, and left the room.

As his heels echoed along the corridor, his mind began to overload with images of Sophie and a faceless man sleeping together behind his back.

How many times had it happened? How many times when Daniel had initiated love-making had she tolerated it, gritting her teeth, thinking of someone else? Perhaps there were even times when they had both made love to her on the same day. The idea made him want to retch and he had to slap his hand over his mouth and make a run for it.

Daniel went straight to Edith's to collect Ben.

Once they were alone inside the house, he held him, hugged him, kissed him and pressed his face against his sugar-smelling hair.

'My boy,' he crooned. 'We'll get through this. You and me. It's going to be okay. Everything's going to be all right.'

Ben threw up his arms and said, 'Biscuits!'

'Yes – you're absolutely right – this deserves some biscuits,' said Daniel, pumping up his spirits for the sake of his boy.

They spent the next couple of hours in and out of the backyard playing Cowboys and Indians, making mud-pies in the sand pit and seeing how many balloons they could blow up and burst.

Finally, Ben flopped onto the sofa. One minute he was talking to his furry rabbit, the next he was fast asleep. Daniel, on the other hand, felt like an aeroplane in a tailspin, not knowing if he was heading for a crash landing.

Sophie had denied sleeping with anyone. She was completely insane. It was the only explanation.

Now there was one more step he had to take.

Chapter sixty

'I need to ask you a favour,' said Daniel without preamble.

'Oh. It's you. I didn't think I'd hear from you again,' she said.

Jody sounded like she was on the move; he could hear her heels in a regular click-clack in the background, together with passing cars.

'Nor did I, if I'm honest, but I think you're the only person who can help. If you're up for it?'

There was a tiny hesitation. 'Depends what it is. I've got myself into a lot of trouble lately by doing favours for people.'

'That's true,' he said, picturing the twist of her jaw which no doubt accompanied the irony.

'What's the mission should I choose to accept it?'

He sketched out his idea, interrupted every now and then with trills of intrigue from Jody.

'How fascinating. Am I allowed to ask why?'

'No,' he said simply.

'When do you need it?'

'As soon as you can. It's a bit of an emergency. That's all I can tell you.'

'And should I be caught or killed, are you going to disavow any knowledge of my actions?'

'Forever the actress, eh?' he said, unable to keep the amusement out of his voice.

'Life is one long TV drama, darling – didn't you know?'

Chapter sixty-one

Jody came good. She turned up on the doorstep looking pleased with herself the following evening.

'That was quick,' said Daniel, sleepy in his lounge gear, ready for bed.

'You said it was important.'

Her hair was elaborately whipped up on her head in a fancy roll and she wore high heels, a long camel-coloured coat and fishnet gloves. She was the antithesis to him; bright eyed, dressed to the nines and raring to go. Obviously one of those people who came alive after 10pm.

He beckoned her inside, but she swung round to the taxi waiting outside his gate. 'I can't stay,' she said. Nevertheless, she insisted on giving him a breathy blow-by-blow account of how she'd carried it off.

'I invited him to a friend's cocktail party last night,' she said. 'In my business there's always someone having a party and I figured if an offer involved free booze, free food and armfuls of attractive women, he'd be there in a shot.'

'Good thinking.'

The velvety chug of the taxi and roar of a passing motorbike meant they had to lean closer to hear each other speak. As she stretched towards his ear, a curl of her hair worked itself loose and stroked his cheek.

'I waited until he'd had a few drinks, then claimed he had an insect in his hair. I decided on a woodlouse – that seemed fitting.'

Daniel laughed.

'I got him to undo his ponytail and pretended to rifle through his scalp to capture it. In the end, I showed him a dead one I'd brought along in my pocket.'

'No hitches?'

'Nope...' She drew her lips into a tight 'O'.

'I'm sure if he'd known, Rick would have appreciated the sleight of hand.'

She handed over the plastic bag. 'I hope there's enough for what you need in there,' she said, a serious edge to her voice.

She must know exactly what this was about, he realised, and privately respected her for not probing.

He thanked her by placing his hand on top of hers. She smiled at him.

'Sorry, got to dash,' she said, turning to the taxi again. 'Got a last-minute interview for *Elle* magazine at eleven o'clock in The Savoy.'

Against all better judgement, he found himself waving her a playful goodbye as she disappeared into the taxi.

Chapter sixty-two

A shrill bell told her it was time for lunch, but Sophie wasn't hungry. Before the ringing stopped, Tanya launched herself off the top bunk, almost standing on Sophie's hand as she clambered down. She gave Sophie an oafish snarl and left the cell.

Sophie stayed on the bed hugging her knees. She dreamt of soft silk trailing against her tanned legs, of running her fingers over the luxury cashmere throw she and Daniel kept at the end of their bed. She craved the flavour of fresh carrots and peas; the only vegetable they seemed to get in here was potatoes. But today she missed, most, the smell of fresh croissants at the local deli, Mr Bubble's bubble bath and more than anything, the act of running her fingers through Ben's hair.

She flinched at the sound of someone being yelled at in the corridor. Inmates regularly swallowed batteries in this place. They swapped nicotine patches for cigarette lighters to burn their own skin. They bit their arms and legs hard enough to draw blood. It wasn't about attention-seeking, it was about diverting the pain into something they could control. Once in here, you lost control over everything else.

As soon as she'd arrived, Sophie had signed up for library duties, had a fitness induction and applied to do a course in first aid. But so far, she'd only made the waiting lists. It meant interminable bleak periods of hanging about, dragging time out in slow motion.

Too much time to think. Mull things over.

She'd replayed her visit from Daniel time after time in her mind. *What had he been talking about?* Accusing *her* of having an affair and going on about Rick punishing him for something. It had thrown her completely off balance.

Their meeting hadn't gone the least bit how she'd imagined it in other ways too.

Daniel had been stand-offish, almost hostile, behaving as if he couldn't get their divorce sorted out fast enough. He'd even pulled his hand away when she'd reached out to him. That tiny reaction had hurt her more than anything.

Part of her had been hoping they could come back together over what had happened. She was prepared to move past Daniel's dalliances with other women, was ready to find a way through this mess.

But he wouldn't have a bar of it.

This couldn't be happening. Her affair? Was Daniel losing his marbles too?

That wasn't all she'd been ruminating on. She still couldn't work out how she'd turned from a capable, radiant woman into a monster in such a short period of time. She simply couldn't relate to the person who had stabbed her husband. There were no words to describe how utterly preposterous and out of character her actions had been.

She'd replayed the months between September and February time after time. Daniel's adultery and his claims that he was innocent had worked its way under her skin in a manner she couldn't comprehend. During those five dark months it had eaten away at every rational thought, chewing at the sensible and loving aspects of her personality, gnawing at all her senses, poisoning each moment from the instant she woke to the moment she went to sleep. She'd seen her GP, started taking antidepressants, but things had only got worse.

An unfathomable mystery.

But she couldn't wipe out or rewrite the past. She was stuck with it. The present was intolerable too, trapped with a woman who sneered at her, grunted whenever she asked a question, but mostly ignored her altogether. Living a lonely, desolate, deprived existence based on penance. All Sophie had was the future – and that held fears of its own.

Her father hadn't been to visit yet; a setback in his condition had led to a spell in hospital and her mother was in cloud cuckoo land; in complete denial about her MS as well as Sophie's situation – sending jolly letters, dictated to her carer, about garden birds and Mrs Dean's whisky marmalade as though Sophie had just started boarding school.

Then there was Ben. Missing him was like suffering a spear in her back every day. The precious life she was meant to be taking care of. The new words he'd be coming out with over breakfast, the newly mastered skills he'd want to show her, the cuts and bruises he'd run to her with. She should have been there to embrace every minute. The giggling, the grouchy tantrums, the tears.

Only she wasn't. He'd been left without the one person who was supposed to be by his side every step of the way.

They *needed* her and she'd let them down completely.

Chapter sixty-three

The process had been remarkably straightforward the second time. Ben had barely struggled as Daniel stroked the cotton bud inside his cheek. 'Tickles…' he'd yelped, giggling.

Then he'd put the other sample in the envelope. He'd sent them off to the same DNA company, but had given his mother's address to avoid confusion with the first test he'd done. Soon after, an email had arrived explaining that an unmarked letter would be sent to the address he'd given within five working days. How very businesslike.

He got the call he was expecting six days later.

'A letter has arrived…' Franciska was trying to be neutral, but sounded like the back of her throat was filled with small stones. 'Is it what I think it is?'

'Will you open it?'

'No Daniel, I don't think I can. I think you need to open it yourself.'

He could hear her shallow breathing.

'I'll come over as soon as I can.'

Forty minutes later, he ripped open the envelope and read the contents. While his mother pleaded with him for the result, he stood rooted to the spot, not saying a word.

He couldn't breathe. He couldn't see. His entire world had just gone black and been smashed to pieces.

He handed her the letter, too broken inside to utter the words out loud.

Ben's DNA was a match.

For Rick. From the strands of his hair.

Rick!

Rick who'd insisted Sophie was too 'stuck up' for him.

They'd slept together.

Just over four years ago, before Rick went to Sydney.

He was listing the stark facts in his head, tracking each one as they escalated into an insurmountable panic of their own. But he couldn't take in what they meant.

Rick and Ben. Father and son.

Daddy…

Daniel needed to throw up and bolted for the downstairs toilet. It all seemed so blindingly obvious now. How could he have been so stupid?

And Sophie. He couldn't even bring himself to think about the part she must have played in all of this.

Lying through her teeth…

A collage of pictures ran their own slide show in his head. Treasured snapshots from a previous life which, from that day onwards, would make him recoil with humiliation. Sophie smiling in the maternity ward, strands of her hair folding the wrong way across her perfect parting as she handed the tiny wailing bundle to him.

Warm, starched towels wrapped around the honeyed baby smell. Everyone congratulating him, and the smile he couldn't keep from his face every time he thought of this tiny person who had made them a family.

It was all one big fat lie.

Daniel dropped his head, utterly crushed. All those times he and Sophie had talked about Ben, been with Ben, the times he'd seen Rick play with Ben – and Rick was Ben's true father all along.

He was a complete idiot. The mortification made his mouth go dry.

As if reading his mind, Franciska handed him a glass of brandy, pouring one for herself.

'Unbelievable…' she kept muttering. 'Absolutely unbelievable…'

In that moment he made a decision.

Apart from Franciska, he wasn't going to tell a soul about this and would certainly not allow the two people directly involved to know the truth. He was going to play this one very close to his chest.

He had no recollection of getting back in the car and setting off home. He should never have had any alcohol, but he didn't think he'd have been able to drive at all without it.

He slammed on the brakes at a zebra crossing to avoid a woman with a shopping trolley who'd left it late to cross, forcing his mind to concentrate on the road.

As he pulled up outside his house, a heaviness dense with outrage and devastation filled his head. There were no words big enough to encompass all the feelings he was trying to deal with, piling up inside him one on top of another.

An energy in his body was pumping his blood around too fast. A fuse had been lit inside him and if he didn't wallop something in the next ten minutes, he feared something in his brain was going to rupture.

He couldn't pull it all together to consider sensible things like 'taking it all in' and 'not doing anything rash'. He had no idea what he was going to do, rash or not, because right now he was having trouble seeing straight and stopping himself from hyperventilating.

He made it inside the house.

What he needed to do most was hit something long and hard. Ideally Rick's face. He checked his watch: 5.20pm. Rick always did something after school. Either straight down to a pub for a drink or to a game of squash, pool or darts somewhere. More often than not, it would be followed by a curry. Daniel thought about leaping back in the car again to find him and flush him out, but he had no idea where to start.

Chapter sixty-four

'Just dropping off what's yours, mate,' Rick said, handing over a thick envelope. 'It's all there.'

It wasn't like him to make the trip all the way up to Camden to hand over Stuart's share, but he had an ulterior motive in insisting he pop round with it. Stuart wouldn't risk being underpaid and as he huddled over the bundle of notes to count them on the table, Rick wandered over to the fridge and slipped the keys into his pocket. Simple.

'This is for the latest job, right? Three hundred quid for both, yeah?'

Rick nodded.

Stuart straightened up. 'Cheap at that price. You happy with them?'

'They'll do.'

'I haven't heard from Hank, yet,' Stuart said, 'but it shouldn't be long. The pocket watch has got the best spot in his window, apparently. Should make the sale any day.'

Rick shrugged. He hadn't intended to mention the watch. Stuart obviously hadn't heard the bad news. That the 'precious find dating back to the sinking of the Lusitania' had already encountered an insurmountable setback. A timepiece collector – one of the world's experts, regrettably – happened to be browsing at the Portobello Market and had stopped at Hank's antiques gallery. Intrigued by the memorabilia, he'd examined the watch, and in those twenty seconds their neat little scam had gone down the pan. Rick knew it was only a matter of time before the police would be knocking on their respective doors.

'No rush,' Rick said.

'Sweet. I'm heading off for a bit,' said Stuart, cradling the wad of twenty-pound notes. 'Me and a mate are heading up to Scotland.'

'Nice. Why all the way up there?'

'His aunt just died and left him a crofter's shack of some kind. Might be worth something.'

'How long will you be gone?'

'Dunno. Ten days, maybe. Play it by ear.'

Maybe Stuart had already heard about Hank's unfortunate visitor and was doing a runner without letting on.

'We're heading up in his campervan,' he said, glancing at the clock above the doorway. 'Should be here any minute.'

Stuart was a happy bunny with dosh in his pocket, about to clear off for a while. Rick nodded and left him to it with a jolly wave. He jiggled the keys he'd pinched in his pocket. Sometimes life just handed you stuff on a plate.

Chapter sixty-five

'Is this about Rick?' asked Louise, cautiously, as soon as Daniel told her who was calling.

'Do you know where he is?'

Daniel heard a sound through the handset that could have been either a sigh or a passing car. 'No. His school rang me. He didn't show up for work this morning.'

'He's not answering his phone.'

'I know. The tenant upstairs said he left the flat carrying bags and a suitcase.'

Daniel didn't like the sound of that one bit.

'You able to meet up?' he asked.

'Meet up?'

'A quick chat. Just coffee somewhere.'

She drew a sharp intake of breath. 'About Rick?'

'Mostly.'

'Do you know Balham High Road?' she asked.

'I can get there in around thirty minutes.'

'I'll see you in Café Réale – it's by the supermarket.'

Daniel parked behind the high street and once he'd reached the main road, he spotted Louise heading towards him. It had been over ten years since he'd last seen her, but the hunched shoulders and short pixie steps gave her away. Her hair was curly, a mousy-brown colour, and still in the same style as in her teenage years; halfway between Bette Midler and a cocker spaniel. She was wearing a purple smock over a denim miniskirt that was both too short and too tight. She could have just about got away with it if it hadn't been for the red trainers. He recalled how there was always something about her that was out of place.

He allowed her to lead the way.

The café was dark and pokey inside and Daniel wondered why, out of all the cafés along the high street, Louise had chosen this place. Daniel looked away as she hitched up her skirt even further and perched herself on a high stool at the window.

'This your local?' he asked, placing the mugs on the grubby ledge.

'It's cheap,' she said, pulling up long hockey-style socks that looked out of place on someone who was thirty-something.

His mug had a chip in it, but he couldn't be bothered to go back to the counter.

'I really need to talk to Rick,' he said.

He locked on to her eyes, but she dropped her gaze and began fiddling with sugar cubes in a dish.

'I told you, I don't know where he is.'

She dropped a cube from several inches into her mug, sending splashes of coffee over the edge. 'What's he done now?' she said with resignation.

Daniel tried to hook his feet over the bar of the stool, but his legs were too long. 'Did you know that Rick stitched me up with some wild scheme to make it look like I was having an affair?'

He wasn't going to reveal the truth about Ben unless he absolutely had to.

Daniel pulled out the digitally altered photographs and put them down, one after another, beside her mug. Louise spluttered as a mouthful of coffee went down the wrong way. She clutched her throat, then composed herself.

'Oh, Daniel…'

'Rick went to considerable lengths to set me up.'

'I didn't know anything about these. Honestly. But Rick has been so odd lately; very secretive, getting drunk all the time, missing Mum's birthday, not turning up when we've arranged a drink. It doesn't surprise me he's doing crazy things. But this?' She pressed her fingers into her temples. 'Actually, he does seem a bit out of control. He's been ranting on about someone who's going to suffer.'

'That's probably me he's referring to – but I don't know what I'm supposed to have done. Do you?'

She shrugged. 'He didn't tell me about these photos. Or about anything else concerning you, for that matter.' Her features took on an earnest expression. 'Something underhand is going on with that Stuart guy, but he won't say anything. You know Rick. Some cockeyed scheme, no doubt. The long and the short of it is he now seems to have disappeared.' She let her legs dangle in mid-air, like a child. 'I think he might need help.'

'Hmm. I've seen a totally different side to him lately.'

'He's been really weird since last summer. Since we cleared out Mum's house. It totally got to him.'

'How do you mean?'

'We had to wade through a load of stuff. Stuff from the past. Dad's books, the little wooden toys he made, old photographs. Mum hadn't even thrown out Dad's old clothes. And then there was Miles's room.'

'Rick told me about that.'

'It brought it all back. Rick's been down, since then. Maybe even depressed.'

Daniel was determined not to let the discussion head off down the road of feeling sorry for him. 'It's not just that, though,' she added. 'He's been cruel. A real bully at times.'

Daniel sighed. 'He's always been shrewd. But, there's shrewd and there's devious and then there's downright malicious. I think he's walked the whole line.'

He was still for a moment as he saw the crestfallen look on her face and knew he'd deeply wounded her. 'Sorry... it's just...'

'It's true. You're right. He's gone off the rails.'

Rain began to spatter on the window pane facing them and the light outside turned a tarnished grey. They finished their drinks in silence.

Daniel got to his feet. 'Let's keep in touch,' he said finally, pushing the stool under the ledge. 'Let me know if your brother contacts you and I'll do the same.' He glanced out into the rain. 'Do you need a lift?'

'No, I only live along here.' She waved her arm vaguely.

When they got outside, the air had already taken on that distinctive acidic wet-pavement smell. She stopped him as he turned to go. 'Do we need to do something?'

'About what?'

'Tell the police or something about Rick going missing.'

Daniel pulled up his collar as the drops fell thicker and faster onto the canopy above them. 'When did you last speak to him?'

'Two days ago.'

'Would you normally expect to be in touch every day?'

'No, but the school…'

'It's only yesterday and today. I'm sure he's bunked off school before. He certainly did when we were younger.' He gave her a wry smile to try to set her mind at rest. 'Let's wait a couple of days, at least,' he suggested, pulling away.

They separated and he put up his hand in a goodbye gesture.

Right now he had other things on his mind.

Chapter sixty-six

'Thank you for what you did.' Daniel was standing on Jody's doorstep.

He hadn't intended to get in touch with her again, but he had a question he needed answering. Besides, she might have picked up a clue about Rick's whereabouts.

She moved to the side to let him through. 'Did it help?' she asked, walking down the hall to the kitchen.

He followed her. 'It clarified things.'

'Not in a good way by the sound of it.'

He shrugged. He didn't want to explain further, although he was certain she must have had an inkling as to why he'd wanted strands of Rick's hair.

She poured two glasses of sparkling water and took them out to the patio. She turned to look at him, squinting into an isolated shaft of sunlight that was breaking through a gap beside the roof next door. 'I didn't think I'd see you again. I thought I'd made up for what I'd done and we were more or less quits.'

'I'm not here to harass you. I won't stay,' he said, settling into a patio chair and taking a sip of the water, nevertheless. He leant forward, studiously tracing the curved pattern in the cast iron table with his finger.

She took a deep breath. 'So what happens now?' He had the feeling she was referring to their relationship, but he skipped around that particular interpretation.

'I need to ask you a question. It's not another favour,' he said, fixing on her eyes for the first time. 'You said you never found what you were looking for at my house, but what was it you were trying to find?'

'Rick asked me to look for Sophie's diaries.'

Daniel knew she'd kept one, on and off, but Jody's words set his mind racing.

'Why?'

'He didn't say.'

'Is that all?'

He dunked his finger in his glass to retrieve a tiny fly that had fallen in. He set it on the table, but it was already dead.

'And any of her medication I could find,' she added. 'Hence having to break the lock on the bathroom cabinet.' She dropped her head, her lips nipped together. 'Sorry about that...'

Little did Rick or Jody know that all of Sophie's medication had gone into the filing cabinet. Although, if he was honest, he'd only kept it because he never seemed to get around to throwing things away.

'Is that also why you got into the loft and went down to the cellar?'

'Yes. The filing cabinet down there was locked and I'd been trying to track down the key.'

Ah. The key. The one he kept on a magnet stuck to the back of the fridge for absolutely no good reason, except that he'd put it there. Jody had never found it. Maybe his scatty nature had worked in his favour for once.

'That was probably the night you left the front door open,' he said, wryly.

She looked genuinely horrified. 'Did I? Shit! I'm so sorry...' She slapped her hand over her mouth. 'Ben... was he okay?'

Daniel nodded, his mind already elsewhere. So Rick was after Sophie's diaries and her medication. He drummed his fingers over his lip. He recalled the restless afternoon when he'd cleared a pile of her stuff away. Various boxes of paperwork had been bundled into the filing cabinet, for certain. Sophie's diaries could easily have been among them. He'd never broken her trust by looking at them.

'When you say medication, do you mean Sophie's insulin or something else?'

'Rick asked me to get hold of anything and everything. He didn't say why. I didn't ask. I just did what I was told, I'm sorry to say. Once I'd started to get to know you, I felt terrible about what I was doing. I just wanted it over with.'

He held her gaze, watching her carefully. 'Rick's disappeared. Do you know where he is?'

She raised her eyebrows instantly. 'When?'

'This is the third day he's missed school, apparently. No one's seen him since he left his flat with armfuls of luggage.'

'That doesn't sound good. What's he up to?'

She sounded almost as mystified as him, but Daniel had to remind himself that she was a consummate actress, after all.

'You look like your mind has gone to the moon,' she said.

'Too many loose ends,' he sighed, as he twisted his wrist to look at his watch. 'I ought to head off.'

'Sure,' she said, giving him a warm smile as though there had never been an issue between them. 'If there's anything I can do, you know where I am.'

Chapter sixty-seven

As soon as he got back, he went straight down to the cellar with the key to the filing cabinet. He'd never thought about looking at Sophie's diaries; it hadn't crossed his mind.

In the bottom drawer of the filing cabinet were a stack of box files; most were for Sophie's work, but there was one without a label.

As soon as he opened it, he knew they were the right papers. Sophie's personal jottings.

He carried the box up the steps and spread out the spiral-bound exercise books on the kitchen table. Each one had the dates clearly marked on the front. With trepidation he peeled open the first page.

I want to preserve as much of these precious years as I can, she'd written in her first entry, *because I know it will fly past in a flash.*

He saw instantly, there was a snag. The first book started after Ben was born. He scuttled back to the cellar and riffled through the rest of the paperwork, but there was nothing more. Then he checked the suitcases in her wardrobe and under the bed. Drawing a blank, he climbed up into the loft and sifted through every box.

Nothing.

The entries from Ben's birth onwards were all there was. He decided to read a few random sections nevertheless, just in case there were references back to Rick, to Ben not being Daniel's son.

There were occasional entries about work, but mostly her notes described cosy, special family times and the delights of motherhood. Pure moments. Not descriptions of what they did and where they went, but tiny gems of love, sweetness, tenderness. Cherished recollections. All wrapped in an overflowing blanket of affection and joy.

I feel like my life has truly begun, she'd written. *When Daniel and I got together I never dreamt I could be happier, then Ben came along and my life took off into another stratosphere altogether! Now I know what love is.*

Every word broke his heart.

He'd traced a few stray comments about Rick, but all of them were disparaging. No covert comments or coy hints about him. No guilty revelations. Nothing about Rick being Ben's father. Nothing about Daniel *not* being Ben's father.

Nothing about hiding secrets or having to lie.

He couldn't bear to read anymore. In any case, it was of no real use to him as the notes didn't go back as far as Ben's conception which would have been the end of 2014. *That* was the period he'd been most keen to read about.

He stopped reading and sat back. Why had Rick instructed Jody to steal her journals? What did he think was there? And did he want to keep hold of what he found? Or get rid of it?

He decided to take a break and made coffee.

Sitting at the table with his mug, he found his eyes returning to the pages. Everything he'd found so far had been testament to a loving and devoted family unit. But what about later? Had she made entries when it had started to go wrong? Is that when her true feelings about Ben's paternity had been documented?

He didn't have long left before he had to collect Ben from the nursery, so he speed-read entries from July of last year until he got to September. That's when the tone changed. He swallowed hard, unsure about whether he could stomach reading on.

He skimmed over all the accusations, the disbelief and anguish about the 'proof' she'd found. He knew all that. He was looking for statements about Rick, Ben, about Daniel not being his true father. He searched and searched, but found nothing. Nothing at all.

Though something else did catch his eye.

Her handwriting seemed different from mid-September onwards; less precise and symmetrical. Over the next six months it got worse and worse, gradually disintegrating into an illegible scribble. This wasn't Sophie. She'd always taken pride whenever she put pen to paper. Even her shopping lists were a work of art.

But it was the description of her emotional and physical state that was most striking.

September 29
Had to leave a meeting at work as I was shaking and sweating. Cassandra said I must be coming down with flu, but it's not that. I've never felt like this before. It's like a raging fire inside my head. And a dread all the time. Like someone is going to jump out at me.

By November, she was talking about her constant fear of waking up in the morning and finding Ben had gone:

Daniel is plotting to abduct him. I know he is. I saw it in his face at breakfast this morning. He and his whore are going to steal him. They're in it together. I've got to watch Daniel all the time. I can't bear to leave Ben in the mornings. I'm terrified he won't be there when I get home.

Then, January 26:

Can't think straight. Pain in my eyes, like pins. My brain... hot. Burning. Can't walk in a straight line. I looked in the mirror and I saw an ugly fish... gaping mouth. Bad smell everywhere. Mustn't tell Daniel or he'll get me sent away... got to be strong for my boy.

And February 1:

Nearly passed out after a meeting this afternoon. Unbearable heat under my skin. My eyes feel like they're on fire. Everyone is staring at me. I'm being watched – I know I am. Followed. Daniel is on to me. He gave me that look again at breakfast, only this time he wants to see me dead. I'll never see Ben again.

The last entry was the day before the attack, February 3. By then, none of her statements made any sense and he couldn't even make out her final words. Finally, her pen had merely dragged across the page in one long flat line.

Chapter sixty-eight

Sophie was reluctant to send him another visiting order at first, until Daniel made it clear during her next phone call that what he had to say could affect Ben's future.

He was led through to the same fluorescent lit visitors' room, bracing his nostrils for the smell of disinfectant, but this time it was Sophie's perfume that greeted him.

She was sitting tall in the chair, her arms folded, primed for a fight.

'You've been reading my diaries?!' she said, hurt clouding her eyes, as he got straight to the point.

'Only a few pages. They didn't go back far enough.'

'Far enough to what?'

He avoided her intense gaze. He wasn't going to mention any dates. He didn't want her to work anything out. Unless she got there first, he wasn't going to mention a thing about Rick being Ben's father.

The prison officer sauntered over to their table.

'We had a hold up on medication this morning,' she said, addressing them both, 'and Sophie didn't have her insulin injection. She needs to come and have it now.' A perfunctory smile followed. 'You'll still get your full hour,' she said, then added pointedly, 'if you want it.'

Sophie left the room without a word and Daniel kept his eyes firmly fixed on the table, not wishing to look like he was taking an interest in anyone else.

He let his mind wander back to yesterday.

After the long stint reading at the kitchen, he'd been glad to bundle everything up and return the papers to the cellar. He'd picked up Ben and spent most of the afternoon playing skittles with him, desperate to push the new revelations about Sophie's radical decline into a dark cupboard at the back of his mind and bolt it shut.

But he couldn't do it. His mind kept pulling him back to the diary entries. Her deterioration was far worse than he'd ever thought. How come he hadn't noticed all her odd physical symptoms? Why hadn't he marched her down to the GP to request a psychiatric assessment or specialist tests to find out what was going on?

Simple answer: she'd hidden as much as she possibly could from him. Not least, because she was afraid she'd look like an unfit mother.

Just before bed, another idea occurred to him. What about emails from around the time of Ben's conception? Daniel grabbed his laptop and scrutinised all the messages he and Sophie had exchanged during the weeks before Sophie discovered she was pregnant. It was the only record of that time he had.

One event in particular grabbed his attention. Daniel had been away one weekend, giving a series of lectures in the soil science department at Reading University. Sophie had mentioned going to a dreadful party. A Christmas do with Cassandra.

He used Sophie's password to get into her personal email account to see what other messages she'd sent at that time. They'd never hidden passwords from each other, although he did feel a twinge of guilt for snooping.

She'd mentioned the party only once, to her friend Greta, describing it as 'excruciatingly boring'. There was even a reference to Rick: *Daniel's oafish school 'mate' was there,* she'd written. *He's a total pain and I couldn't get out of there fast enough.*

Daniel had called Cassandra and asked if she could remember the event. She was her usual brusque self.

'Work thing. Don't remember much,' she said.

'Can you remember who was there?'

'I'm sorry Daniel. It was over four years ago. Book people, I really don't know. I'll play it over in my mind… see if anything comes back to me.'

'Where was it?'

'Er… Islington, I think.'

'Were there any bestselling authors there? Did anyone take photos?'

'I doubt it. Just an in-house excuse for staff. Although, a bunch of gatecrashers turned up I seem to recall, and it got a bit rowdy.' She paused. 'Sophie didn't hang around – she left early.'

'Did she? Why?'

'Well, that kind of loud bash is hardly her thing, is it? In any case, she didn't feel too well, I think. I really can't remember.'

But to her credit, Cassandra came good. She'd rung back. After asking around in the office, she discovered that someone who'd been leaving the company had taken short bursts of video footage of the gathering on her phone. It had been uploaded onto one of the office computers and forgotten about.

Daniel made the journey over to the publishers straight away to take a look.

He had to scour every frame, but once he found it, there was no mistaking him. Rick had certainly been there. He was leering in the background, wearing a pair of red Rudolf antlers on his head and holding a can of lager.

The approaching voice of the prison officer pulled him back. Daniel heard the click-clickety-click as her key fob banged against her thigh as she brought Sophie back in.

His wife approached him with that familiar, alluring glide that she'd lost in the past few months. Surprised by a tingle of adrenaline, he had a momentary glimpse of the way things used to be, before the juggernaut dressed as Richard Fox had blasted its way through their lives.

'Do you remember a party?' he asked, once she'd settled. 'A Christmas get-together in Islington for work. It was in 2014.'

Daniel couldn't move. He held his breath, dreading what she was going to say next.

She fiddled with her lip and stared into space, then slowly shook her head. 'In 2014? Why? Should I?'

'You went with Cassandra. It was a bit boisterous apparently. She said there were people who weren't invited...'

'Oh, wait. I remember.' She crumpled her nose. 'It was awful. People were drunk and rolling around the place. I left early. I'd been sick and felt awful.'

'Apart from Cassandra, do you remember who else was there?'

'Why? What's this about? You said it could affect Ben's future.'

'Was Rick there?' His words punched the air louder than he intended during a tiny hiatus when the rest of the room had fallen quiet.

She thought about it, her face clear of any shadows. 'Why would *he* have been there?' Her voice came out in a whisper.

'I don't know.'

Was she going to deny it?

'Wait...' She tutted and threw her eyes to the ceiling. 'He turned up – I remember now – with some people from the theatre. He was wired. On something, I think. He was raucous and pestering me and I didn't feel well. So I left.'

'With Rick?'

'God, no! I slipped out when he was halfway through telling some vulgar joke.'

She must have slept with him around that time. Had she no shame?

'You were away at some conference or other,' she said. 'Like I say, I had a bug or something and was feeling very sorry for myself. I remember really missing you and longing for you to come back.'

'Really?'

'You got back the day after, you remember? Late in the evening. Your train from Reading was delayed and I'd just got out of the bath...'

Yes – she was right. A wave of warmth flooded through him, bringing with it the ghost of remembered passion.

'How does this affect Ben's future? Was that a lie. So that I'd agree to see you?'

'No, it wasn't a lie. Can you bear with me? It *is* about Ben's future – about all of us, but I don't know for sure how everything fits together yet.'

She didn't protest.

'That time was a special one for all of us,' she said wistfully. 'I was on the pill, but I'd been sick at that dreadful party. When I counted back the days *that* was the moment Ben began his tiny life, smaller than a particle of dust.'

His lips barely formed the words. 'The day after the party?'

Daniel wiped a trickle of moisture from his cheek, not knowing if it was a bead of sweat or a tear.

'Yes,' she said, a glow spreading across her cheek, 'the night you got back…'

Chapter sixty-nine

After he left Stuart's, Rick wandered to the local pub to bide his time. Sure enough, when he strolled back to the end of the street, a campervan had pulled up outside Stuart's flat.

Rick leant against a wall on the corner and pulled out his phone, pretending to check for messages. Every so often he glanced along the road as Stuart and his mate bobbed in and out of the gate with boxes and bags. It looked like they were carting off enough stuff for a family of six to last a fortnight. Rick yawned. It was taking ages.

A tinny rendition of *Blow the Wind Southerly* made him jump as an ice cream van came careering around the bend, almost mounting the pavement. Rick was tempted to flag it down and buy a double 99 for the hell of it, but didn't want to risk being spotted. Just as well, as Mr Softee was stopping for no one. He sped off and by the time he'd rattled through his jingle again, the campervan had gone.

Rick took the newly-acquired keys out of his pocket and strode along in search of his new courtesy car – thanks to Stuart's inadvertent hospitality. Having shuffled behind the wheel, he fired up the engine and drove the blue Fiesta over to his own flat. He picked up what he needed and headed towards a little secret spot not far away from his place – namely an abandoned shed in the local allotment. Hardly the epitome of luxury, but that wasn't a priority at this moment in time.

From his safe vantage point, he waited a few days to see if anything kicked off. He kept his eye on the local news, sent one of his teenage acolytes from school over to Portobello Road and checked in with the tenant who lived upstairs to see if he was getting any callers dressed in navy.

But in the event, it was all clear.

No police snooping around. No one on his tail. No obvious trouble heading his way following the scam with the fake pocket watch. Hank must have done a good job at covering their tracks. Although, it was in his own interests to turn woolly and forgetful over exactly how, when and from whom he'd got hold of it.

Ignoring pleading calls from his sister and with the stirrings of fresh ideas for the final stage in his plan simmering in his mind, he made his way through the streets of London. He had one humdinger of a shock to put into place for Danny-boy, then his work would be done.

Once he was outside the city, he kept clear of the motorways, choosing instead to weave through a web of back roads with no security cameras. He pulled onto a farm track and stopped. He'd left the items Stuart had so expertly made for him under a suitcase on the back seat. A pair of extremely credible fake number plates for the princely sum of three hundred pounds. Rick clipped them neatly to the front and back of the car and got back on the road.

He joined the M4 and drove for miles until he reached the remote village deep in the Welsh countryside. Stuart had bragged about his swish 'holiday home' several times and Rick had been careful to jot down the exact location. You never knew when that kind of information might come in handy.

Chapter seventy

When Daniel drove up outside the house, he was unnerved to find a police car taking up his usual parking space. It had been left at an angle, sticking out into the road as though it had arrived in a hurry.

Was this about Rick? Had Louise called the police in the end?

He left the car a few doors down the road and was walking back when Edith shot out of her front gate at full pelt towards him.

'I'm so sorry, Daniel...' she sobbed, stopping in front of him, her hand clamped to her forehead. 'I didn't know. It's all my fault... I'm so sorry.'

Daniel spent all evening walking the streets trying to find his son.

Edith had made a terrible error of judgment.

'I came out of the nursery and Ben wanted to be in the buggy, so I took him the park way – you know, along West Street?' She blew her nose loudly into a tissue. 'My phone rang, just as he spotted a puppy inside the side gate. He wanted to stroke him. You know what he's like.'

She'd already told the police everything. They were already out scouring the bushes in the park and the streets around the nursery.

Daniel wanted to shake her, slap her even, but instead he reached out and clasped his arms around her shoulders in a shared moment of anguish.

'I only took my eyes off him for one second while I found my phone,' she muttered, tearfully, into his collar. 'And when I looked up, he'd stepped momentarily out of sight. I went straight after him, into the park. The puppy was rolling in the grass with a teenage boy, but Ben wasn't there... he wasn't anywhere.'

Franciska must have driven like the wind to get to Daniel's house in such a short time.

'No traffic,' she said, avoiding his wide eyes.

She threw her jacket over a chair in the kitchen like she meant business.

'There's no sign of him,' he told her.

'We'll find him,' she said decisively, as she placed two steaming mugs of sweet tea between them.

He didn't share her optimism. He trembled and nearly dropped the mug as he tried to pick it up, as if all the muscles in his body had lost their strength.

'It's Rick. I know it is. He's snatched him.' Daniel kicked the kitchen door shut to be out of earshot of the police officer who was winding things up with Edith. 'That was why Rick was so keen to save Ben at the beach, wasn't it – you remember? Why he's been hanging around. He wants him for himself, don't you see?'

'But Ben's nearly four years old. Why would Rick wait all this time?'

'Maybe he only found out in the last few months that Ben was his child. Perhaps that's why he's been turning up all over the place. It's not Sophie he wants, it's Ben!'

Daniel strode out into the hall and without telling the constable why, told him he had reason to suspect Richard Fox was involved.

'We've fallen out recently,' he said, hoping that would be sufficient.

'Over what?'

'I'm not sure. He won't tell me. He set out to ruin my marriage.' He gave him the sketchiest outline possible about the altered photos. At this stage the details didn't matter. The biggest priority was to find Ben and bring him home.

Daniel told him about Louise. About how she'd been worried ever since Rick failed to turn up for work. How a fellow tenant had seen him leaving with his belongings.

On his way out, the constable explained that a family liaison officer would be visiting the next morning and told Daniel to stay put. But he was having none of it. Once the officer had left, he grabbed his jacket.

'You stay here,' he'd said to Franciska, holding both her hands in his, 'in case there's any news.'

At around four in the morning, he returned from trawling the local streets to see if there'd been any updates. He must have drifted off on a kitchen chair for a few minutes, because he woke with a snap, wondering where he was.

This couldn't be real. This couldn't be happening.

And Sophie? Had they told her? What state would she be in? Of all the incidents likely to send someone over the edge, someone who was already hovering at the precipice – surely this was it.

He spread his toes and pressed them into the floor. His feet no longer felt attached to the earth and the earth around him seemed to be moving.

Chapter seventy-one

The Sat Nav took ages to direct Rick to the right area, so he finally pulled up at the gate of a remote abandoned farm. True to form, Stuart had somewhat embellished the facts. There was no cottage at all, only a caravan. A poky one, at that; dragged into the mud and left to rust. It would never be going anywhere again.

'Swish holiday home', eh?

As he'd driven over, Louise had left another text to ask where he was. She also told him that a couple of police officers had just turned up at his flat. Ah. Things weren't so cool, after all.

He opened the gate and brought the car onto a patch of grass under the cover of an oak tree. Before he got out of the car, he switched off his phone. Thank goodness he'd planned to lay low for a while. He'd claim he didn't know the police were looking for him. He couldn't cope with any of that right now.

A few days to get his head straight and work out the final details of his ultimate strike should be enough. Then he might think about getting some fake ID from Stuart, if the old bill hadn't already tracked him down. If the worst came to the worst, he might have to bunk off on a plane back to Sydney.

But not yet.

He unlocked the door to the caravan, pulled down the handle and gave it a shove. Two things hit him as he stepped inside. Firstly, it stank of so many different odours it was hard to work out which one was the most offensive: the rotting fish, the mould, the rancid butter or the stale urine. He tried to force open the window, but it was jammed shut. He propped the door open with an aluminium deckchair and hoped for the best. The second thing was how cold it was. Even though the temperature outside was well into the high sixties, it felt damp and chilly inside.

No longer such a great choice for a getaway, he thought, cursing Stuart's blatant lies about how swanky the place was. This wasn't going to be the exclusive glamping retreat he'd had in mind.

He returned to the car and pulled out a box of provisions from the back seat. He went round to the boot, then changed his mind. He'd leave the warm bundle where it was for the time being and come back for it once he'd unpacked. What was wrapped inside was in no fit state to make a fuss, in any case.

Back inside, he opened the fridge door and slammed it shut again. He'd deal with that later. At least there was gas. He put the kettle on, switched the portable radio on and began to whistle along to the pop music.

Within the hour he was starting to feel at home. He'd shoved all Stuart's bedding under the caravan and replaced it with his own duvet and pillows. After cracking open a can of lager, he checked the map for the nearest pub. It was about five miles away and would do nicely for an evening meal. He chose a name for the night: Bob Walker. Impossible to trace. He'd tie up his hair, too, and tuck it in under the flap cap he'd brought. Blend in with the locals.

He stretched out on the bunk, starting to feel pleased with himself. He'd bought some useful time. He could chill out in complete safety and decide what to do next. Sod the crap watch. And Stuart, too. He and Hank were on their own. Bunch of sodding amateurs. He deserved better. Right now, he needed to focus on the next stage: the unfinished business that needed taking care of. The final act of his cleverly constructed play.

He drank from the can and belched loudly, then went outside to the car to pick up what he'd left in the boot. He brought it inside, and seeing the blood oozing from under his fingers, he left it on a sheet of newspapers on the draining board.

'If Danny-boy thinks everything is over he's in for a rude awakening,' he said, addressing the lager in his hand. 'Give it a few days and it'll be time to drop the final bombshell.'

He rummaged through his rucksack in search of a pen. 'I'll have a nap in a while,' he said, continuing his running commentary, 'but in the meantime, I've got another postcard to send.'

Chapter seventy-two

It came to him while he was searching the streets for Ben, just as wisps of orange began flooding the inky sky at dawn. While Daniel's eyes darted from shadow to shape back to shadow again, his mind was a tangle of inner turmoil, replaying the words from Sophie's most recent diaries. Until finally, he could spit it out. Like a cat getting rid of a furball.

Of course, it was such an obvious explanation.

But time was not on his side. He needed to speak to Sophie again – urgently. He knew the prison wouldn't permit another visit – he'd already used up his limit for that month – but he had to speak to her, just once more.

Back at home, he rang Kew to explain why he wouldn't be turning up. Given the situation, he was granted compassionate leave straight away. With that out of the way, he paced up and down the hall, chuntering to himself, desperate for his wife to call. Surely, she'd ring as soon as she could to find out more about Ben's disappearance. She *had* to.

Sophie finally called from the payphone using the special PIN card prisoners were given.

'Have they found him? Is he okay?' she pleaded.

'Not yet.'

'Why aren't you out there looking for him?!'

'Because I've looked every single place I can think of and I'm just getting in the way. The police have dogs, trained people who know what they're looking for, ways of covering every inch of a local area.'

'What about the boy with the puppy?'

'They haven't found them, yet.'

'So, what other leads are there? Did anyone else see him in the park?'

He'd exhausted himself with these very same questions. 'The police are doing what they can,' he said wearily.

'My boy...'

'I know. Mine, too,' he said, feeling the weight of irony in his words.

'That silly, dizzy-headed girl – what was Edith thinking?' Sophie snatched a breath. '*She* hasn't taken him, has she?'

'Edith?'

'I've seen the way she looks at you. I imagine having me out of the picture has been a nice bonus for her.'

'Don't be ridiculous. She's been great. I admit... she might have a bit of a thing for me, but it's completely in hand.'

'You don't think she might have taken him somewhere?'

Could Edith be involved? It didn't seem to fit. 'I really don't see why,' he concluded.

He told her he'd been called to do a press conference and would be making an appeal on television. 'Someone must have seen him,' he added.

Sophie dissolved into sobs.

'Hold yourself together, please. Don't hang up, stay with me, okay? It's really important.'

He could hear the usual commotion in the background. Sophie had told him that using the phone was always a nightmare – aside from the complete lack of privacy, invariably a long queue stretched down the corridor and other inmates jeered and heckled when anyone spent more than a few minutes on a call.

Daniel got straight to the point. 'I need to ask you more questions. Not about Ben, about something else. It's really important.'

He heard her sniff.

'Can you think back to when you first thought I was having an affair? Right at the start, *before* you were sent the photos at your office. The first little clue.'

He'd already read her account of that time in her diary, but he didn't mention that. Nor did he mention that, only a few hours ago during those solitary hours on the barren streets, he'd begun to realise their implication. It could turn everything upside down. It was all there. Now he needed to hear if what she had to say backed it up.

'It was in September. I was looking for tea lights and found that love letter in the pocket of your gardening jacket. I was in total shock. I didn't know what to do, so I just started keeping my eyes open and checking.'

'Did you notice any changes in how you were feeling physically at all?'

'How do you mean?'

Daniel breathed heavily. He didn't want to put words into her mouth; it was crucial that she remembered for herself. Moreover, he didn't want her to realise how significant her replies would be. He had to keep his tone light and casual. 'I mean... any changes in yourself... your moods?'

'Well, of course. I felt jittery and anxious, because I was upset. There were times when I felt almost paranoid. I had to be watching you all the time.'

'Anything else?'

He held his breath. How she answered his next few questions could make all the difference between staying behind bars and being released from prison.

She hesitated. 'I thought you were going to take Ben away from me.' There was a clunk as she changed the position of the receiver. 'This is going to sound stupid, but I even thought you might want to hurt me. At one point, I got it into my head that you were planning on suffocating me.'

'Did you explain all this to Dr Marshall?'

'Of course. That's why he kept asking what I was taking. And whether I'd used recreational drugs.'

'He asked me that, too.'

It made complete sense. Daniel waited, silently urging her to say more.

'A couple of friends at work said I seemed edgy… and my leg was bouncing up and down all the time.'

'I remember that happening at home, too.'

Everything she'd told him tallied exactly with her diary entries from September onwards.

Everything.

'Where are you going with this?'

'You know how surprised Dr Marshall was at your fast recovery? It's been playing on my mind.'

'Yes, he did seem shocked by that.'

Daniel bit the bullet.

'Okay. I have a theory. I think it's possible that you *might* have been drugged for weeks without knowing. Substances to make you agitated and volatile. It would explain your outbursts, your physical symptoms…'

Her response nearly deafened him. 'What? That's incredible!'

'Rick's degree was in biochemistry. He'd know about drugs, about how to get hold of them.'

'But the items I found; the love letter, the condoms, the lingerie – they were *real*. They weren't hallucinations, honestly. I swear on Ben's life…'

He waited for the inevitable question.

'Why would Rick resort to something like that?' she hissed.

Before he could reply, there was a clunk and he thought they'd been cut off.

'No… no…' he cried. 'Sophie, are you still there?'

There were sounds of a scuffle, shouts – then a whistle blew which sliced into the uproar and brought about an abrupt silence.

'I haven't finished yet,' said Sophie politely, speaking to someone beside her.

'Sophie?'

'I'm here,' she said, her voice breathy. 'I'll have to be quick.' She took a moment to compose herself. 'You're saying I was *given* something in the months before my outburst?'

'Yes.'

'I remember starting to feel very weird soon after taking the antidepressants from my GP, but I thought maybe I'd get worse before I got better.'

He slapped his palm into his forehead.

'Whoa – of course. That probably made everything far worse. Maybe mixing antidepressants with whatever Rick was giving you created a lethal cocktail. It could explain what tipped you over the edge in the kitchen that day.'

'But, why didn't the psychiatrists and doctors pick it up when I was committed? Wouldn't I have had traces of an alien substance in my blood?'

He glanced up at the kitchen clock. 'I'm going to look into that. I think they did run some tests, but not straight away.'

'What can we do, Daniel?'

He blew out a blast of air. 'Leave it to me.'

'And find Ben,' she cried, 'you must find Ben.'

Chapter seventy-three

Outdoor life in the rat-infested dump of a caravan was overrated and Rick only lasted three days. The police were looking for him, but everything was under control. Louise had left various breathy messages on his phone, but he didn't trust her. Little sisters were fine for some things, but not this.

He wondered at what point Stuart would realise his car was missing. With any luck, he'd already gone into hiding in Scotland for as long as he could.

He sang tunelessly to himself as he replaced Stuart's bedding, now damp and covered in mouse droppings, back onto the bunk and made a point of not clearing away any of the mess he'd made. Give Stuart something to think about if he ever made it back there.

He was tempted to leave the place unlocked and throw away the key. Let some down-and-out make use of the fleapit. But he changed his mind. He might still need Stuart to dig him out of a hole in the future and couldn't afford to burn all his boats. He might even get his car back in place before anyone knew it was missing.

His heart raced as he thought about what was ahead of him; one final stage in his plan before he disappeared for good. He couldn't wait! The look on Danny-boy's face when everything exploded before his eyes. It was going to be priceless!

He left the inert bloodied bundle in the blanket where it was, on the bunk bed; give Stuart a nasty shock when he made his next visit.

Rick chuckled at the look of horror and befuddlement it would bring to Stuart's face when he tried to figure out how the hell it had got there.

He revved the engine, grated the gears and pulled out onto the squelchy track. He felt like he was on his way to pocket the jackpot on the lottery.

Chapter seventy-four

'Come in, Mr Duke,' said DCI Watson, shaking his hand. 'You've become something of a private eye, it would seem.'

After he'd spoken to Sophie, Daniel had dug out all her old medication from the filing cabinet in the cellar where he'd previously dumped it. As well as out-of-date insulin phials, there were antidepressants and a half-empty nasal spray.

Daniel had been sitting about in the waiting area for some time, but on entering the interview room felt unaccountably out of breath. He placed the diary and the medication, wrapped in a plastic bag, on the desk.

'I take it there is no news about my son?'

'I'm sorry, Mr Duke. We're doing all we can.'

Daniel winced at the familiar words, then let out a long, tired sigh. 'I've got new evidence concerning my wife's case.'

Watson glanced at the items. 'So you said on the phone.' He hitched up his trousers before sitting down. 'You think someone drugged your wife in the lead up to the attack on you, is that right?'

Daniel didn't fail to pick up the DCI's tone of weary condescension, as if he was feigning interest in a child performing a song badly off-key for the umpteenth time.

'Sophie gave me permission to bring her record of that time,' he went on, regardless. 'In the margin... see... I've made pencil marks beside her references to feeling disoriented, suffering intolerable headaches, hallucinations and delusions. And here...' He pointed to an entry she'd made the day before the stabbing. 'I'll read it out, if I may?'

DCI Watson half-smiled and sat back, folding his arms.

'Feb 2. Felt really weird and scared this morning. Had to lie down at work – saw beetles coming out of my stomach. All around me on my clothes. Is it the antidepressants? Am I going mad? What is happening to me? Daren't tell Daniel. Must get back to the GP.'

Daniel swivelled the book round, so Watson could get a good view, and flicked through more pages, pointing to his pencil marks. 'You can see how her handwriting disintegrates over time from being neat and precise into this messy scrawl.' He straightened up. 'I've spoken to my wife in prison and we both believe that when she stabbed me, it was following months of being drugged by Richard Fox.'

Daniel touched the plastic bag. 'And I have her medication from that period, too.' He pushed them towards him. 'If you could test them, it could show they've been tampered with.'

As the words tumbled out after his long wait, Daniel had the horrible feeling he sounded not only desperate, but deluded. Having put it into words, his 'evidence' looked feeble and flimsy at best. He was clutching at straws.

DCI Watson drew a long breath and addressed his response to the items on the desk. 'Even if you're right, Mr Duke, it's purely circumstantial.' He shut the spiral-bound book and tapped the cover. 'I'm not saying she did, but your wife could have written all this *after* the attack. You yourself could have tampered with the medication.' He pushed them away. 'It doesn't point the finger anywhere, I'm afraid.'

Daniel silently cursed himself – he'd even forgotten about fingerprints, had slapped plenty of his own all over the containers.

'But, Rick... Mr Fox... knew my wife needed insulin every day. He joked about it once, when he saw it in the fridge. Then after Christmas, she started taking an antidepressant from the doctor. Venlafaxine.' Daniel glanced up at the detective to check if he was still listening. 'Mr Fox could have come into contact with any of these – and the nasal spray. He came to our house and joined us at several social gatherings from September onwards on some pretext or other.' Daniel screwed up his eyes. 'He would have had access to the fridge, to my wife's handbag.'

DCI Watson remained impassive, but Daniel kept going. 'He could have left replacements and Sophie would never have known.'

'Mr Duke, we're not in a position to host a treasure hunt.' He placed his hands on the desk, ready to stand up.

'But… surely, this needs looking into? I checked online and antidepressants mixed with other drugs can have a radical impact. Isn't it worth checking with the psychiatrist?'

He knew he sounded pathetic.

'It's all speculation, Mr Duke. We work with evidence,' DCI Watson said with a conclusive shrug. 'Clear, hard evidence. And this isn't it.'

DCI Watson stood up just at the moment Daniel realised he'd blown it.

'I can see how preferable it would be for this to be the reason for your wife's behaviour, Mr Duke. Far better that your wife was suffering some drug-induced derangement than she attacked you in her right mind. But…'

He left his last word hanging in the air.

That night when he climbed the stairs, Daniel forgot for one nanosecond that Ben wasn't there. He'd been keeping the night light on in Ben's room since his disappearance, like a beacon calling him back home. Tired and not thinking straight, he stepped inside the room just as he'd always done.

This time he stared at the empty cot.

Night after night, he'd stood in awe as the night light threw a gentle beam over Ben's face. He'd watched the little white stars as they slid over Ben's cheeks and eyelids, then ran across the wall and ceiling. Then he'd waited for his son's little body to rise and fall in the dim light.

Only, not this time.

Chapter seventy-five

Louise dropped everything when she got Rick's message and made her way to Borough Market. It was closed on Wednesdays; the entire area deserted apart from stacks of slatted vegetable boxes and barren trestle tables. She moved from one spot to the next trying to shake off the smell of rotting vegetables and stale milk.

He came out of a side street and moved swiftly in her direction. It was a mild day, but he was wearing a thick scarf that covered his mouth and a woollen hat pulled down over his eyes. Louise barely recognised him. From this distance, he looked like a tramp.

'Rick? What's going on? Why are we meeting here?' She looked up into the rows of shadowy railway arches.

'Shh. Don't use my name. I'm lying low.'

'Why?' she sighed. 'What's happened?'

'Everything's fine. I'm just keeping a low profile, that's all.' He ushered her into an alleyway. He was unshaven and looked like he'd been sleeping rough.

'You didn't answer my calls. Where have you been?' She stared into his eyes, but they were darting around, wary, like a trapped animal. 'Daniel said you'd set him up. He said you'd done something to make people think he was having an affair.'

'Yeah, well. That's only part of it.'

'But you *lied* to me. You said he'd done something awful and he hasn't.'

Rick laughed, but it wasn't joyful. Instead, it sounded weary and cynical.

'Believe me, Daniel is going to pay big time for what he's done.'

She was confused. 'So, what *has* he done?'

'He's poisoned everything. Sullied and degraded our family.' He spat on the pavement.

'What are you talking about?' She tried to take hold of him, get him to face her, explain properly, but he pulled free.

'He's in for a nasty shock, that's all.'

She turned full circle, frustrated, unable to make any sense of what he was saying.

'Look,' he said. 'Just say you haven't seen me, if anyone asks, okay?'

'Are you going home? When will I see you?' A sick feeling was bubbling away in her stomach. Rick didn't look well; he was twitchy, shifting from one foot to the other as though the pavement was on fire.

'No. I won't be around for a while. I'll contact you. But, let me know if Daniel gets in touch, okay. It's really important. Will you do that?'

'Yes – okay,' she replied, grudgingly.

'It shouldn't take him long.'

'Long for what?'

'He should have had a couple of postcards by now.' He strode off, not waiting around to answer her pleas for an explanation. 'Don't follow me,' he hissed. 'It'll all become clear soon, believe me.'

She stood there, not sure what to do. Someone barged into her, carrying a sack of potatoes, and by the time she looked up, her brother had disappeared.

Chapter seventy-six

After being asked to hold the line, and then enduring several renditions of 'The Blue Danube', Daniel eventually got through to the right ward.

He explained the situation as concisely as he could.

'I can't imagine we'd still have any of her medication, Mr Duke. Normally when a patient leaves us, those items are incinerated.'

'This could be a police matter, so I'd be very grateful if you would go and check.' He hoped that dropping in the 'p' word might shake the nurse up a little. 'But please don't handle anything directly, it could be evidence.'

'I'll go and see. I'll call you back.'

'No, no, please, I'll wait.' He heard the clunk of the receiver hitting the desk and hung on.

It could equally go either way: lead to Sophie's release and Rick's arrest, or lead to a pile of dust long since swept away from the grate of an incinerator.

'Mr Duke?'

'I'm here.'

'You're in luck. Her original medication is still here.'

He pumped his fist in the air. Thank goodness for the inefficiency at Maple Ward.

He called the police straight away, insisting he had extremely important information and would only speak to DCI Watson. Eventually, he was put through.

'I've been in touch with Maple Ward,' he said, tripping over his words. 'They still have the original medication that Sophie was using when she was admitted. There's a nasal spray and more insulin. It should have been destroyed by now, but luckily it wasn't.' Watson was silent. 'If you could at least get in touch with them and run checks on it?' There was still a horrible silence from the other end of the line, and so Daniel felt the need to beg. 'Please! My son is still missing… Richard Fox has disappeared… it could all be linked.'

Another silence. Then DCI Watson cleared his throat.

'Let's see what we can do,' he said eventually.

Within the next hour, DCI Watson had sent a team to the hospital to collect Sophie's original medication and take statements from Dr Marshall and the nurses.

Soon after, Daniel had a call to say the forensic laboratory would be running tests. Only, it would take days. He was told to keep his phone close by and wait.

During that first night he found himself plagued by images in his mind's eye of the white ball dancing on a spinning roulette wheel. Relentlessly, it clattered from red to black, red to black.

Chapter seventy-seven

With Ben still missing, Daniel didn't dare leave the house more than he had to. He needed to be there for that glorious moment when the police brought his son home.

Any other outcome was unthinkable.

Uniformed officers and the family liaison officer had been in and out, day after day, but they always offered him the same two dismal words: 'no news.'

He asked his boss to send him figures to analyse in the hope that it would distract him for short periods. But, all he could see before his eyes was Sophie's frenzied handwriting and all he could hear inside his head was his little boy calling, 'Daddy, Daddy, where are you?'

He bought a map of his local area and stapled it to a cork board he found in the cellar, so he could mark out all the areas he'd personally scoured looking for Ben and keep up to date with the police search. Every time he stabbed a pin into the chart, he imagined piercing another sensitive part of Rick's body.

Where have you taken him you piece of shit?

Franciska had brought fresh milk and provisions over for him, but she'd forgotten bread, so Daniel slipped out to the local deli. When he returned another postcard awaited him on the mat. Daniel recognised Oxford University; a different shot this time. Unlike the last one he'd received. However, there was a message:

You treated her like dirt... and I don't mean your wife.

It was Rick's handwriting. Definitely.

What the hell was he getting at?

He checked the postmark, but it was smudged. Sighing heavily, he stared at the picture, then back to the words. The police needed to see this.

He took a picture of it on his phone and raced to his car.

Chapter seventy-eight

His mobile rang early the following morning.

'Mr Duke, we fast-tracked the tests and we have preliminary results from Mrs Duke's original nasal spray when she first entered the psychiatric facility,' said DCI Watson.

'And?' Sweat instantly began to form in Daniel's palm, so much so that he almost dropped the phone.

'Early indications show positive signs of contamination with another drug.'

A rocket of euphoria shot though Daniel's body.

'Wow! So what happens now?'

'We do further tests and consult the relevant specialists to see what effect this combination of drugs could have had on your wife.'

'So, you'll be able to tell whether this was the cause of my wife's outburst?'

'It won't be an exact science. We'll know the likely physiological outcomes of the combination of drugs your wife was taking, Mr Duke. I can't say more than that for now.'

'And Ben… any news?'

He knew the DCI would have mentioned this first had there been anything to report.

'I'm so sorry. The family liaison officer will be back with you later today to give you a full update, but we can't give you the news you want to hear at this stage.'

'Have you found Richard Fox?'

'Not as yet… we're working on it.'

Why hadn't the police been able to track Rick down?

'Is there anything more I can do?' he asked in desperation.

There was a sad smile hidden in the DCI's voice. 'You've done a great deal already, Mr Duke. We'll be in touch.'

Chapter seventy-nine

Daniel entered the crowded café on Hampstead High Street to the loud hiss of the coffee machine. It suddenly stopped and was replaced by voices calling out orders and clinking crockery.

The smell of warm dough from the Danish pastries made him feel hungry for the first time in days. He found a seat by the window.

Pacing up and down at home was driving him nuts. He couldn't sleep, couldn't work, couldn't face the barrage of concerned phone calls, couldn't sit still. He needed to be doing something positive and the only thing left was to follow every lead he had to try to track down Ben.

He didn't have the energy to put his hand up and wave when Jody rushed in. Instead, he watched her scour the faces, looking for him. Her hair was tossed in all directions as though she hadn't had time to brush it that morning. Daniel found that just the sight of her lifted his spirits. He chased the warm feeling abruptly away. They could never even be friends after what she'd done.

'Sorry I'm late,' Jody called out, flopping down into the well-worn leather armchair next to his. 'Any news about Ben?'

'Nothing. It's been six days.'

Yesterday, he'd sent an impulsive text asking to see her, then questioned why he'd chosen Jody when there were others he could have turned to.

He told himself it was because she might have some clue as to where Rick might have gone, but it was more than that. He'd missed her sparky conversation, the way she genuinely listened to what he had to say and, more than anything, the fresh, warm glow he felt in her company. In spite of everything.

'You must be out of your mind. I can't imagine the torment...' She cupped her hands over his, then swiftly pulled them away.

'I feel like I'm drowning,' he said, closing his eyes against imminent tears.

How come she always seemed to draw out his innermost emotions, without even trying?

'Thanks for coming,' he added. 'I'm sure you've got better things to do.'

'I'd only be at home learning lines,' she said, her eyes bright as she looked at him.

He left her to order two cappuccinos, then brought her up to date with the news about Sophie. 'They still need to do more tests. I'm waiting to hear.'

'I imagine you can't even think about that with Ben still missing. Have they found Rick, yet?'

He shook his head. 'Have you heard from him? Heard anything through the theatre about where he is?' He shifted his jaw, felt his teeth grind together.

'I wish I had. Total arsehole. I asked around at the theatre. That guy he goes around with, Stuart, he's gone AWOL too. He was due to start making an Egyptian sarcophagus for the next show, but he didn't turn up.'

'Can you think of anywhere Rick might have gone? Anywhere he mentioned? Somewhere he could take a child?'

She swallowed. 'Relatives? Friends?'

'The police have got those covered.'

She frowned. 'You really think he's got Ben?'

'If he has some kind of secret vendetta against me, what better way to torture me?' He threw his arms up. 'He's already gone to ridiculous lengths to poison Sophie against me – literally! Now, why not take the closest thing to my heart?'

She nodded, staring at her coffee cup. 'It would make sense.'

Daniel aligned the salt and pepper pots at the centre of the table and reached into his pocket. He brought out the two postcards the police had returned to him. Apparently, they'd made a note of them, but said there was no action they could take.

'Rick sent me these. I don't know what to make of them. Did he mention anything to you about them? About Oxford?'

She scrutinised them in detail and handed them back. 'Weird...' she said, shaking her head.

'I just don't know what he's getting at.' Daniel tapped the cards on the edge of the table. 'I feel like I should know what they mean, but I haven't a clue. I keep thinking that if the penny dropped, they might lead me to Ben.'

She read out the words on the card, intently.

You treated her like dirt... and I don't mean your wife.

'Who is he referring to?'

He slapped his hands on the table with exasperation. 'I have no idea.'

'Is this the same scenario as before? Accusing you of something you didn't do?' she said.

He sighed. 'Isn't he tired of all that by now? Sophie went to prison. My life's a mess. Isn't that enough?'

Jody pulled an impassioned face by way of reply as Daniel sunk back into his chair.

Then his phone began to buzz on the table in front of him.

'It's the police,' he said, getting to his feet. He hurried outside, ended up standing on the other side of the glass pane from Jody. He watched her questioning face glued to his, as he responded to the DCI's words. Then he scrabbled in his pockets for a pen and jotted a few words on the back of his hand.

'Okay,' he said breathlessly, returning to their table. 'Sophie was given a low dose of a drug called Iperatine; it can cause paranoia.'

'Wow...'

He sank back into the armchair. 'It was mixed with the insulin. Incredible. Some of the phials also had something called...' He held out the writing on his fist. '... crystal methamphetamine – it's a street drug; cheap and easy to find. Watson said it creates a tremendous rush, but it can also have effects like agitation, paranoia, confusion and can cause violent behaviour.'

Jody puffed out her cheeks. 'Why didn't they test her for drugs when they arrested her? Couldn't they tell she was high?'

'She was tested, I checked, but not straight away. The drugs she'd been given had already left her system by then, so no one picked it up. She didn't show any obvious signs of drug use – no needle marks in her arms, no damage in her nose or gums. Her father told them the discreet needle marks in her stomach were for insulin and that she'd never touched recreational drugs. She didn't fit the profile, so they didn't check soon enough. Big mistake on their part. They put her behaviour down to mental illness.'

'But wasn't she continuing with the same medicines at the hospital?'

'No. Once admitted, they reviewed her meds and she was given fresh prescriptions. I was out of it at the time, but apparently the paramedics took Sophie's handbag with them when she was taken to the hospital. It had her daily medication inside, but it was put to one side for reference only.'

'So what happens now?'

'Watson thinks there's a real chance the court will consider the conviction unsafe and quash it.'

'So, she could be released?'

'It's possible, but that's still some time away.'

Jody clapped her hands together. 'Even so, that's amazing.'

Daniel's glimmer of shared euphoria subsided like a punctured dinghy. 'There's still Ben...'

Chapter eighty

'Okay. Let's look again at what we've got here,' said Jody. 'This is the latest communication from Rick, right?'

'Yes.' Daniel scrunched up his nose. 'Only the postmark is smudged.'

'Never mind. Let's look at it at face value,' she said with authority.

Daniel felt his shoulders slide down. At last, someone else was taking the lead, for once.

Jody carried on. 'This is about a woman that Rick knows, who *he thinks* you have treated badly, who has some connection with Oxford, yeah?'

He pointed to the postcards. 'These are pictures of his college; he did a degree there in biochemistry.'

'Does anything else ring any bells?'

Daniel shrugged. 'Rick and I were brought up in Oxford and used to see a lot of each other as kids. I visited his college a couple of times once he'd started.' He folded his arms. 'I don't know what I'm supposed to be looking for…'

Jody looked out onto the street and Daniel followed her line of sight. A boy was attempting to lean his bicycle against the window of the café and someone behind him was shaking his head and pointing further up the road.

'I don't know if it's in any way connected, but when I bumped into Rick at the memorial for Mark, he said something really odd about you not being squeaky clean.'

'Oh, great,' said Daniel, throwing his wooden stirrer into his saucer. 'Why didn't you mention this before?'

'I thought he was just trying to wind me up. He mentioned a cemetery near Barnes Bridge.'

'What?' Daniel screwed up his face in disbelief.

'He said there was a gravestone that I should be interested in, in connection with you.'

She glanced down into her lap. He knew from her hesitation that there was more.

'I went there. To see for myself.' Using a discarded napkin on the table, she mopped up a spill of coffee in a way that suggested she was making light of the information. 'I didn't want to bother you with it. It didn't make any sense to me, but... yes, I went to check.'

'And what did you find?' He was on the edge of his seat.

'A headstone for a boy called Miles Fox; Rick's brother, I assume.'

'Oh, yeah.' Daniel rubbed his eyes. 'You asked me about him. He died young.' He started nodding his head as the truth dawned on him. 'I see... you must have found the grave by then – that's why you were so interested in what I had to say about him.'

'Yeah, that was just after I'd been there. You seemed so relaxed about it, so I dropped it. I didn't want to worry you.' She looked directly into his eyes then swiftly away again. 'I put it down to one of Rick's bizarre antics.'

'Jody, what else is there I should know? What else have you kept from me?'

'Nothing – that's it, honestly.'

She sounded so innocent and artless. He stretched his eyebrows apart with his thumb and middle finger, still unsure whether or not he trusted Jody.

She picked up her bag and pulled out her phone.

'Look, I've got a picture of the grave on here.'

Daniel looked at the words carved into the stone. He nodded. 'Yeah, he died in 2011.' He rested his elbows on the chair arms, propping up his head. 'Really sad, he was still a child.'

'And he died of a brain tumour you said. What could that possibly have to do with you?'

Daniel covered his eyes with his hands. 'I don't know…'

'Okay, our biggest priority is to find Ben,' she said with renewed purpose. 'What else can we do?'

Seduced by her concern, he heard the words coming out of his mouth before he could stop them.

'I'm not Ben's biological father,' he said.

Jody shot round to face him 'Not his—?'

'The DNA test… think you knew.'

'I didn't want to pry.'

'The long and short of it is I found out that not only is Ben not mine, but his real father is…' He spat out the word, 'Rick…'

She visibly shuddered. 'S-H-I-T – are you sure?'

'Yes. It all ties in, don't you see?'

'But, Sophie…' He could see Jody's mind running through the ramifications.

'She went to a party when I was away once. She said Rick was pestering her and then she felt ill and threw up. The dates tally. Now we've got proof he was drugging her from September, I think he drugged her then, too.'

Jody's eyes peeled wide. 'What an utter bastard. Do the police know all this?'

'Not the last bit, or about Rick being Ben's father. I don't think it will help at the moment. I just need my boy back.'

Daniel started to cry. He dropped his head, smudging his tears with the heel of his hand.

Jody reached out to him, pulled him towards her and he sank into her sturdy arms, unresisting.

She gritted her teeth. 'We'll get him back. We'll find him. Where's Rick's family? Are they still in Oxford?'

'His father died, but his mother is still there, I think. His sister lives in London.'

'Is he close to his sister? Have you been in touch with her?'

'I saw her last week. We've been in touch since then.'

'We've got to go and see her,' she insisted.

'She doesn't know where Rick is,' he snivelled. 'The police have been questioning her.'

'Has she seen these postcards?'

'No.'

'Right. Let's see if *she* can shed any light on them. Rick's dangerous. We need to talk to her today.'

Chapter eighty-one

Louise opened the door to her flat before Daniel had the chance to ring the bell.

'I heard footsteps,' she said, standing in the doorway. 'I thought it might be Rick.'

The three of them stood looking at each other until Louise realised she'd need to step aside and let them in.

'This is the living room,' she said, as though they were prospective buyers with an appointment to view her property.

On the way over, Daniel had described Louise to Jody. The words 'skittish and impulsive' had come to mind.

'She sounds like a jolly, but benign version of Rick,' Jody had surmised with great accuracy.

Louise looked like she hadn't had much sleep, but unfortunately had enough energy to hum along to a loud rendition of 'Funky Gibbon' coming from the kitchen.

'Drinks?' she offered. On her way to the kitchen she surreptitiously shoved a packet of toffees down the side of the sofa. A washing machine began to rumble as it gathered speed during the spin setting, drowning out the music.

She returned carrying a Mickey Mouse tray with three tall glasses of lemonade, having failed to determine which drinks they actually wanted. They sat around a pine dining table tucked into an alcove. From the sixth floor there was a clear view of a nearby netball pitch and carpark.

'Thanks for agreeing to see us,' said Daniel. 'This is all a bit awkward.'

'I still don't know where he is,' she said defensively. She pulled up the neckline of her smock to cover her ample cleavage. 'He didn't say.'

'You've seen him? When?'

'No,' she said, looking away. 'He left a message saying you were in for a nasty shock. He didn't say what you're supposed to have done. I'm worried about him, to be honest.'

Alongside the upright piano, a collection of Samurai swords mounted on the wall were catching the light, as were several twirling mobiles hanging from the ceiling with multi-coloured umbrellas, butterflies and fish dangling down. An orange monkey sat on the sofa arm and rows of framed posters of Batman, Spiderman, Flash Gordon and other comic heroes cluttered the interior. The entire place looked like a small toy shop.

Daniel and Jody exchanged a glance.

'You know Ben is missing, don't you? My boy?'

'Yeah,' she said with a grimace. 'The police were asking if Rick had mentioned him.'

'And?'

'No,' she said with conviction. 'No, he hasn't.'

A silence sucked out the air between them.

'We wondered if you might be able to shed some light on these.'

Daniel pulled the postcards out of his jacket pocket and placed them on the table. Louise took a quick look, turning them over.

'They're from Rick. What's he getting at?' Louise asked.

'That's what we hoped you might be able to tell us?'

Daniel swirled the straw around that Louise had plonked in his glass, making the ice cubes clink. He wasn't sure how much she knew about the recent criminal revelations. He wasn't going to waste time bringing her up to speed. She'd find out soon enough.

'It's Rick's college, isn't it?' Louise asked, taking a second look. 'But I don't know what it means.'

Daniel shot a glance at the door. 'What's that?' He froze to the spot with his finger in the air.

'It's a baby crying,' said Jody.

'It's Ben,' he yelled, launching to his feet.

He scuttled out of the door and into the corridor, waiting for the sound again. Jody and Louise followed him.

'There are loads of kids in this place,' Louise told him.

'Shush!' he hissed, putting his finger to his lips. He began striding stealthily along the corridor, hovering outside each door, listening. 'There it is again.' He shot to the end of the corridor into the stairwell, but there was no one there.

'Ben? Ben?' he yelled into the empty echoing space below.

He was certain there was a cry abruptly muffled. He stood still, straining to listen.

'It's him!' Daniel yelled.

Louise sank her weight to one hip and looked pointedly at her watch.

There were around seven other doors and a lift on that floor, so Daniel slowly wandered past each of them as Louise huffed and puffed. When the wailing came again, he stopped outside the third door along. He rapped on it hard with his knuckle, before noticing the bell at the side, then pressed it furiously.

A woman answered with a distressed girl of around three in her arms.

'What?' she barked at him.

'Are you...? Is this your only child?' he asked, straining to look past her.

Louise hurried to his side as the little girl opened her lungs for another round of wailing. 'Sorry, Elaine – he's lost his little boy. He thought he heard him.'

The woman stared at Daniel with the kind of look usually given to people who let their dogs foul in the street.

'You're hypersensitive, you want it to be him,' said Louise brusquely, pulling him away as the woman closed the door in his face. 'Any child is going to sound like Ben.'

Daniel dropped his head and backed away. Louise ushered him back to their seats without another word.

'Why did you come, exactly?' Louise said. 'Is it just to show me these postcards?'

'No,' said Daniel, 'there's something else. Rick told Jody to find Miles's gravestone.'

Louise's shoulders fell at the mention of her dead brother's name. Daniel glanced up at the framed portrait of him by the window, smiling gleefully through crooked teeth.

'Poor Miles… what's he got to do with anything?' she said, rubbing her arm as if she was cold, even though she was standing directly in the sunlight.

'Did Rick ever mention anything odd about Miles, about his death,' continued Daniel.

She frowned.

'Was Rick ever angry with me… in connection with Miles?'

Louise turned her palms upwards in a gesture that said, *search me*.

Jody cut across them. 'Let's look at the dates,' she said. She put her phone on the table between the postcards so they could see the saved shot from the cemetery.

Louise rested her finger on one of the postcards. 'When would this have been, Daniel? When was Rick studying at Oxford?'

Daniel rubbed his chin as he worked out the exact dates, but before he could reply there was a sharp metallic rattle behind them. Jody jumped.

'It's the letter box,' said Louise, getting up. 'More junk mail, probably.' She brought back a blank white envelope and put it on the table. It didn't look like junk mail and Daniel and Jody stared at it, wondering if Louise was going to open it.

'Don't mind us,' said Jody, pretending to look for a tissue in her bag. Louise opened the envelope, Swore loudly, then bolted out of the flat.

Chapter eighty-two

There was no one in the corridor and no sounds of running footsteps.

Louise had thrown the envelope containing a single photograph onto the table and rushed out.

She knew it was Rick who'd dropped it off. He was like a child playing a never-ending game of tag and she was fed up with it. If only he'd stand still for one minute and have a proper conversation.

She heard the lift clank into action and noticed the green light had been activated from her floor. She waited for it to open, but when the silver doors juddered apart there was no one inside. She ran to the staircase and peered down over the banister, but there was no one there. And no response when she called out his name. Instead her voice echoed into the space below like a hollow cry down a deserted mine shaft. She tutted and retraced her steps.

On hearing movement from within the flat, Rick backed away from the letterbox and made a hasty dash for the lift. He pressed the button and when the mechanism failed to come to life immediately, he ran for the staircase. The tightly sprung door flapped shut behind him and instead of heading down the stairs, he climbed up two flights, then stopped and listened. He stood away from the centre stairwell, leaning into a window bay out of sight from below.

He could hear distant footsteps and then his sister calling out his name twice, but no sounds to indicate anyone was investigating further.

He turned to look out of the window. Down in Balham High Road, people meandered in and out of shops, trooping behind one another living their small-scale lives. A group was bunched around a bus stop and as the number 155 squealed to a halt, Rick saw a youth push in front of an elderly woman who was clutching bulky carrier bags. No style, he thought to himself. If you're going to get ahead mate, you need more than elbows.

Rick pressed his nose against the window and watched his breath fog up the glass.

I've got everyone on the back foot. I've got them all in a spin.

It was a powerful feeling – a feeling he'd been waiting to experience for a long time. He wanted to savour it.

He spat out the gum into his hand, rolled it into a ball and pressed it onto the window frame. He decided to give it another five minutes. That should be long enough for the shit to hit the fan.

Chapter eighty-three

Jody picked up the creased photograph that Louise had taken from the envelope.

'I'm not sure we should be—' Daniel began.

'It's you,' said Jody, pushing it towards him on the table.

Daniel took a moment to take in the scene and locate the occasion in his memory. It showed a room full of people – someone's sitting room – with bottles and cans strewn over the carpet.

His heart was thudding fast. 'That's Oxford,' he said, holding it up to get the best light.

'Is there anything on the back?' she asked.

Daniel turned it over.

'This…' He showed her the writing in faded pencil: *30 March, 2002.*

'You remember it?'

He lowered his eyes. 'I remember the girl – don't remember much about the party.' He pointed to the woman wearing a frilly apron side-on to the camera.

'Who was she?'

Daniel drummed his fingers on the table.

'Good question.' He squinted at the blurred shape. 'I can't think of her name.' He shrugged. 'It was a long time ago. She was serving drinks.'

'One of your infamous teenage parties?' she said, without judgement.

'Probably.' He was finding it hard to look Jody in the eye.

'Did you and she…?'

Daniel tugged at his shirt to circulate some air.

'Yeah. Only that one time. She was… she was something, I tell you. I remember I wanted to see her again, but she brushed me off.'

There was a sound at the door and they both turned as Louise arrived back, out of breath.

'It's Rick, I know it is.' She turned to check through the peephole. 'He knows you're here.' She pulled a guilty face. 'I left a message for him. I thought we could all talk things through together, like proper adults – and sort out whatever it is that's going on.'

'Where is he?' asked Daniel. 'Has he got Ben?' But Louise didn't seem to hear and turned to Jody when she spoke.

'Did you take a look at this photograph?' Jody asked.

'Yeah…' she replied, nonplussed. 'It must have been at some function she was waitressing at…'

Daniel felt acid rise in the back of his nose. 'She? You know her?' he asked.

Louise waved her finger over the figure wearing the apron.

'Of course. It's Mum!' she said, as if it was obvious.

Daniel shot up as if a firecracker had gone off under his chair.

'This was your *mother* serving the drinks? Rick's mother?'

He stabbed at the picture, gasping for air. 'Oh, God.' He slapped his palms on the table and squeezed his eyes shut.

Jody let out a noisy breath.

'What's wrong? What's the matter?' cried Louise, snatching the picture from the table to get another look. 'Who's that standing beside her?' Louise held up the photograph and narrowed her eyes. 'Oh… is it you, Daniel?'

He was on his feet pacing the room.

'Is this you?' Louise asked again.

'Are you sure that's your mother?' he demanded, his voice suddenly hoarse. 'It's hardly a clear picture.'

'Of course I'm sure!'

'What's her name?'

'What do you mean?' asked Louise, consternation twisting her face.

'Her name. What is it?' His brain was spinning, like he was about to tumble over the edge of a cliff.

'Jenny – Jenny Fox,' she said, as if he should have known.

'Jennifer,' he whispered. 'Oh God, we were...'

'What happened, Daniel?' Louise asked, her voice high in pitch.

He swivelled round to face her. 'Jennifer and I... we slept together. I didn't know...'

'Daniel!' screeched Louise. She took two swift steps towards him. 'You slept with my *mum*?'

Jody stepped between them.

'Hang on a minute here. Let's try and calm down.'

Jody coaxed Daniel back into his chair.

'When did it happen?' asked Louise, her arms folded, refusing to sit down.

'It says here: *30 March, 2002,*' said Jody.

'It's the same year,' said Louise, her voice faltering.

Daniel quickly did the maths and put his hand over his mouth.

'Miles was born on 31st December... the *same* year,' she said, tailing off.

He got to his feet again, unable to keep still. 'Oh, shit!' he muttered.

Louise let out a hysterical laugh. 'Well, it would explain why Miles didn't look anything like the rest of us.'

Jody looked at Daniel, then Louise. 'Surely he could still have been your father's child,' she said.

'Dad had stomach cancer by then... they had separate rooms.' Louise dragged her fingers over her forehead, wiping away dribbles of sweat. 'I really don't think—'

Jody was about to speak when there was a crash at the front door and a figure burst in.

'I'm so glad you've finally worked it out,' Rick said, smirking.

Chapter eighty-four

'Where's Ben?' shrieked Daniel.

'How the hell should I know?' Rick replied flippantly. 'That's not why we're all here.'

Rick grabbed the chair that faced the piano, spun it round and sat on it back to front. He was wearing grubby denims and a lime-green T-shirt that looked like it had been left to dry in the washing machine.

Daniel surged towards him. 'What have you done with him, you bastard!?'

Rick looked genuinely taken aback.

'I seem to have missed something while I've been on my little holiday.' He looked to Louise for an explanation, but it was Jody who spoke.

'Ben was taken last Thursday from a park near his nursery.' She took a step towards him, squeezing her fists as if she was about to land a ferocious punch in his face. 'Was it you? Did you take him?'

Rick stayed put, his arms flopping over the front of the chair, the epitome of nonchalance. His skin was blotchy, as if he'd been drinking. 'Well, all I can say is now *you* can have a flavour of what it's like to lose your own nearest and dearest.' He glared at Daniel.

'If you've got blood on your hands… I'll…' Daniel drew back his clenched fist.

Rick put up a hand in surrender. 'Listen mate, the only blood on my hands is the pheasant I knocked down on my recent trip to Wales. I was going to have it for supper but taking out all those frickin' feathers looked too much like hard work. I left it behind for someone else.' He sniffed loudly. 'I don't know anything about your kid.'

It was Daniel's turn to be confused. Did Rick really not know where Ben was? And, more remarkably, not know that Ben was actually his own son?

'*This* is why we're here,' Rick announced, pointing to the photograph on the table.

'When did you find out?' Louise demanded.

'When we cleared out the old house. I found the snap in a posh frame in a box of keepsakes. In Mum's loft.'

'September?' shrieked Louise. 'You've known for months?'

Rick brushed some dust from the toe of his shoe with the flat of his hand. 'Come on, it was obvious Miles wasn't Dad's child.' He pointed his finger at no one in particular. 'We all knew back then that Mum and Dad weren't sleeping together.'

'You never said a thing...' whispered Daniel, 'all this time... pretending we were buddies.'

Rick ignored him. 'I knew there had to be a reason why Mum kept this lovely shot of her and pretty-boy.' He turned to Daniel and raised his eyebrows. 'And anyone can see by the look on your face that the deed had already been done. I had a little chat with Mum... and Zip-a-Dee-Doo-Dah... it all added up.'

Daniel stared at the herringbone pattern of blocks on the floor. 'I don't know what to say. I didn't know it was your mother.' He shook his head. 'I'd never met her when we were kids. We never went to your house. I never came across her in all the time you and I have known each other.'

'That's no excuse,' said Rick, slurring the syllables together so they came out as one word. 'Death came into our house and stayed forever because of you.' His voice shot up in volume. 'Their marriage collapsed after Mum got pregnant. Did you know that?'

Daniel shook his head.

Rick picked a nugget of mud from a groove in his sole. 'My father knew the child wasn't his. He lost the will to live. You made a mockery of him. You practically killed him!'

'I didn't know,' Daniel reiterated.

'Did you know he was suicidal once he realised what had happened?' Rick spat the words at him. 'Not only was he dying, but his beloved wife – our *mum* – had been unfaithful.' He jabbed his finger at Daniel. 'You led her astray and broke his heart. You tore our family apart.'

'Daniel said he didn't *know*,' said Jody.

'*You* keep out of it,' Rick hissed back at her.

'What were you doing with a woman twice your age, to start with?' asked Louise. 'She would have been… what, thirty-nine in 2002.'

'I was nearly twenty – she didn't seem that much older. And she came on to *me*!'

'Didn't you realise she was married?' Louise was red in the face, looking like a toddler on the verge of a tantrum.

'She wasn't wearing a wedding ring and to be perfectly honest, we… she… didn't mention it.'

'A bit naïve, Daniel,' said Louise, as if she was the epitome of maturity.

'Well, we all know now,' said Rick. He was staring at Daniel, but looked like he was having trouble focusing.

'It's a terrible shock… for everybody,' said Jody calmly.

'What is it you want from me?' Daniel cried.

'It's not enough, but seeing your wife imprisoned for attempted murder and watching your fairy-tale romance sink into divorce is a pretty good start.'

Daniel lurched forward, but Jody grabbed at his arm.

'Don't, Daniel, this is what he wants… he's goading you.'

Rick leant back and slammed his right arm down on the piano keys. A low-pitched discord reverberated around the room.

Louise flapped her arms, looking flustered. 'We all need time to let this sink in,' she said. 'Let me get you a drink, Rick.'

'I don't want a bloody drink.' He stood up straddling the chair. 'I want revenge.' He stabbed a finger at Daniel. 'I want *you* to pay the full price you owe my mother – the guilt and shame you caused her – and for the bitterness and grief my father went through.'

He took a step forward, then wobbled and fell back against the wall, ending up at eye-level with the largest of the Samurai swords. In a single move, he wrenched it from its bracket and swung it experimentally from side to side. It made a swishing sound like a skater's blade on ice. He took two paces towards Daniel.

'Stop this now!' cried Louise, parking herself between them, blocking Rick's path.

With Rick focusing on Louise, Jody felt for the phone in her pocket and discreetly slid it halfway out. She tapped in 999 and when the call was answered, she waited in silence, then pressed 55. Enough to alert the police.

Louise kept her eyes on the sword and made a grab for it. 'Rick, put it down. Someone's going to get hurt.'

'That's the idea,' he scoffed, shoving Louise aside with his elbow.

'Stop. Please STOP!' she screamed at the top of her voice, taking them all by surprise. 'There's something… I need to come clean,' she said, staggering towards the door.

Chapter eighty-five

Everything went quiet.

When the door to the flat opened again, the figure who came rushing inside wasn't Louise.

'Ben!!' Daniel hurtled across the room and scooped the boy up in his arms. 'Are you okay? Are you all right?'

He clutched him to his chest, muttering into his hair. Ben's cheeks were on fire and swollen with tears. He was muttering, '*Daddy, Daddy*' over and over, clinging onto him.

'What have you done to him?' cried Daniel, running his fingers through what was left of Ben's hair. It should have been thick and curly, but had been shorn into a crew cut.

Louise gritted her teeth. 'Sorry. I had to make him look different from the photos on the news.' Her shoulders slumped forwards. 'You were right. Elaine along the corridor had him just now. I said he was my nephew and not to say anything if—'

'That woman…?'

'He's been with me until an hour ago, when I knew you were coming,' she said, dropping her head. 'I took time off work to look after him.'

'You just took him? For *six* days?'

'I thought Rick might hurt him, so I took him out of harm's way. Rick had mentioned where you lived so I followed you to the nursery. Then I turned up at the gates at closing time. Ben's name was on his rucksack.'

'Why the hell didn't you tell me? Why hide him from *me*? Don't you realise what torture you've put me through?'

'It wasn't just that I thought Rick might take it out on Ben. Rick said you'd done something terrible to our family, something unforgiveable that I wouldn't believe.' She bit her lip. 'I didn't altogether trust you after that. I thought I'd wait until I knew exactly what you'd done before giving Ben back.'

Giving Ben back?! She made it sound like a playground tiff.

'He isn't hurt or anything,' she insisted. 'We've had a great time. Everyone says I'm brilliant with kids.'

Daniel had no words left. He hugged his boy, taking in his smell, nuzzling his face until Ben was struggling to get down.

'Don't fuss, Daddy,' he said, sounding just like Franciska. Ben wiped his runny nose on the cuff of his sleeve and reached out for the orange monkey on the arm of the sofa. 'Hungry, Daddy,' he said. 'Need sweets.'

Daniel laughed and was momentarily distracted. The resilience of kids… In that split second, Rick stumbled forward and grabbed the boy, the sword still in one hand. Ben giggled, thinking it was a game.

'What better way for Daddy to suffer than to watch his beloved son get caught up in a very tragic accident,' he hissed. He turned to Louise. 'Thanks, sis – superb timing. Didn't know you had it in you.'

'You're mad,' spluttered Louise.

'Don't…' implored Daniel, edging towards him.

Rick plonked Ben down on the edge of the table. 'Look what we have here,' he said enticingly.

'Big sword,' said Ben, reaching out for it.

'Yes, very big sword,' he said. 'The kind of sword you could do a lot of damage with.'

'Let him go!' cried Daniel. 'Ben, come here!'

Ben's bottom lip started to quiver, but he stayed where he was, confused.

Rick's face was tight; his eyes bright with a combination of rage and jubilation as he brandished the sword above Ben's head.

Rick would never do this to his own son. He can't possibly know.

Daniel drew a breath to tell him the truth – to save Ben – but there wasn't time. Instead, he threw his full weight into

Rick's thighs. Knocked off balance, Rick took two unsteady steps backwards and careered into a tropical fish tank standing on a narrow table. The force sent it toppling over and a colossal crash followed as the glass shattered on the bare floor, accompanied by gushes of escaping water.

Ben pointed at the mess, uncertain whether to laugh or cry.

Rick swiftly began clawing his way to his feet amidst shards of broken glass, but didn't have enough time before Jody rushed out of the kitchen clutching a damp duvet cover from the washing machine. She flung it over Rick's crumpled body, pinning him down.

Before anyone could speak, the door swung open to the cries of 'Police!'

Two officers stormed in to find the three of them crouching over a soggy mound in a pool of water – and a small boy sitting on the table, looking bemused, swinging his legs.

Chapter eighty-six

Daniel took the day off work to bring Sophie home. It was windy and wet, just as the weatherman had predicted. The morning sun had got lost behind a haze of overlapping clouds, and in spite of the breeze there was an odd kind of stillness, like liquid gradually seeping into fabric, making it heavy and damp.

As he sat in the reception area waiting for forms to be signed and her belongings to be handed over, the acrid smell of bleach made him nauseous. He shuddered as distant heavy iron gates slammed shut. A guard came through, a radio crackling at his hip, and Daniel wondered what impact being incarcerated here would have had on his once graceful and radiant wife.

A clock on the wall laboured with every second and rain spattered against the window, leaving trails like forlorn tears. Beside it, a green poster hung with the words, 'What are you going to do when you leave prison?' He wondered if Sophie had seen it and what her response would have been. *Go home and give their marriage another go? Go home and pack her things?*

He hadn't prepared himself for Sophie's release at all. Every ounce of energy had been directed towards Ben; checking to see if he was emotionally scarred by his recent ordeal, spending every minute watching him, attending to him, giving him everything he wanted.

Daniel had given little thought to what could happen next. Not in any detail, anyway. He just wanted peace and an end to all the hostility and hurt. And no more surprises.

Sophie appeared, looking pale and thin, and a surge of despondency caught him off guard. He dropped his eyes, let them fix on the tiled floor. As they drifted together towards the door, he was forced to slow down to her pace. He was unsure whether to link arms with her or not, if only to keep her upright. Although fragile, Sophie looked self-contained and determined, like a new-born fawn standing on spindly legs for the first time.

He got out of her way. She needed to do this part on her own.

Once in the privacy of the car, they said little. He listened to the windscreen wipers beating a steady pulse like the rhythm of a life-support machine. Best to wait for her to speak. He didn't want to overwhelm her with questions or glib reassurances and she'd never been one for small talk.

Taking his eyes momentarily off the road, he followed her gaze as she silently watched life unfold and reacquainted herself, no doubt, with a world that had been out of bounds for months.

The dreamy familiarity of dripping umbrellas, pushchairs and green and white striped shop awnings slid past. People seemed to know where they were going; crossing the road, huddling at bus stops, rushing against the rain.

As the car pulled into their street, she turned and stared at the mini-supermarket that was now evolving into a wine bar. He remembered that since she'd last been there, speed ramps had been introduced and the laundrette had been boarded up, too.

Sophie hesitated on the doorstep; dread and excitement tugging her in both directions as she re-entered her former life. Once inside, Ben flattened himself against her legs, giving her no chance to reflect further. Edith muttered hello and goodbye in one garbled sentence, grabbed her bag, then slipped out to give them some privacy.

All of Sophie's trepidation was squeezed out by Ben's tiny arms when he wrapped them around her. Sophie lifted him to eye-level and wept silent tears as she tenderly rocked him, telling him how sweet and wonderful he was, guiding his face into her neck so she wouldn't upset him.

Daniel left her bags on the landing; it was up to her as to whether she chose the spare room or not. Then he let her be, so she could find her bearings.

She took a long time to take those first steps into the kitchen, and when she was finally ready, she did so holding Ben's hand. Daniel had moved the table and shifted the fridge-freezer, added a wine rack and a shiny new wall clock. It was a different room. A different life.

She was unable to imagine taking up the same physical space as the figure who had once stood there, holding a carving knife. That day was a scene from a film, with an actress who didn't even resemble her.

Nevertheless, her eyes were drawn to the spot on the floor where the horrifying pool of blood had expanded, but she could find no trace of it. Seeing it erased in the physical world allowed her to imagine for a split second that she might be able to wipe it clean from her memory. Perhaps they all could.

But in her next breath she knew it would be impossible. The damage had been done, even though everyone had finally agreed it wasn't her fault.

Rick had been arrested for contaminating her medication. With his degree in biochemistry and connections with the underworld, it hadn't been difficult. He was charged with administering noxious substances with intent to endanger life and cause bodily harm. He was looking at six years for that alone; there were the other offences to take into account too. The possibility of attempted murder hadn't been ruled out.

Rick was also the one who'd left the vanishing trail of so-called 'evidence' of Daniel's affair designed to cause so much pain. None of that was in her own head!

At last, it was so good to be believed.

Daniel sliced vegetables for a simple pasta dish for supper while Sophie took a bath. She spent a long time putting Ben to bed and afterwards joined Daniel in the kitchen as he dished up.

They ate in silence, barely making eye contact. Daniel glanced up at her now and again, wondering what she was thinking, wondering if she had questions she was desperate to ask or details she wanted to explain – but like him, didn't know where to start. Or perhaps she was reliving those moments in this unremarkable room when their world turned inside out.

Instead of reflecting on the past, Daniel was thinking about the future. About Ben. About burying secrets. About what was the right thing to do and whether that was also the *best* thing to do. Daniel knew he'd always live in fear of the day when Ben showed similar traits to Rick. Condemned to watch and wait; he would carry that dread with him forever. Or perhaps nurture would outweigh nature. Only time would tell.

Sophie pushed a pile of unwanted penne to the edge of her plate and sat back. He'd spent hours rehearsing this moment. There was so much he needed to tell Sophie, but now the time had come his mind was numb. He couldn't imagine finding any of the right words.

His phone vibrated. A text message. He turned it over, so the screen faced him. It was Jody.

I'm thinking of you. Thinking of you all.

Daniel sighed, and when Sophie looked up, he struggled to smile.

'We need to talk, don't we?' she said.

Daniel swallowed hard, then opened his mouth.

THE END

About the Author

A J Waines is a number one bestselling author, topping the UK and Australian Amazon Charts in two consecutive years, with *Girl on a Train*. The author was a psychotherapist for fifteen years, during which time she worked with ex-offenders from high-security institutions, gaining a rare insight into abnormal psychology. She is now a full-time novelist with publishing deals in UK, France, Germany, Norway, Hungary and USA (audiobooks).

Her fourth novel, *No Longer Safe* sold over 30,000 copies in the first month, in twelve countries worldwide. In 2016 and 2017, the author was ranked in the Top 10 UK Authors on Amazon KDP (Kindle Direct Publishing).

AJ Waines lives in Hampshire, UK, with her husband. Find out more at www.ajwaines.co.uk. She's also on Twitter (@ AJWaines), Facebook and you can sign up for her Newsletter at http://eepurl.com/bamGuL.

Lightning Source UK Ltd.
Milton Keynes UK
UKHW010001240922
409344UK00002B/171